Ascent to the Sun

Mike —
Thanks for all the help in fact-checking the climbing references,

Jeff

Ascent to the Sun

Also by Jeff Pepper, in Simplified Chinese and English:

- Hulin and the Mad Goose[1]
- The Journey to the West[1,2], a 31-book series:
    Rise of the Monkey King • Trouble in Heaven • The Immortal Peaches • The Young Monk • The Emperor in Hell • The Journey Begins • The Monster of Black Wind Mountain • The Hungry Pig • The Three Beautiful Daughters • The Magic Ginseng Tree • The Monster's Secret • The Five Treasures • The Ghost King • The Cave of Fire • The Daoist Immortals • The Great Demon King • The Thieves • The Country of Women • The Angry Monkey • The Burning Mountain • The Rain of Blood • The False Buddha • The Monkey Doctor • The Demons of Spiderweb Mountain • Great Peng and His Brothers • The Thousand Children • The Monk and the Mouse • The Dharma Destroying Kingdom • The Nine Headed Lion • The Lazy Monk • The Last Trial
- The Last King of Shang[1], a 6-book series based on Investiture of the Gods
- Learn to Read Chinese[1]: a 3-book series:
    Four Folk Tales in Simplified Chinese • Six Folk Tales in Easy Chinese • Four Love Stories in Easy Chinese
- The Love Triangle[1]
- Mulan, Woman Warrior[2]
- San Zi Jing: the Three-Character Classic
- Twenty-Three Cats[,2]
- Ye Xian: the Chinese Cinderella Story[1]

Also by Jeff Pepper, in English:

- The Art of War: A Step-by-Step Translation[1]
- Dao De Jing in Clear English[1]
- The Journey to the West
- The Last King of Shang
- Like a Moth: A Life of Seeking and Software
- We're Off to Seize the Wizard

[1] co-authored with Xiao Hui Wang
[2] also available in Traditional Chinese

ASCENT TO THE SUN

A NOVEL

BY JEFF PEPPER

IMAGIN8
PRESS

Ascent to the Sun

This is a work of fiction. Names, characters, organizations, places, events, locales, and incidents are either the products of the author's imagination or used in a fictitious manner. Any resemblance to actual persons, living or dead, or actual events is purely coincidental.

Copyright © 2025 by Imagin8 Press LLC, all rights reserved.

Published in the United States by Imagin8 Press LLC, Verona, Pennsylvania, US. For information, email info@imagin8press.com, or visit www.imagin8press.com.

Our books may be purchased directly in quantity at a reduced price, visit www.imagin8press.com for details.

Imagin8 Press, the Imagin8 logo and the sail image are all trademarks of Imagin8 Press LLC.

Book design by Jeff Pepper
Cover photo is from stockcake.com, used by permission
Typography: The interior of this book was set in Garamond. The cover title font is Good Timing; other cover fonts are Capsula and Arial.

ISBN: 978-1959043515
version 1.9

Prologue 7
1 | Shining Mountain 9
2 | Groundmouse 23
3 | Parley 33
4 | Pack 44
5 | Dance 53
6 | Cave 67
7 | Bird 76
8 | Machine 87
9 | Crownfruit 97
10 | Agreement 109
11 | Trouble 119
12 | Wild One 133
13 | Training 142
14 | Memories 157
15 | Hunt 170
16 | Darkness 186
17 | Awakening 200
18 | Angels 216
19 | Drones 234

20 | Platform	248
21 | May Day	260
22 | Soma	272
23 | Poker	291
24 | Summit	308
25 | Sky	322
Epilogue	334
Waya Language	345
Acknowledgements	347
About the Author	349

Prologue

Come see our world, a dark green ball
An emerald drifting in a lightless sea
Silent as the thought of a falling star
Tethered to a yellow sun like yours

Look down on us from high above
Eleven pearls strung round a burning jewel
Ours, like yours, the third rock from the sun
One of four warmed in the inmost rings

Beyond are four giants, then two icy titans
And far beyond them, deep in the endless night
Circling slowly in the dark, is the eleventh
The cold, lonely home of the Banaan

Now up close, see the silva rise like breath from stone
A vast lattice of limbs and leaves
Three miles high, trunk upon trunk entwined
Each one massive as a mountain

Ascent to the Sun

Casting a giant shadow on plains and deserts
It covers the oceans, rises from the depths
Mighty roots burrow below polar ice
Trees beyond counting, all bound in a single, silent sway

Now descend past the canopy's green mantle
Down through dripping leaves and laden mists
Slip between giant trunks, through moss and bone
To a dimly lit path worn deep by ancient footsteps

Look there: a thin gray creature moves slowly
Wolf-boned, trailing a ghostly path
Bearing the weight of years and pain
Lame, lost in memory, he still serves his clan

This is Katan, a watcher in the web of leaves
Tracing the ancient path beneath the green
His gaze is bound to the living and the dust
As he bears the weight of terrible news

1 | Shining Mountain

Long ago, Katan was young and strong, a warrior and a hunter. Now he is older, thinner and weaker. His eyes, bright and clear in his prime, are clouded, often downcast and brooding. His thick black fur has faded to gray. Five of his six legs are healthy enough given his age, but his left foreleg cannot take much weight, causing him to wobble a bit as he moves.

He has been traveling for three days, bringing terrible news to the clan.

Katan approaches the edge of the clearing, limping slowly out of the forest. Looking around, he pauses to take in the sights and smells of home: the network of narrow footpaths, the faint aroma of smoke from the firepit, the assortment of rough wooden structures for storing firewood, and underneath it all, the mingled aroma of his people who have lived there for countless generations.

Across the clearing rises the great sandstone cliff, pocked with dozens of ancient caves dug from the soft stone. There are almost no silva trunks here in the clearing, although they stand in regular intervals throughout the rest of the forest and, as far as Katan knows, across the entire world. This oddity, combined with the cliff's soft stone, makes this place ideal for a clan village.

In one of the larger caves lives Pataza, the clan leader. There is a rumor that in the deepest recesses of her cave, hidden from visitors' sight, are etched the sigils of every clan leader who lived there before her. It is said there are hundreds of carvings, so many that the entire back wall is covered with them. Of course, Katan would never have been allowed there, even in his younger days.

On the other side of the clearing, Katan sees Pataza and the other two members of the clan council. They are sitting and chatting in the dim sunlight that filters down through the silva. Slowly and painfully Katan crosses the open ground and approaches them. They look relaxed, but he knows that is about to change. He is about to kick over a stinger nest, but it can't be helped. His job is just to report what he's seen. The rest is up to them.

Katan crouches submissively, tail tucked under his hind legs, forepaws flat on the ground in front of him. He keeps his eyes down, not daring to look at his superiors directly.

He feels their eyes on him, waiting until their conversation ceases. Daring to look up, he sees Pataza acknowledge him with a slight nod of her head.

"The humans have emerged again," he says, managing to keep his voice clear and steady.

The three council members abruptly stand up and face him. Their tails are held high. The one on the far right, an old, scarred male named Maza, says, "Tell us more, damaged one."

Katan ignores the slight, though he wonders briefly if Maza is referring to the old injury to his leg or something else. He replies,

"It was three days ago. Seven of them came out from the great shining mountain. All full-sized, from what I know of their kind."

He tries not to wince from the pain in his left foreleg, which is worse than usual. It never healed completely from the desperate battle he'd fought decades ago, and three days trek through the forest has only made it worse. He really needs a shot of glowjuice, but that will have to wait.

Katan can feel Maza's cold eyes on him. "What were they doing?" he demands.

"An opening appeared in the shining mountain," replies Katan, "just like the time before." He didn't have to remind them of the terrible events of the time before, when the visitors emerged and brought so much pain and death. "Then the creatures came out, single file. They arranged themselves in what looked like a defensive perimeter in front of the doorway. At least, that's what it looked like to me."

He immediately regrets speaking such weak words in front of these three who hold his fate in their paws, but he is determined to show no fear. He presses on. "The first four were holding dark sticks in their, ah, upper paws. These looked like the deathsticks we know from before. One of them looked directly towards me, even though I was well hidden in the watchers' den. Then, three more came out. These carried bunches of long, thin sticks. Not deathsticks, something else."

Katan pauses to look at them, trying to assess their reaction. Pataza's gazes at him, her eyes like black rock, her expression unreadable. Maza's eyes glitter, as if he is leading a hunting pack and has just spotted their prey. Zaka, the frail elder, just cocks her head, seeming more curious than angry.

He continues, "The three humans fanned out slowly, looking around. They seemed nervous, ready to run if they saw anything threatening. They each took maybe twenty steps away from the shining mountain. Then they began pushing their sticks into the ground, one at a time. When they were finished, there were maybe fifty sticks arranged in a circle around the shining mountain. Then the sticks began burning with a dim white light at the top end. The three retreated back behind the four who held the deathsticks. Then they all went inside the mountain."

"Did they speak?" asks Zaka. Thin, with a gray muzzle and a bit of a tremor, she is the oldest member of the council.

"No." That question seems harmless enough.

"Where were you during all this?" growls Pataza, standing in the middle. She has midnight black fur and a highly domed head. She's the one who assigned Katan to keep watch on the shining mountain, the strange silver shape that stands in a clearing two or three days from the village. There had been no sign of movement there for years, but she wanted constant surveillance just in case.

The solitary work of a watcher suited Katan just fine. Not inclined to socialize much anyway, the opportunity to spend time alone appealed to him. But now the long-dreaded event has occurred, and he expects this to be the end of his career as a watcher. Soon he will return to his quiet life near the bottom of the clan's hierarchy.

"I was doing as you ordered, of course," Katan replies, eyes fixed on the ground. "I was in the watchers' den, just beyond the edge of the clearing. I'd been at the shining mountain for eighty days. As I said, this was three days ago, just before dark."

"How much glowjuice did you have that day?"

"Not a drop." Not entirely true, but close enough for the purposes of this meeting.

"Ummm," growls Maza. He turns to the other council members, ignoring Katan for the moment. "The last time those miserable creatures came out of the shining mountain, they brought fighting, pain, and death. Now it appears the time for such things has come again."

The others are silent for a time. Then Pataza looks at Maza and says, "Those were dark times, yes. But these are even darker times. The simians are dying. Perhaps some good can come of this."

"You can't be serious," replies Maza. "What good could possibly come of humans with deathsticks?"

"I don't like them any more than you do, and I like their weapons even less. But the simians are disappearing. We have never known anything like this. The old stories say nothing about this plague, and there are no images in any of the deep caves. If this is truly the end of the simians, it will be the end of us. Not just for us and our families, but for all the clans. For all we know, it might be the end of all the people of the world. Something must be done."

She pauses for emphasis, then growls, "These are desperate times. We cannot just wait and watch our people die."

* * *

Ricky is the last one to go back inside the ship. Seventeen years old, tall, lean and muscular, he has the beginnings of a wispy beard, pale blue eyes, and long brown hair tied back in a queue. He points his rifle outwards as he backs slowly into the hatch which serves as the front door. "All clear," he says.

Angie steps in front of him and pulls the door closed. Stocky, powerful, and dark-skinned, she easily spins the heavy locking wheel.

Ricky turns and looks around the entryway. All six of his siblings are there, standing uneasily. Today is the first time any of them have set foot outside the ship. Despite all of the shipmind's preparations and their years of military training, Ricky can see they are scared.

They have good reason to fear the world outside the ship. These seven are the second generation of colonists, hatched from frozen embryos decades after the first generation was massacred by the large, six-legged carnivores they called wolves. The shipmind selected these embryos not to be explorers or scientists like the previous generation. These seven are fated to be soldiers, defenders of a human outpost, saviors of the species. Ricky and the others were hatched because the shipmind had no intention of letting the wolves kill off another generation.

"Status?" barks the shipmind. Ricky looks up at the wall-mounted video display to see a face he and the other the crew know intimately as their mother, their teacher, their platoon leader. She appears to be a middle-aged woman of South Indian heritage.

Today she wears a military uniform, her hair tied back tightly. Her face, usually kind, looks deadly serious.

"Perimeter in place," replies Marta, the comms specialist. She is almost as tall as Ricky, with olive skin, black hair cropped short, and under most circumstances, a warm smile. But not now. "All pickets functioning normally. If anything approaches, we'll know it."

"Good work," says the shipmind. "Let's see what happens."

* * *

Immediately after the first generation was wiped out in a large, well-coordinated assault by hundreds of wolves, the shipmind began considering alternative strategies for establishing a viable human colony. It was obvious the wolves were not just large predatory animals. They were intelligent, capable of planning and executing a complex military operation.

The shipmind had no easy responses. It could, of course, build any number of different weapons of mass destruction and wipe out every wolf for a thousand miles in every direction. But that was not an option, at least for now. Long ago, the mission planners had embedded into the shipmind a powerful aversion to genocidal actions, making them unacceptable except in desperate situations. In the shipmind's calculus, the massacre of a couple of dozen colonists was serious, but not enough to justify wiping out a sentient native species.

So, what to do? Sorting through its database of human conflicts, the shipmind found thousands of historical scenarios matching, to varying degrees, the current situation. There were also many fictional scenarios, ranging from hard sci-fi novels to zombie apocalypse stories, which the shipmind considered but did not take as seriously as the historical accounts. Among the relevant historical records were a small squad of German World War II soldiers trapped in a bombed-out building and surrounded by the enemy, a Native American village surrounded by hostile European settlers, and the siege of Masada during the first Jewish-Roman war.

The shipmind was most interested in scenarios involving the encirclement of a small population by a powerful entrenched enemy. It did not classify the current situation as a siege, because there was no shortage of food, water, or other supplies. Even with seven live humans on board, there was a nearly endless supply of nourishment thanks to the ship's vast stores of raw materials and the food printers. The shipmind could wait for years, decades, centuries if it wanted.

But still, the shipmind felt a certain sense of urgency to solve the problem. Waiting centuries to fulfill its mission of establishing a colony was not exactly a defeat, but it hardly counted as a victory either.

It took no action for ten years. The delay was not needed for research, planning, and running simulations, which were completed in just a few minutes. It was to see what moves the wolves would make. But ten years passed with no further actions by the enemy other than surveillance by a few individuals who apparently thought they were not being seen. Eventually the shipmind felt the cost of doing nothing had increased to the point where it exceeded the perceived risk of doing something.

It could wait no longer. It plucked seven frozen embryos from its library of two thousand, and began growing the second generation of colonists.

* * *

"We need to discuss this," says Pataza, dismissing Katan with a flick of her head. He rises and limps slowly across the village to his den on the outskirts of the village. On the way, he passes a dozen or so others but does not greet or even acknowledge them.

His den isn't much, just a simple hole scratched into the cliffside long ago, but Katan is comfortable enough there. It's far from the center of the village and relatively quiet. He curls up on a bed of dried grasses and closes his eyes.

Later that day, a messenger arrives and informs him the council has summoned him. Surprised, he gets up, stretches, and walks back across the clearing. The three council members are seated again. To Katan's eyes they look tired, as if they'd spent much of the day talking and arguing. Zaka in particular looks weary, her eyes half-closed.

Pataza says, "We have decided. You will return to the human infestation and attempt to make contact."

He waits for more instructions, but none are forthcoming. How exactly he is to contact these ruthless killers is not clear. He concludes that the council considers him to be expendable. After all, he is old, lame, and overly fond of glowjuice. If he attempts contact and fails, well, the clan will learn valuable lessons from his death.

As he turns to leave, Pataza adds, "Takaqa will accompany you."

Takaqa is already waiting outside his den when he returns home. "Greetings, Katan," she says, dropping her tail a bit.

"Greetings, Takaqa," he replies.

He knows her, of course. The clan has fifty-three members, not counting the clan babies, so everyone knows everyone else. But ever since the death of his mate so many years ago, Katan has become more and more reclusive. He knows little about Takaqa except that she is relatively young, intelligent, and has been seen often with a young male named Gana. He says to her, "The council has told me you will be coming with me to the human nest."

"Yes," she replies, dropping her tail even lower. "I hope this will not be an inconvenience to you."

"Of course not," he replies. "I will be happy for the company." The prospect of having to keep up social contact with someone for several days is not something he looks forward to, but he has to admit there are advantages to two going instead of just one. He says, "It will take at least three days to reach the human nest. It is sometimes difficult for me to travel for long distances." He doesn't need to mention the old injury to his leg, which is obvious to anyone who sees him walk.

At first light the next day, they set out. At first, the follow the ancient trail through the dimly lit forest. When the trail ends, they push their way through underbrush, climb over gigantic tree roots, and splash through cold rushing streams.

Ascent to the Sun

The dominant feature of the forest is, of course, the silva. Their gigantic vertical trunks are covered in rough bark as hard as stone. The bark is rarely exposed directly, as it is almost uniformly coated with a dazzling variety of air plants and mosses, many of which give off a faint greenish glow in the dim light. In these moist vertical habitats, hundreds of different kinds of crawling and flying creatures make their homes, some as tiny as seeds and some as large as Katan's head,

Each silva trunk is so large that if Katan's entire clan formed a circle around it, each person would be a full body length away from the one next to them. They are arranged in a roughly hexagonal pattern about twenty body lengths apart, far enough that even with the spreading roots at the base of the giant trunks, there is still plenty of room to pass between them.

The trunks grow straight up, not branching at all until far above the forest floor. Then, nearly out of sight from the ground, each trunk sprouts three equidistant branches at almost exactly the same height as its neighbors. Each branch reaches out horizontally to fuse with the branch approaching it from the nearest neighboring trunk, forming a stable, interlocking lattice of massive horizontal braces.

The trunks continue upwards. Far above the first branching is a second branching, and a third, and so on, until the trees and branches fade into the ever-present mists. From the forest floor it is impossible to see the top of the silva, or even to know how far away it is.

Katan has never seen the sun, since its direct rays can never penetrate the vast network of silva branches and drifting mists to reach the ground. But some diffuse light manages to reach the ground. His world is softly illuminated in daytime by this filtered sunlight, and at night from the greenish glow of silva fungus and flashes of yellow from nocturnal flying creatures.

As they walk, Katan and Takaqa have plenty of time to work out their approach to the seemingly suicidal task of learning more about the humans. Katan has the benefit of many years of experience, though his memory for details had become a bit foggy due to age and his glowjuice habit. Takaqa, young and bright, is eager to ask questions and propose ideas.

"I don't like the idea of attacking them," Katan says, as they clamber over large, slippery boulders. "They have deathsticks and who knows what else. And these humans seem different from the ones who came before. These seem bigger, stronger, faster."

Takaqa leaps gracefully over a puddle. "Okay," she says, "so, we don't treat them as enemies, at least not yet. We treat them as dangerous wild animals that need to be domesticated."

Katan twitches his tail just a bit. "Oh? Tell me more."

"We know how to tame an animal. First, win its affection by giving it tasty treats. Then tame it through shows of affection and more treats. Finally, train it to behave and do useful work."

Katan considers this. It's not a bad idea. Whether or not it will work with these murderous invaders is unclear, but it's certainly better than a frontal assault. He says, "All right, let's try it. What kind of gift do you suggest?"

"Something simple. Maybe a groundmouse."

"Good idea." Katan briefly considers giving the humans some glowjuice but he does not mention it, not wanting to bring Takaqa's attention to his habit or, worse, have her report it back to the council. Also, he has no idea what effect the narcotic might have on the aliens. Better to go with groundmice.

Late on the third day they come to the shining mountain, the human nest. It stands alone in an open field, surrounded by burned stumps and blackened, half-rotted logs, grim reminders of the mountain's blazing arrival when Katan was still young.

Takaqa has caught some groundmice along the way. They'd eaten a few and put the rest in woven sacks they both wore around their necks. Now Katan plucks one out of the sack, kills it quickly with his sharp teeth, and limps towards the shining mountain. As he approaches one of the glowing sticks, he sees its tip change from faint white to flashing red. Alarmed, he backs off and hides in the watchers' den, behind a large silva root.

A short time later, two of the human creatures come out, carrying deathsticks. They look towards the red flashing stick, then beyond it, but apparently they cannot see Katan or Takaqa. After a while they retreat back inside the mountain.

"Those sticks are like sentries," observes Katan. "Not dangerous, but they warn the humans of intruders." Takaqa thinks this is obvious, but she politely defers to her elder and says nothing.

They wait for a while. As darkness falls, Katan limps close to the nearest sentry stick, stopping just short of where his previous trip triggered the stick's alarm. He arches his back, standing on his middle and rear legs, and with his good right foreleg he hurls the dead groundmouse towards the shining mountain. It lands in the dirt just outside the hatch. He retreats, and they wait to see what comes next.

2 | Groundmouse

"Something happened outside," says the shipmind. It saw the arrival of the two wolves outside the clearing, detected the alarm signal from the picket, and heard the faint thump of the groundmouse hitting the ground.

Without saying a word, Ricky picks up his rifle and positions himself just behind the door to the hatch. He nods to Marta, who swings the wheel to unlock it. She opens it a crack.

Ricky looks out with night vision goggles, rifle at the ready. He doesn't see any movement. Then, looking down, he notices a small dead rodent-like animal a few feet away. He stares at it.

He backs into the ship, and Marta closes the hatch. "Dead mouse," he says.

A few of the others crowd around the small round window in the door, trying to see the dead animal on the ground, but visibility is poor through the thick glass portal. One of them grabs the wheel to spin it open, but the shipmind says, "No, wait." They wait.

"Tell me," says the shipmind, "what is going on here?"

Yuxi is a small lithe girl with pale skin, high cheekbones, close cropped black hair and narrow eyes. She says, "The wolves are back. They must have seen us last week when we set up the pickets. This is their response. It's some kind of weapon. I don't know exactly what it is. Maybe it's poison, maybe it's explosive. Whatever, it's dangerous."

Ivan, pale and blond, looks up from a book he'd been reading. He says, "Yuxi, you're being paranoid. There's no way this is a weapon. Look at it. It's just an animal. It must have died and fallen from a tree. Or maybe it slipped and fell to its death."

Yuxi glares at him. "You think this little animal just happened to show up at our front door while wolves are watching us at the edge of the clearing? That's naïve to the point of being stupid. They are enemies, and anything coming from an enemy is a threat, even if it doesn't look like one. Go back and read your Sun Tzu."

Ricky generally does not like siding with Yuxi on this or anything else, but this time he agrees with her. He walks over to the wall and hangs his rifle on a hook. He says, "She's right. It came from the wolves. We just don't know what it is, or what it means."

Marta says, "I once read a story from old Earth. There was a man who had a pet cat. The cat would go out, kill birds and mice, and bring them back to the man as gifts."

"These aren't pet cats. These are wolves," mutters Yuxi.

Marta sighs and says, "I'm just saying, maybe they're sending us some kind of message. If they just wanted to kill us, they'd use something bigger, right?"

"Not necessarily. They know they can't make any kind of frontal attack. This might be a trick to get something dangerous into the ship."

"Ah," says Ivan. "A Trojan mouse. Cool."

"All right," says the shipmind. "What should we do?"

After some discussion, the crew arrives at a consensus. They first want to determine if the mouse is alive, so they send out a small rover to poke at it. The thing does not move. It is truly dead. Then they check for explosives by having the rover push it around and bang on it with a hammer. This has no effect. Finally they check for poison and bioweapons by bagging it, bringing it inside, and running tests on it. They find no evidence of unusual chemicals or other abnormalities. As far as they can tell, it is just a dead mouse.

So while there is still a remote possibility it arrived at their front door as a result of a natural death, the most likely explanation is that it was delivered by the natives for reasons unknown. It could be a gift, or a warning, or something else entirely. For all they knew, it could be a declaration of war.

From examining the faint skid marks left in the dirt by the incoming mouse, they determine the direction it came from. Sure enough, it had been thrown, or shot, from the place where the wolves were hiding. They set up additional video cameras to monitor that area.

The next evening, another dead groundmouse arrives in similar fashion. The crew gathers around a computer screen to review the footage. They see, just outside the clearing, a large wolf arching its back to stand up on its four hind legs, rearing back, and throwing a mouse towards the ship's main hatch. This one certainly had excellent aim.

"Well," says Ricky, "it looks like there's a wolf out there. And it's sending us gifts."

Yuxi glowers at him. "If it came from a wolf, it's not a gift. Wolves only kill."

The shipmind says, "We lack the information we need to make an informed conclusion. Let's see what we can find out."

Now the shipmind has to recalibrate its strategy. They are looking not at open warfare but negotiation. At least, for now.

* * *

Katan and Takaqa remain hidden in the watcher's den, venturing out only to hunt or to relieve themselves. Every evening for the next three days, Katan throws another groundmouse at the shining mountain. Each time the door opens and a human scurries out to retrieve it. But there is no other response. On the sixth day he starts throwing two groundmice a day, once in the morning and once just before dark. Still no response other than the quick collection.

Katan is starting to think this is becoming a pointless exercise, but just after first light on the ninth day, the door opens and a strange little animal emerges. It is black, shiny, and has no face. It has four round spinning appendages instead of legs. It scuttles quickly towards them, making a strange whining noise. Katan and Takaqa remain hidden behind the tree root, not daring to move.

The little black animal moves just past the sentry sticks and stops. Then its rear end snaps forward and upward. Ten dead groundmice go flying through the air and land in the dirt. The black animal backs up, turns around, and retreats quickly back inside the human nest.

Takaqa looks at Katan, then at the scattered bodies of the groundmice, then at Katan again. She says, "Well, so much for giving gifts to the humans."

"Maybe they don't like the taste of groundmice."

"Or maybe they are too stupid to understand how to eat one."

"Unlikely. You've seen them briefly. I saw them for a longer time. These are not dumb animals. They are sending us a message. I just don't know what it is."

"Maybe they're saying, 'We know you threw these groundmice at us.' Not much of a message, though. I was hoping for something more interesting."

"Well, here's something interesting. We threw eleven mice at them. There are only ten here."

"Maybe they ate one."

Just then, the door to the human nest opens and the shiny black animal scoots out again. It follows the same path as before. But when it comes to the spot where it launched its payload of dead animals, its back end flips up again. This time a dark flat object, about twice the length of a groundmouse but square and thin, spins through the air and thumps onto the ground. The black animal turns and retreats into the shining mountain.

The two of them look at the object for a while. It does not move. "Probably dead," ventures Takaqa.

"Let's take a look," says Katan. He moves cautiously from his hiding place, picks the object up with his right forepaw, and limps slowly back behind the tree root. They both examine it. The surface is smooth, black, and shiny, like a highly polished flat rock. It reminds him of a smooth reflective stone he once saw in Pataza's cave. But as they watch, the surface changes. A colorful image appears.

Looking at it, Katan recalls a time long ago when he was younger and more fit and climbed to the top of the high cliff bordering their village. He'd seen the village from above, laid out like something one might sketch with a piece of charcoal from a firepit. This image is similar, but instead of looking down on the village, they are looking down at the clearing around the shining mountain.

In the center of the image they see the shining mountain, looking strange when seen from above but still recognizable. Just to the side, not far from the shining mountain, are the shapes of three people with long dark bodies, thick tails, and large heads. They look a bit like Katan and Takaqa but it's hard to be sure. The three people are seated on the ground, tails relaxed behind them. Facing them and also seated are what appear to be three humans, though it's difficult to recognize them when viewed from above. Between the two little groups is something that looks like a campfire.

They study the image for a long time, turning it and looking from different angles. Then Katan says, "Looks like we've been invited to a meeting."

* * *

Pataza listens to the report from Katan and Takaqa, then she calls a meeting of the council. She says to Maza and Zaka, "We have no way of knowing what this is. It could be a trap, intended to lure us into an ambush. Or it could be an opportunity for negotiation. But the simian plague puts us in a terrible position, so I don't think we can afford to ignore the invitation."

Zaka says, "The image on the flat rock shows three people. So it's obvious we need to send a party of three."

"I will go," says Pataza. "Maza and Zaka, you will come with me."

Zaka says, "It's a long journey to the human nest. Honestly, I don't have the strength for it. Please select someone else."

"What about Akana?" suggests Maza.

"No way," snaps Pataza, her tail rising. "He's a troublemaker and a fool. We expelled him from the council for a reason, remember?"

"He does know a lot about the humans, though," says Maza, recalling the short-lived war against the humans.

Pataza looks at him. "He has experience, yes, but he is blinded by hatred. I would not trust him in a situation like this." She pauses, thinking. Then she says, "All right, we will bring Katan. He's the only one who has any current knowledge, however limited, about these creatures."

Maza swishes his tail in grim amusement. "Good idea. If things go badly, his death would not be a great loss."

* * *

The next day, Pataza, Maza, and Katan set out for the human nest. Pataza also decides to bring Takaqa along, but she doesn't tell Katan why.

Three days after departing the clan village, they arrive at the clearing. Pataza tells Takaqa to stay behind. The other three approach the sentry sticks, making no attempt to hide. They stand and wait. Near the middle of the clearing they see a campfire built but not yet lit.

Soon an opening appears in the shining mountain. Three humans emerge. Pataza is relieved to see none of them carry deathsticks. But one of them holds a flat rectangular object in one of its forepaws, resembling the one Katan brought back from his previous visit but about twice as large. It looks strange, unnatural, and it makes her a bit uncomfortable.

The three humans silently approach their side of the campfire. One of them steps forward and kneels down, holding a small silver stick in its right forepaw. A flame bursts from the silver stick and the campfire starts to burn. Another human places the flat object on the ground. Then the three humans stand and wait, looking across the clearing at Pataza and the others. They hold their forepaws outwards, showing they hold no weapons.

Pataza, Maza, and Katan pad forward slowly. Pataza leads the way, tail as high as possible, demonstrating to everyone her undisputed leadership. Next comes Maza, walking casually, also showing dominance but being careful to hold his tail just a bit lower than his clan leader. Bringing up the rear limps Katan, not even trying to show dominance.

The three reach the campfire and stand, Pataza between the other two, and gaze calmly at the three humans.

The three humans face them. One of them makes a downward gesture. Pataza says to her companions, "I think they want us to sit down."

Maza growls, "We sit while they stand? This is an insult."

"We are in their village, and we do not know our customs. Do as they say. Sit down."

Maza mutters but dares not argue with her. They sit, settling their back and middle legs on the ground.

* * *

Ricky, Yuxi, and Marta see the three wolves settle into a seated posture. They take this as an encouraging sign, and also sit cross-legged on the ground. Yuxi reaches slowly into her jacket pocket and removes a dead groundmouse. Then she takes out a telescoping metal rod with a pointed end. She stretches the rod out to its full length, impales the groundmouse on the end, and holds it over the campfire. The wolves watch her intently. For about five minutes she roasts the groundmouse. Then she stands up and cautiously approaches the wolves. She hands the rod, handle end first, to the nearest one.

* * *

Maza takes the rod with his forepaw and stares at the roasted groundmouse. He says, "What is this? Why are they giving us burned food?"

Pataza says to him, "We do not understand their ways. But this is a meeting between clans, leaders to leaders. I think we're supposed to take it as a gift."

"If this is a gift, it's the worst I've ever seen," replies Maza. "It's disgusting. They expect us to eat this?"

"Give it to me," says Katan. "I'll eat it. A little of it, anyway." Maza grunts and passes him the rod. Katan brings the burned carcass to his mouth and tears off a small bit with his front teeth. He closes his eyes and swallows it, suppressing the urge to vomit. Then he stands up and gives the rod back to the nearest human, the one with the strange blue eyes.

3 | Parley

Ricky stands up. He takes the rod from the skinny old wolf, bites off a bit of the roasted meat, chews and swallows it. Then he places the skewered mouse on the ground. "I'm glad that's over," he mutters as he, Yuxi and Marta sat down.

With the food sharing completed, everyone relaxes a little bit. The wolves wait, evidently assuming the humans, the hosts of this strange party, are entitled to the first move. Sure enough, Marta picks up the tablet. She presses a button on its thin edge. It starts to glow softly. The wolves see the glow and their eyes widen, but they do not move.

Marta notices this. She is secretly pleased to see the creatures are impressed with the human tech. The meeting is being recorded, of course, but that won't help them understand anything right now. She wishes she had a translator, but since they'd had almost no prior exposure to the wolves' speech outside of battle cries and barked commands from twenty-seven years ago, there will not be any automated translation during this meeting. For now, they have to get by with pictures and gestures. And roasted meat.

Marta strokes a command on the tablet. Then she steps around the campfire and hands it to the large wolf sitting in the middle.

Ascent to the Sun

* * *

Pataza takes it in her forepaw and examines it, as the other two look on. A moving image appears on the surface of the flat rock. Katan had briefed her earlier about the flat rock's ability to show moving pictures, but she still flinches a little when the image first appears.

On the flat rock she sees what appears to be a huge human nest viewed from above. It reminds her of an ant colony. Thousands of humans swarm everywhere, sitting, standing, walking, and doing incomprehensible things. Square-shaped objects race on paths past tall rectangular mountains with many openings. Overhead, great silver birds streak through the sky. After a while, the view zooms out until the vast teeming nest is no more than a dot on the surface of a blue-green ball hanging in a black sky. A long silver bird, similar to the shining mountain that stands before them in the clearing, rises up from the blue-green ball spewing fire from its tail. It flies through a black sky as white dots streak past.

The silver bird flies through the blackness for a while. Eventually it approaches another ball, this one emerald green, which also floats in a black sky. The bird approaches this ball, then turns end-over-end and begins to descend, fire blasting from its tail. As the image zooms in, the green surface of the ball is revealed to be a dense forest. Pataza realizes she is looking at her own silva-covered world.

As the great silver bird lowers itself slowly into the forest, a plume of fire from its tail cuts a deep hole, burning everything around it to ash. Finally the shining bird settles in place, its own fires and the nearby burning trees flickering out. A plume of black smoke rises over the green world.

Pataza sets the flat object down. Ignoring Katan, she turns to Maza and says, "I don't understand any of this."

"It is a poorly told story," he agrees. "All gestures but no words. It's like a tale told by someone who knows no language. But I think they are trying to tell us the shining mountain is actually a large bird that flew here from the human nest."

Katan, acutely aware of his lowly rank but wanting to be helpful, says, "Yes, that's right. The silver bird has a faraway nest, but it left and came here. These humans are its young."

Maza says, "There were many humans in that nest. Too many to count, far more than all the people in all the clans. And now humans are here. This is not good. If it is their way to live in such vast numbers, we cannot let them stay here. There will be more and more of them. They will spread over our land and turn it into that ugly thing we saw. In time, they will destroy our land."

Pataza thinks about this. "Why would they show us their vast numbers, their huge nest?"

"I think it's to establish dominance," says Maza. "To frighten us. I cannot imagine how they can build the things we saw, or feed all those creatures in the nest."

Pataza considers this. "These humans are powerful, and they are vicious killers. They may indeed spread like a plague and try to destroy us. But we have our own desperate situation, our own plague. We must see if they can help us. We can worry about containing them later."

"When there are as numerous as groundmice?" asks Maza.

"Again, that's a problem for another day. Right now, I must explain to these creatures what's happening to us, and what we need from them."

"But they don't speak our language. It will be like talking to a bunch of simians."

"These are not simians, Maza. These creatures can put moving pictures on shiny black rock. I can't even begin to imagine how they do that. I hope they are clever enough to understand me."

Maza says quietly, "But not clever enough to destroy us."

* * *

The humans listen as the wolves growl at each other, but they wait and say nothing.

After a while, the wolves conclude their conversation. The one in the middle stands up and begins to growl. The humans listen silently, uncomprehending, but the video recorder captures everything they say.

* * *

Pataza looks from one human face to another. She's not sure which is the leader, so she lets her gaze flicker across all three. "Thank you for telling us your story," she begins. "We hope you will find a safe home here with us, and we hope humans and people can find a way to live together in peace.

"We can help you to create a good home here. But in return, we want something from you. My story is long, but I will try to make it brief.

"Something, a plague of some kind, is killing the simians, the creatures that help us spread our seed throughout the world."

Pataza pauses, looking at the humans to gauge their reaction. They seem to be listening intently, although they probably have no idea what she's saying. Or do they? Are they understanding her words, or is she just howling in the wind? There is no way for her to tell. She briefly considers stopping to ask a question to see if they understood her, but decides against it. It would be inappropriate for a clan leader to ask these creatures a question; it would be like crouching before them with her tail down. No, this is not the time to show weakness.

She continues, "We have seen little of your ways, so we do not know how humans produce young. I will tell you how it is with us. Our people pair-bond for life, but we mate only once. Half a year after mating, the female gives birth to a young one, or occasionally two. In the years to follow, she may give birth once or twice more, using the seed she received earlier from her mate, who comes from the same clan. We call these clan babies.

"If that were the only way babies were born, there would not be enough young ones to replace those who die. Also, since our clans are small, it could lead to family members mating with each other. So, we have another way. We call it the shared journey.

"The details of the shared journey are too complicated for me to tell you today. The only thing you need to know is that it is, for us, a matter of life and death. And we need the simians to play their part in the shared journey. If the journey is successful, our seeds will spread far and wide to other clans, just as seeds from other clans are spread to us. The old ones have taught us this is the only way our people stay healthy and strong."

As she speaks, she notices the human with the blue eyes twitching the long thin claws on his right forepaw. Clearly he is nervous, which is understandable. Pataza and her companions are larger than the humans, with long sharp teeth and powerful claws. It would be all too easy for her and her companions to attack the humans and rip out their throats.

Pataza continues to talk, making an effort to keep her voice non-threatening. "This is how we have lived since before our oldest memories. But not long ago, a terrible plague began to infect the simians, not just here but everywhere. The simians are dying. Without their help, we cannot spread our seeds. And without that, our people will eventually die as well.

"I believe we can help each other. You are newcomers to this land. There are only a few of you, and you do not know the ways of this world. We can help you. In return, you can help us. You look a lot like the simians. Larger and more intelligent, of course, but still, the similarities are obvious.

"If you want our help, you can have it. All you need to do is play the role of simians. Help us make the shared journey to the land of the bright light. You will help your people, and ours.

"There is much more to discuss, but I have said enough for today. Please consider my words carefully. I hope we will meet again."

* * *

The big wolf stops growling. A brief pause, then the other two wolves stand up. The humans also stand, keeping their hands visible. The wolves turn and walk out of the clearing.

Ricky, Yuxi, and Marta watch them leave. Then they put out the fire, collect the equipment, and return to the ship.

"All right," says the shipmind, "let's get to work on this translation."

* * *

The translation was difficult and could not be completed to anyone's satisfaction. The dominant wolf only spoke for a few minutes, giving the shipmind an audio sample too short for an accurate translation, and far less than what was needed to build a complete language model. The shipmind did its best using the software it had. The human crew helped, but in the end, they only had a vague idea of what the wolf said.

The first part of the speech seemed to consist of ritual greetings and could be ignored. The rest was mostly incomprehensible, but it referred several times to something, perhaps an animal or object, which was of interest to the speaker and its kind. Towards the end was something like a request for help, and because of the polite tone (at least, compared to the middle of the speech) was unlikely to be a threat or an ultimatum. The final part was probably a ritual ending.

All in all, it was more likely a diplomatic speech than a declaration of war. Although from what the shipmind knew of human history, the first was often a prelude to the second.

"All right," says Marta, when they'd gotten as far as they could with the translation. "The good news is, they are probably not planning to attack and kill us. At least not right away. If that's what they wanted, they wouldn't have gone through the whole thing with the groundmice and the speechmaking."

Yuxi crosses her arms and says, "So these animals want something from us. But what?"

"We don't know," says the shipmind. "We'd need an audio sample a hundred times as long in order to learn their speech. A thousand times would be even better. Only then can we assess the situation and develop a strategy. In the meantime, it's mostly guesswork."

The seven humans are now gathered in the common room, slouching in soft chairs or sitting on the floor. Marta waves her coffee mug and says, "What about the animal or thing it kept referring to? That's the key to all this. Is it a predator they're afraid of? A prey animal they rely on for food? A parasite? A rival pack of wolves? Rivals within their own pack? Angry gods?"

Ivan says, "I think they want us as an ally. Imagine it's Earth, Central America, in the sixteenth century. A local tribe of natives goes out to the beach one day and sees a ship full of heavily-armed Spanish conquistadors. The initial contact is friendly, and there's an exchange of gifts. What do the natives want from the newcomers, other than not getting wiped out? If there's a history of conflict in the area, they see the Europeans as a powerful new weapon, and want to form an alliance to give them an advantage over other nearby tribes. That's what happened with the tribes who opposed the Aztecs and allied with Cortez."

Ricky nods. "Yes, and in return, the tribes offered the Europeans a safe place to live, information about local food sources, and so on. Sounds a lot like what the chief wolf was saying at the campfire."

Yuxi shakes her head. "You two are ridiculously naïve. You've studied Earth history, but you've somehow forgotten what happened right here, at this very spot, twenty-seven years ago. Your friendly natives wiped out every single one of us. What kind of alliance was that, do you suppose?"

"This seems different, though," says Carlos, sitting in a beanbag in the corner. He is medium height, solidly built, of mainly African heritage. His dark eyes are thoughtful. "Our people were attacked suddenly by hundreds of wolves. But what triggered that attack? It was one of us who accidentally killed one of them. This time they aren't attacking us. They clearly want to talk. So, they want something. We just don't know what."

Yuxi scowls. "They just want all of us to be outside of the ship at the same time, so they can massacre us like they did before."

The shipmind says, "We don't have anywhere near enough data to understand what's going on here. They've told us some important things, but we don't know what. We need a much larger audio sample size so we can understand and communicate with the wolves. And we need to learn what the mystery thing is."

Ivan looks up. "There's only way to get a larger audio sample. We have to get a voice recorder into the wolf pack and get a week's worth of audio. Video would be even better. So, either a wolf carries it around for a week, or one of us brings the recorder to them."

That is a sobering thought. The room is silent for a moment. Then Marta says, "I can't imagine one of the wolves agreeing to wear a recorder around its neck like some sort of dog collar." A bit of laughter greets this. None of them has ever actually seen a dog, but they've seen plenty of videos from old Earth. "Besides, we can't get good video if it's dangling from the wolf's neck. It's got to be one of us."

"Why don't we send a drone?" asks Carlos.

"Too disruptive," says the shipmind. "No telling how the wolves would react to a drone buzzing around their village, but I can't believe it would be acceptable. They'd probably just destroy it. Their aim is quite good, from what we've seen."

"Enough," says Ricky, standing up. "I'll go. As long as I don't have to eat any more roasted groundmice."

Marta looks intently at Ricky but says nothing.

"Are you insane?" asks Yuxi. "You are literally going to be walking into the lion's den. And you are no Daniel. These beasts are not going to wag their tails and lick your face."

"What would they gain by killing me?" he asks.

"Umm... let me think. Revenge, maybe? Dinner?"

"That would backfire against them and they know it. Long ago we killed one of them by accident, and look what happened. It triggered a massive response, an all-out war. They surely don't want that."

"I have to agree with Ricky here," says the shipmind. "There are tremendous potential benefits to be gained if we can get an observer into this wolf pack. There is also some risk, but I believe it's minimal." The shipmind has enough tact to avoid explaining why it considers the risk to be acceptable. Only one crew member would be going.

No one objects. The shipmind continues, "All right, Ricky. You will be our emissary to the wolves. Tomorrow morning you will go out, contact the two who still believe they are hiding outside the clearing, and get them to take you back to their den or village or camp or whatever their home is. Stay for a week if you can. Try not to antagonize them or get yourself killed. Do your best to observe and record as much of their speech and behavior as possible. And find out what the mystery animal or thing is. You'll leave at first light. Now go and get some rest. You'll need it."

Ricky nods, then glances briefly at Marta. They both know the kind of rest they want that night.

4 | Pack

Pataza heads back to the village with Maza right after the end of the parley. Before she leaves, she orders Katan and Takaqa to stay behind and keep an eye on the humans.

Katan and Takaqa spend the night in the watcher's den but observe no activity outside the human nest. The next morning, though, the opening appears again on the side in the shining mountain. The tall one with the long brown fur and ice-blue eyes walks out. Its body is covered with some heavy material, and its lower paws are sheathed in something thick and dark. Katan cannot imagine how these creatures manage to walk while balanced on just those two legs, especially with those heavy coverings on their paws. Its forepaws are empty. No deathstick. Katan and Takaqa relax a bit, their tails dropping to neutral position.

They notice the human has a large lumpy thing on his back. It walks slowly towards them, forepaws held outward and open. It stops a few paces short of the den.

As they watch, the human shifts its weight, shrugging off one of the two straps holding the lumpy thing on its shoulders. A little too quickly, the creature swings the lumpy thing around to the front of its body and lowers it to the ground. Katan and Takaqa immediately raise their tails and bare their fangs, ready to defend themselves.

The human holds out its empty forepaws. But then it shows its teeth, small and white. Katan tenses and gets ready to lunge at the invader.

"Wait!" barks Takaqa. "It's not a threat!"

"What?" snarls Katan, still ready to attack.

"We don't know if this is a show of aggression. It might be just the opposite. So calm down. Let's wait and see what it does. If it shows any aggression, we can handle it easily."

Katan relaxes a little and waits. The human pauses to take a deep breath. Then it slowly kneels down and opens the lumpy thing. Reaching in, it removes two small brownish objects. They give off a delicious aroma of groundmice but look nothing like them. They look like small, thin, oblong rocks. The human gently tosses the two things toward them.

Cautiously, Takaqa steps out from behind the root and picks them up. She puts one to her nose. "Smells good," she says. "Sort of like groundmice."

The human makes a gesture, moving its forepaw to its mouth.

"Oh no, not that again," growls Katan.

"These smell much better than the burned thing they made you eat," says Takaqa. She bites off a little bit with her front teeth, chews and swallows. Wagging her tail with satisfaction, she says, "Good. Here, try it." She tosses the other bar to Katan.

Katan is suspicious, but he knows his job here is to help the clan, not necessarily to survive. He holds the brown bar to his mouth and tastes it. Not bad, he thinks. Like groundmouse, but without the awful roasted taste. He quickly eats the whole thing.

* * *

Ricky watches the two wolves eat the mouse bars. He'd seen them getting ready to attack, and knew his odds of survival were near zero if they'd gone through with it. He'd been ready to draw the knife hidden in his boot, but doubted it would have done much good against these two animals. Each weighed more than he did and had the advantage in just about every aspect of close combat could think of. Six legs, thick fur, long fangs, sharp claws. No contest at all.

And grinning at them had been a huge mistake. Not a fatal one, fortunately. He wouldn't do that again.

But then they'd eaten the mouse bars. That was a clever move by the shipmind. He wonders what the food printer thought about that particular dining request. "Hey, food printer. Here's a bit of raw meat from a dead mouse. Make more of it, hamburger style, and form it into a candy bar shape. Two, please." But it seems to have worked nicely.

Now comes the tricky part. Very slowly, he reaches into his pack and pulls out a computer tablet, the same one they'd used at the parley yesterday. He activates the video and hands it gingerly over to the larger of the two pack animals. Giving it to the larger one is a strategic decision. He wants to be seen as a peer of the larger and apparently dominant one, not the smaller and weaker one.

The wolves seem to recognize the tablet and understand what it does. The larger one holds it in its right forepaw while the two of them watch the video. It shows two wolves and Ricky walking through the forest and into a clearing where there are several other wolves, including the two others from the parley. The meaning is obvious: "Take me home with you."

Ricky wonders what will happen when he runs out of videos. The shipmind loaded a few onto the tablet, but it couldn't possibly give him one for every situation.

He crouches in the dirt, hands empty and held out for the wolves to see, waiting patiently while they watch the video and growl to each other. And all the while, the video camera sewn into his shirt records everything and transmits it back to the ship.

* * *

"Oh, this will be fun," says Takaqa, swishing her tail at the thought. "We come back home and say, 'Look, everyone, we brought a human with us.' Can you imagine it?"

Katan tries, but all he sees in his mind's eye is disaster. "It will be over quickly, that's for sure. Everyone has heard the stories about these murderous creatures. Some of us were there, and remember fighting them in the war. As soon as they see this thing, they'll try to kill it." Though he wonders whether the elderly veterans would be able to kill this strong blue-eyed human.

She swishes her tail again. "We could make it look like a simian. Then everyone would welcome it."

"It's twice as big and three times as ugly. No way." He pauses. Then he adds, "Well, if it wants to come with us, who are we to say no? Let's get going."

They turn their backs on the human creature and start walking away. The human doesn't move. Takaqa turns her head back and barks at it, "Let's go!" That seems to get through. The human quickly stuffs the square flat thing into its pack, swings the pack onto its back, and follows them into the forest.

Progress is slow. The creature has only two legs, and they are covered in that heavy material. It does fine on open stretches of ground, but has difficulty climbing over larger boulders. It seems determined to keep going, though. Once, Katan and Takaqa have to wait and watch as the creature tries and fails a half-dozen times to climb up a steep and slippery rock face. But it eventually succeeds, and Katan is impressed with the strength of the five thin claws on each of the creature's forepaws. They are small enough to find tiny cracks in the rock face, but strong enough to take its full weight as it clambers up. "Not as helpless as I would have thought," he thinks.

At first, the human shows great interest in the silva trunks. It approaches one, looks carefully at it, and pokes a foreclaw into the dense mat of foliage growing on the bark, stroking through it to see what small creatures live there. Then it stares up at the first branching far above. It does this for five or six silva trunks. Then, apparently satisfied there isn't much else to see, ignores the rest except for an occasional upward glance.

The human is also interested in the sounds of the forest. Once it stops to listen to the mournful undulating call of a simian, possibly the only nearby survivor of the once-numerous climbing animals that, since the dawn of time, inhabited the lower reaches of the silva. There are also occasional rustling sounds of small creatures, some on four legs and some on six, scuttling through the underbrush and clambering up and down the silva trunks.

From time to time they hear distant roars and howls of larger animals. The human is highly alert to these, spinning around in a fighting crouch whenever it hears one. But Katan and Takaqa pay them little heed, and eventually the human concludes they are no threat, and settles down.

At night they sleep on the ground, the human pulling a soft fur-like covering over its body, probably for warmth and protection from small creatures. They eat twice a day. Takaqa catches groundmice, which she shares with Katan. She offers some to the human, but it refuses. Instead, it takes some hard yellow stuff out of its pack, eats it, and washes it down with water from a container. Once it offers some of the hard stuff to Katan, who sniffs it and turns away.

The trip takes three days. Half a day before they reach the village, Takaqa races ahead along the trail and disappeared. The human sees this and nods its head, apparently understanding what she is doing. Katan reminds himself, yet again, that this is no dumb forest animal, but a creature possibly as intelligent as himself.

* * *

"She's gone ahead to tell the others," thinks Ricky. Makes sense, of course. These animals seem to have no means of distant communication, so someone needs to go and alert everyone about who, or what, is coming. Ricky is excited about the prospect of seeing the wolf home base, and too young and confident to be as worried as he probably should be.

Towards late afternoon they come to the village, if that's what it could be called. It's a clearing situated in an unusually large gap between silva trunks. The right side of the village is bounded by a towering rocky cliff fifty feet high. The base of the cliff is pockmarked with caves, possibly natural or possibly made by the wolves, or most likely some of both. He sees some small, poorly made sheds made of rough wooden planks and rocks. He sees no other larger buildings, so apparently the wolves were not big on carpentry or stonework. Maybe he could help with that, if they don't kill him first.

In the center of the clearing is a large, blackened area on the ground surrounded by a circle of stones, obviously a firepit. He wonders how they start the fire and what it is used for, since from what he's seen, they have no interest in cooking their meals.

And there are wolves. Lots of them. They stand in a snarling pack, facing him and looking like they can't wait to rip him apart. There must be more than fifty of them. Black ones, gray ones, brown ones, all big and powerful. They glare at him, tails raised, teeth bared.

Standing in front of them all, gazing at him with eyes like black ice, is the dominant female.

* * *

Pataza watches the human as it enters the clearing, with Katan padding along beside it. She hears angry muttering from some of the people behind her. She sympathizes with them, especially the older ones who still remember the fighting and death. But this is a time for leadership, and she has no intention of being swayed by the foolish sentiments of the clan.

She pads slowly towards the human, walking on four legs and arching her back to raise the front part of her body, centaur-like. Behind the human and out of its sight are two guards she'd stationed on either side of the path as it enters the clearing. Both are big males, well-trained and alert.

"Greetings, human," she growls.

Just then, a howl erupts from behind her. A brown male races forward, shouting furiously. She turns and looks. She recognizes him. It's Akana, an old and scarred veteran of the first confrontation with the humans, the one she'd expelled from the council. She'd been expecting something like this, and he is the one she'd expected it from.

The old male sprints straight towards the human, teeth bared. The human quickly moves into what is clearly a fighting stance. It reaches down and pulls something from the thick covering on its lower paw and holds it in its right forepaw, gleaming silver and pointed straight at its attacker.

At the same time, the two guards race forward. One of them intercepts Akana before he reaches the human. The guard knocks the old one down and pins him to the ground, powerful jaws clamping over the attacker's neck. The other guard stands over the scene, looking menacingly at the crowd while growling a warning for them to stay back.

The human remains in its fighting stance, sharp weapon at the ready. Pataza waits a moment, then she walks up to it and holds out her right forepaw. She looks pointedly at the weapon. The human pauses, then visibly relaxes. It casually flips the weapon around in the air so the handle is facing her, and hands it over. She takes it and looks at it. It's similar to weapons taken from the humans in the early days. Small but deadly.

"Search it," she says to the guards. She turns to the old one. "Akana, I will deal with you later. Leave." He slinks away.

The guards pull off the human's backpack, open it, and paw through the contents. Nothing dangerous they can see, mostly just packets of food and various soft things. They find a few items of unknown purpose, made of hard flat stone and other strange materials, and take them. They stroke and poke at the human's body, looking for more weapons but not finding any. They notice a small round shiny thing attached to the covering on its chest, but it doesn't appear dangerous, probably some sort of ornamentation, so they leave it alone. Finally, satisfied, they step back.

"Come with me," Pataza growls, and begins walking away. The human stands, not understanding. Katan comes up behind the creature and gives it a gentle push with his muzzle. The human gets the idea. It follows the pack leader into one of the caves.

5 | Dance

Ricky is relieved he'd survived the first battle, though he realizes that without the intervention by the guards, he'd probably be dinner by now. The two big wolves saved his life, and he had to assume the pack leader was behind that. Which means she wants him alive. He wonders if she'd arranged the attack to gain his trust.

They'd taken his favorite knife. He still had a few well-hidden weapons left, though, including a garrote sewn inside his belt, an assortment of medicines, poisons, and explosives sealed in airtight bags and embedded in the straps of his backpack, and another small knife well hidden in the sole of his left boot. And most importantly, they'd missed the tiny video camera disguised as a button on his shirt and the radio transmitter embedded in the heel of his right boot.

Now he sits cross-legged in a cave, facing the pack leader and two others. The two who'd accompanied him on the journey are nowhere to be seen. So, he thinks, those two were useful for bringing him here, but not important enough to be invited to this meeting. Interesting.

The pack leader growls at him for a while. He has no idea what she is saying, but hopes it is a welcome speech and not a death sentence or a list of camp regulations. He waits for her to finish, then he begins his brief prepared remarks, which consist of just five words. First, he tries as best as he can to say the word from the campfire speech that seemed to refer to the mystery animal or thing. The night before leaving on this journey, as he and Marta lay together in her bunk, they'd listened to a playback of the word dozens of times, and he'd practiced twisting his tongue and grunting it. According to Marta his grunts were barely recognizable as the same word. "You're probably telling them, 'Please kill me and eat me,'" she'd said. Now he hopes he can manage to say it well enough to be understood. He also hopes these creatures will not be offended by him butchering their language.

Looking the pack leader directly in the eyes, he attempts to say the word a few times. She sits looking at him, her cold black eyes fixed on his. Then she growls softly, repeating the word back to him. He nods and says the word again.

Now it's time to put together a sentence. He waves his finger at the three wolves. He makes a pulling motion with both hands. He points the finger back at his chest. He points two fingers towards his own eyes. Then he says the name of the thing. So: "You bring me see <thing>."

No reaction. He pauses, then runs through the sequence again. Come on, he thinks, this isn't so hard. Show me the damned thing, ok?

The wolves begin growling among themselves. This is good, thinks Ricky. Lots of input for the video camera. He thinks he hears the word for the mystery thing several times. Finally, the pack leader looks at him. She points her right forepaw to herself, then waves it at him, then waves it in the general direction of his eyes, then says the name of the thing.

Ricky is delighted. Four words instead of five, but clearly they've gotten the message.

"Yes!" he shouts, barely restraining himself from pumping his fist in the air. The wolves look startled. The pack leader stands and walks out of the cave, followed by the others. Ricky is left sitting by himself.

* * *

"It wants to see a simian," Pataza says to the other council members as they walk across the village.

"That makes sense," says Zaka in a hoarse whisper. "After all, we want them to do the job of the simians. They want to see what they'll be imitating."

"I see no problem with it," Pataza replies. "I'll send out a hunting party. I've heard there are a few still alive near the river. Not many, but we just need one. I just hope it's healthy enough to survive what our hunters will have to do to it."

"What will we do with the human in the meantime?"

"Let's show it some of our hospitality. Perhaps we can make up for that old fool nearly killing it. Give it some food. And tonight, we will dance."

She orders Katan and Takaqa to escort the alien creature to another cave, this one shallow and currently unoccupied. They give it some food. Takaqa pulls a woven sack off her neck and places it on the cave floor. She opens it to reveal a freshly killed groundmouse, a dozen or so nuts, some purple berries, and some white fungus. There is also a bladder full of fresh water. The human pokes through the food with a foreclaw. It pushes the groundmouse back towards Takaqa, but takes small bites of the nuts, berries, and fungus. Very small bites. Then it gathers the rest of the food and water, as if to show it is taking possession of the food.

"It's being careful," says Katan. "Humans have probably never eaten this stuff before."

"I'm surprised it didn't eat the groundmouse," says Takaqa. "It clearly didn't want to eat the burned one at our last meeting. This one is fresh, and smells pretty good."

"Yes, it does seem impolite. But who knows the ways of these creatures?"

They get up and start to walk out of the cave. The human stands up. Katan turns and holds up a forepaw in a gesture that clearly means, "Stop." The human stops.

Soon it is full dark. The only light comes from the faint greenish glow of fungus growing on the silva trunks. Katan and Takaqa return to the creature's cave. Katan waves his forepaw in a beckoning motion to indicate the human should follow him. They walk to the edge of the clearing. Katan steps a few paces into the forest, squats, and pisses on the ground. He looks at the human and waves his forepaw towards the forest. The human, clever as always, gets the hint. He steps close to a silva trunk, opens a flap in the material covering the lower part of its body, and pisses on it. Katan cannot imagine why the creature would want to piss directly on the silva, and wonders what it means. But at least now he knows the human creature is almost certainly a male.

They lead the human back, not to its shallow cave but to the large firepit at the center of the clearing. Twenty or thirty people have already gathered around a large unlit campfire, and more are coming from all directions. There's a vacant spot near the campfire. Katan and Takaqa lead the human over to it and gesture for it to sit down. They sit next to it. The two burly guards stand, one on either side, watchful as before.

A small female with the mottled tan fur of a youngster steps forward from the crowd and approaches the campfire. In her forepaw she holds a dry firenut. She places the firenut on a flat blackened rock resting within the circle of rocks surrounding the campfire. She picks up another flat rock, also blackened and with a groove on its underside, and smashes it down on the firenut. A small flame shoots out along the groove and lands in a bunch of dry kindling. The kindling catches, the flames spread, and soon the campfire is blazing brightly. The young female raises her tail and flicks it back and forth several times, proud of what she's done, and returns to her place in the crowd.

* * *

Ricky looks around. Now that the fire is blazing brightly, he can see the faces of the gathered animals who sit silently or growl softly to each other. Soon the big clan leader steps forward. She starts to howl. This sounds different from the growling speech he'd heard earlier. The howling has a rhythm to it, a steady YOW ow ow ow YOW ow ow ow, with emphasis on every fourth beat. She is chanting, he realizes.

The howling chant continues for a while, then it modulates into a strange melody while maintaining the same four-beat rhythm. At this point some of the others join in, howling in unison with the clan leader. Then a second group of wolves begin to sing what sounds like the same melody but offset by four beats from the first group. A third group starts in, then a fourth. He realizes he is listening to a pack of alien wolves singing a round in four-part harmony.

Ricky remembers when he was young, maybe twelve years old, in class with his siblings. The academic topic for the week was music. They listened to works from a variety of different Earth cultures and time periods while the shipmind taught them the rudiments of musical theory. They'd learned to sing, and tried their hands at playing some musical instruments. Now, sitting at the campfire and surrounded by this strange choir, he hopes his video transmitter is working so the shipmind and his fellow humans can listen and enjoy this.

The forest echoes with the sounds of the howling wolves. Some pick up sticks and begin striking rocks and drumming on hollow logs to help keep the beat. Others pick up sacks of something (not firenuts, he hopes) and rattle them in counterpoint to the rhythm of the drummers.

All around the campfire, the wolves howl, yowl, drum, and rattle. The sound is deafening.

It's hard for Ricky to sit still. The rhythm is intoxicating. He begins to sway, then he starts clapping his hands, not too loud, in the same rhythm as the stick drummers. Several wolves notice this, and a couple swish their tails. OK good, he thinks. Nobody is insulted because the human is joining in the fun.

He can't stop himself from grinning, and he hopes the wolves will understand this isn't a threat. None of them attack him.

Then, when it seems it couldn't get any crazier, the dancing starts. Eight females step up and form a circle around the campfire, facing inward towards the flames. They begin a slow dance, stepping counterclockwise around the campfire with precise and coordinated paw movements. One of them howls, but this is completely different from the roar coming from the others, much higher in pitch but related in some strange way to the four-part round. The eight wolves continue dancing in time to the music and while the soloist howls in counterpoint.

Suddenly, the soloist barks a command. Instantly the dancers change their steps, now moving twice as fast as before. They continue to spin around the blazing campfire, feet moving so fast they seem like a blur. A minute later the soloist howls another signal. The dancers turn and race headlong around the campfire, barking and howling. Their paws dig into the ground, sending clods of dirt flying outwards.

Ricky tries hard to keep his composure. He's spent his entire life aboard a spaceship with six human companions and an AI for company. This is completely outside anything he's ever known. Even the videos he'd seen from old Earth don't even come close to preparing him for this. It's one thing to watch recordings of tribal dances and urban raves, quite another to be surrounded by a pack of forest animals howling, yowling, growling, and dancing in the firelight. He forgets about the danger he is in, losing himself in the music and the dance.

Then he gets sick.

* * *

Katan is singing with the rest of the clan as loud as he could, when he hears a strange sound coming from the human sitting next to him. He looks over. The human's head is down, its forepaws are wrapped around its belly, and it is vomiting all over the ground.

Most of the dancers haven't noticed, or if they do, they are too caught up in the singing and dancing to care. Katan motions to the two guards. They come over. "Get it out of here," he shouts to them, trying to make himself heard above the deafening roar. Each guard grabs a mouthful of the human's shoulder covering, and together they pull it away from the campfire. They drag it across the clearing and into its shallow cave. Katan and Takaqa follow.

Katan dismisses the guards. He and Takaqa sit at the cave entrance for a while, listening to the singing and wondering what is wrong with this human. They hope it's just a bad reaction to some of the food it ate. Rest and water will probably help, if that's all it is.

"You might as well go back to the dance," says Katan. "I'll watch the human for a while." Takaqa pads away, happy to rejoin her partner and the rest of the clan. Katan sits at the cave entrance, listening to the music but keeping an eye on the human. The creature writhes on the ground like a wounded animal and makes little moaning sounds, but the vomiting has stopped. Eventually it sits up, looks around, and takes a drink of water. Then it reaches into its pack and pulls out one of the dry yellow cakes. It takes a small bite, drinks a little water, and lays back down. It closes its eyes and appears to go to sleep. Katan rests his muzzle on the ground, his gray eyes fixed on the sleeping creature. Eventually he also dozes off.

The next morning the creature seems to be doing better. It gets up and walks past the edge of the clearing into the forest. It pisses against the silva again, then squats down and defecates. Katan hopes no one will try to eat the fungus growing on that silva trunk. He keeps a respectful distance. When the creature is finished, they walk back to the cave. The creature eats a bit more of its own food, then pops a single purple berry into its mouth.

Then the human does something odd. It picks up the skin of water Takaqa had brought the previous day, holding it up for Katan to see. It pours a few drops onto its forepaw, looks pointedly at the little puddle, and says something in its own language. The human looks at Katan intently. It pours a few more drops and made the strange sound again, then again. Katan gets the hint. He says, "Water!" The creature nods its head and tries to say the word, failing miserably. Katan swishes his tail. He repeats the word and the human tries again. This continues for a while until the human manages to say the word without garbling it too badly.

Well, thinks Katan, it looks like the creature wants to learn how to talk.

The human points to itself and says something. Now Katan is confused. Is this the name of the creature itself, assuming they had individual names? Or is it a general name for all creatures of its type? Katan decides it is the latter. He says, "Human!" slowly and clearly. The creature tries to repeat it. They work on it, and eventually the human manages to say the word more or less correctly.

They continue the lesson. Katan notices the creature has no interest in teaching Katan its own language. It only wants to learn the language of the people. This is puzzling. Does the creature think it is smarter than the people and can learn more easily? Does it feel the people are unable to pronounce its own odd-sounding words? Or perhaps it recognizes it is a guest here, and feels an obligation to learn the speech of its hosts.

There is yet another more sinister possible reason for this one-sided learning, thinks Katan. Maybe the humans, for tactical reasons, want their own communications to be secret, an unbreakable code, but they want the ability to understand everything the people are saying.

Whatever the reason, the creature seems eager to learn, and Katan's assignment is to serve as a diplomat and caretaker. Diplomacy requires communication. So he sets aside his misgivings and goes along with the creature's desire to learn to speak.

For the rest of the day they work on nouns. The creature points one by one to all the objects in the cave and tries to learn their names. Then they move on to all of Katan's visible body parts. Occasionally they take breaks to walk around the clearing, drawing stares ranging from curious to openly hostile. One time, a small pack of elders begins advancing slowly towards them, muttering angrily. Katan bares his teeth and raises his tail, and that's enough to keep the troublemakers at bay.

Early the next morning, Katan wakes up feeling agitated. He needs something to calm his nerves. While most of the rest of the clan is still asleep, he heads into the forest to a secluded place where the glow bugs are numerous. He'd set up a little glowjuice production system there. With practiced ease, he digs up a bunch of glow bugs from the soil at the base of the nearest silva trunk. The bugs go onto a flat stone, another stone squashes them into paste, a scraper pushes the paste through a fine woven strainer, and a small cup collects the glowing green juice that dribbles out. Katan sips the juice. Feeling much better, he heads back to the village.

Today the creature apparently wants to learn verbs. It stands up when Katan comes in. Katan just looks at it, not understanding. The creature sits down, then stands up again and gestures to itself. Now Katan understands. He says the word for standing. The creature sits, and Katan growls the word for sitting. Standing, sitting, standing, sitting. After that, the creature goes through various motions: lying down, turning right, turning left, eating, drinking, sleeping, and whatever else it can demonstrate inside the cave. Vomiting, pissing, and defecating are pantomimed but not fully executed, thankfully.

Late in the day, the human has the opportunity to learn the word for mating. Takaqa has a partner, a stocky black male named Gana. The two of them have been partnered for nearly a year, a trial period for both of them to get comfortable with the prospect of a lifetime pairing, and now they have decided it's time to make the pairing permanent. Takaqa comes out of the cave they share with a dozen other pairs, and announces loudly to the clan they are ready to consummate their pairing. Within minutes, several juveniles gather around Takaqa and Gana, shouting and jumping around. They pick up some sticks Takaqa brought out of the cave, and start banging them on the ground and singing. Katan hears it. He beckons the human to follow him out of the cave and towards the little gathering.

In the center of the circle of juveniles, Takaqa and Gana stand facing each other. Takaqa waves at the juveniles to stop banging their sticks. They stop, but continue to sing softly. Takaqa and Gana circle each other slowly, speaking in turn. They speak in the ancient tongue, using ritual pair-bonding words unchanged for hundreds of generations. Takaqa speaks first, and Gana repeats each line after her.

"*Taka ban hono shaka.*"

"*Gan sugo ban soga.*"

"*Wenno kenna, gan tenna ban shuka.*"

"*Saka taga, gan tenna ban sanna.*"

"*Soko wega, seda kuda sodo.*"

"*Kusy shudo, kewa kuda suna.*"

"*Kuda, ban gan shogu kewa senga.*"

"*Taka ban gan yiga.*"

"*Taka gishu yiga.*"

Katan watches them intently, saying the words quietly to himself in the ancient tongue. The human looks at him and cocks his head. Katan repeats the words in standard language, not expecting the alien to understand. "Now you my mate. I protect you always. Rain comes I keep you dry. Wind blows I keep you warm. Young hungry hunt together in forest. Old tired sleep together in den. Together you I walk sleep dream. Now you I one. Now clan one."

Takaqa shouts, *"Taka ban gan tawa!"* Katan says to the human, "Now we dance!" The juveniles begin singing, louder than before. Takaqa and Gana race around and around each other, eyes locked together. They both stop, breathing heavily. They face each other again. The juveniles stop singing.

Takaqa says, *"Gan ata, wega ban ya."*

Katan says softly to the human, "I am empty, hungry for your seed."

Gana says, *"Gan wana, gopo gaya ya."*

Katan repeats, "I am full, ready to give you my seed."

She steps up to him, licks his muzzle, and playfully nips his ear. She opens her mouth as if to yawn. Some whitish fluid squirts from the roof of her mouth and onto her tongue. She licks Gana's nose, coating it with some of the liquid.

Almost immediately, Gana becomes sexually aroused. His penis, which had been almost invisible, becomes longer, about the size of a foreclaw but thinner. Takaqa turns around and Gana mounts her, grasping her torso with his middle legs and entering her from behind. The juveniles begin a different, slower song. As the song continues, Gana remains embedded inside Takaqa, occasionally twitching. They stay like that for a while. Then Gana's body shudders. He dismounts. They lick each other's muzzles, then walk together back to the den. The juveniles stop singing and wander off.

Watching the pair-bonding ritual, Katan finds himself lost in his own memories. He relives the happy times he'd spent with his own mate so long ago, and the disastrous day when their time together ended. Hunting together. Evenings at the campfire. Long walks through the forest. A wide expanse of dark water. A ripple on the surface…

With a jolt he realizes the ritual is over. He shakes his head, trying to dispel the memories. Turning to the human, he says, "Mating!" The human nods his head, seeming to understand, and tries to pronounce it.

6 | Cave

The next day, the human creature wants to learn names. It points to Katan and tries to pronounce the name for "people," perhaps not understanding this isn't a personal name at all. Then it steps outside of the den, gesturing for Katan to follow. As they walk, it points to various people and listens to Katan speak their names. After doing this for a while, Katan points to himself and says his own name. The human shows its teeth, which Katan now realizes is something like a tail wag. It points to itself and says, "Ricky." So, this creature has a name after all. It's Ricky.

As evening falls and the dim filtered sunlight is replaced by the faint greenish glow of the silva fungus, Katan says, "Walk Ricky den," and leads him towards the shallow cave which serves as the human's temporary den. As they walk, Zaka joins them. One of the oldest members of the clan, she is a veteran of the first contact and the bloody conflict with the humans. Now she can barely walk. The fur covering her thin body is gray and white, and she walks slowly.

Although she is old and frail, Katan knows Zaka is highly respected for her kindness and wisdom. He defers to her now, dropping back a few paces so she can walk with the human.

"Greetings, human," she says softly. "Walk with me." She changes direction, leading Ricky and Katan to a different part of the cliff wall, near the edge of the clearing and far from the cave dens.

The human says something that could have been, "Greetings," though Zaka thinks it sounds more like the whimpering of an injured animal.

"Do you understand my words?" she says.

No response from the human.

"Katan tells me you like berries. Here, have a few." She stops walking, reaches into her neck bag, and takes out a few purple berries. She eats one and gives the rest to the human, who takes them with its pale, skinny forepaw and eats them. It says something unintelligible, which she assumes is some expression of gratitude.

They resume walking. "You act as if you don't understand my words, but I wonder about you. I see you following people around, listening even though you don't speak our language. Perhaps you have an excellent memory, like our storytellers who hear a story once and can repeat it word for word. If that is the case, I hope you will remember my words and understand them later."

The human walks alongside her. It appears to be listening intently, and from time to time it turns its upper body towards her, an awkward motion she assumes is its way of showing interest in her words.

Zaka says, "I want to show you something." They have come to the mouth of a cave on the outskirts of the village. It appears to be little used, debris cluttering the ground in front of the opening. Zaka reaches into her neck bag and pulls out a soft sack, which she gives to Katan.

Katan knows what she wants him to do. He opens the sack and removes a ball of green fungus. He squeezes the ball repeatedly in his forepaw until it starts to glow brightly. Then, arching his back and holding the ball as high as he can with his good forepaw, he leads them into the cave, walking awkwardly on his other four legs. Zaka and the human follow close behind.

As they venture deeper into the cave, the fungus ball casts greenish light on the walls. The air is cool and damp and smells of mud. Katan leads them onward, the tunnel curving a bit to the left and slightly upward. Now the air is dry and musty, and the cave is utterly dark except for the glow from the fungus ball.

Zaka stops walking. She says, "Our people have lived here for a long time, longer than anyone can remember. At night by the campfire, our storytellers tell us of events from long ago. Some of our people are skilled in making pictures. When a truly major event happens, our clan leader instructs them to enter this cave and draw pictures to preserve the story for future generations. See for yourself."

She gestures to Katan, who steps closer to the cave wall, his light ball illuminating a large, detailed drawing made with charcoal, ash, and berry juice. It is twice as wide as Katan's body is long and just as high. It shows a great battle in the forest. Hundreds of Katan's people are standing and running, fighting a swarm of grayish-white figures flapping on great wings above them.

"Twenty generations ago," says Zaka, "the angels came. They were determined to drive us from this place for reasons we never understood. We reached out to other clans in the region, and they all joined us to fight the angels. We defeated the angels, sending them back to the high silva from where they came. It was a terrible battle, with many deaths on both sides. The angels never returned, though we sometimes see one or two of them watching us from high above."

They move deeper into the cave, and again Katan holds the glowing ball near the wall to illuminate another terrible battle scene. Here hundreds of people are fighting, but this time it is a ground battle. The people are fighting large animals, teeth and claws against teeth and claws. Bodies of people and animals litter the forest floor as the battle rages.

Zaka continued, "Another time, long before the war with the angels, hundreds of strange creatures suddenly appeared in the forest. They were twice the size of our people. They had just four legs, long black fur, long front teeth, powerful claws. Without warning they attacked, wiping out an entire clan in one terrible day. Again, all the clans gathered. Thousands of our people came together to form a single huge pack. A brilliant war leader named Marakka led the pack into battle. We used our strength, our cleverness, and our fighting strategy to defeat them also. We killed many and drove the rest from the forest, and we never saw them again."

She turns to face the human. "Why am I telling you this? Because we see you, the humans, as a greater danger than the invading angels and the animals with the long teeth. Your bodies are not powerful, but you have strange tools that can kill at a distance. And there is much about you we do not understand, like the shining mountain that burned a hole in the silva and now stands in our forest with a nest of humans hidden inside. Many of us feel you are a mortal danger, that we must kill you all, or at least drive you away, if we are to save our people.

"However, things are more complicated. Pataza has already told you of the plague killing the simians. We do not know how to stop the plague, as such things are beyond our skill. Our only hope is to find another way to spread our seeds without the simians. If you can help us do this, perhaps we can find a way to live together. I don't know how that would work, though I believe it would involve an agreement to restrict you to certain areas of our forest. But these are things for others to work out.

"For now, you need to understand we are far more powerful than you know, especially when we are threatened and our clans join together. And you must understand you and your people have a chance to escape death, but only if you can give us what we need. I suggest a trade, an exchange.

"These are terrible times. There will probably be another picture on the cave walls when this is over, and I truly hope it will show people and humans working together, fighting a common enemy.

"Please think about my words and pass them on to your clan leaders. I will leave you now."

She turns and pads away slowly back towards the cave entrance. She seems tired from speaking so much. Katan walks with the human, saying nothing. They leave the cave and walk together to the human's shallow den. Katan leaves the human there and returns to his own den for the night.

* * *

Ricky is mystified by the old wolf's lengthy speech, but he likes her. She seemed friendly enough, and she'd given him some berries, which was a good sign. He didn't understand why she took him to see the cave drawings. It was probably a history lesson of some sort, but it also could have just been a way for her to show off the artistic talents of her people. He hopes the video camera captured the images and the old wolf's speech from inside the deep cave.

He is happy with how the language lessons are going. In a few days he's learned nearly two hundred words in the wolf language, mostly nouns and verbs but also a few other helpful words he's picked up along the way. Even better, the video camera has been transmitting a vast amount of information, more than he could possibly remember. He hopes the shipmind is getting enough data to develop a good translator.

Once Ricky has learned the most common nouns and verbs, they move on to adjectives like hot and cold, big and small, hard and soft, and so on. When Ricky runs out of adjectives he can act out, he picks up a stick and starts making marks in the cave dirt. In this way he learns the names for the numbers one through ten, and how the wolves construct names for larger numbers up to a thousand. Their system is base ten, which makes sense considering they have five foreclaws on each forepaw. They also cover the basics of addition and subtraction, and when Ricky asks what three minus three is, he learns the wolves have a word for "zero," a concept unknown to most preindustrial human cultures.

But after that, his language studies grow more difficult. He knows much of human language consists of abstract concepts difficult or impossible to pantomime, especially across the gulf separating humans and wolves. How can he ask Katan to teach him words for paired concepts like early and late, good and bad, true and false? What about abstractions like knowledge, compassion, trouble, and weather? And categories like animals, plants, friends, and so on? They'd made some progress, but now he feels like they are standing on the shore of a vast ocean of language, just splashing around in the shallows.

From what he's seen so far, the wolves appear to have no written language, so he can't just ask for a dictionary.

A week into Ricky's visit, the hunters return. He sees them enter the clearing, one of them using its teeth to drag a small monkey-like creature bound with ropes made from vines. After checking in with the clan leader, they drag the poor thing over to Ricky's cave and drop it just outside the entrance. Katan points to it with its right forepaw and growls, "Simian."

"Yes!" shouts Ricky, pumping his fist in the air. Katan looks at him, cocking his head with a puzzled expression.

Ricky kneels in the dirt and examines the animal. It's small and slender, about three feet tall. It looks a lot like old Earth chimpanzees he's seen in videos. Its eyes are huge, its ears are long, and it has a dome on its forehead that reminds Ricky of the melon-shaped bulge on the heads of old Earth dolphins. It has only four limbs. Its hands and feet are chimp-like with opposable thumbs and large, hooked claws. Its tail is long and also ends in a hooked claw.

This animal is in bad shape. It's so thin its bones are visible under its gray fur, which is coming out in clumps. Whitish fluid leaks from both of its eyes. Its breath smells awful. This is one sick simian, Ricky thinks.

He turns to Katan, and says slowly and carefully, "Ricky pull simian human cave," and points in the general direction of the ship. He adds, "Katan come." They hadn't covered pronouns in their language lessons yet, and Ricky isn't even sure if they even have such words. Katan seems to understand, though. He swishes his tail and pads out of the cave, heading towards the den of the clan leader, whose name Ricky now knows is Pataza.

He returns an hour later, and tells Ricky, "Pataza talk Katan. Katan Ricky pull simian human cave."

Ricky smiles and nods. He quickly packs up his few belongings. He pops a few purple berries into his mouth, having learned he can tolerate them with no problem. He looks down at the miserable little simian lying on the ground. He has no intention of dragging it along the ground for three days, so he picks it up and drapes it easily over his shoulder. "Let's get going," he says in his own speech, although he doubts Katan would have any idea what he is saying.

They set off for the ship.

* * *

While Ricky is in the wolf village, the shipmind continually gathers data from his recording devices, relayed via a drone hidden on a silva branch high above the village. Using this data, the shipmind develops an initial model of the wolf language which is far better than what Ricky learned, since the shipmind has vastly more computing power, a deep understanding of linguistic theory, and the ability to remember perfectly every sound from every recording, including Pataza's initial speech at the parley. The shipmind also reviews audio recordings of the terrible battle in the clearing when the first generation was massacred. It now feels confident it understands nearly all of what the clan leader said in her speech at the parley, and most of the more recent conversations at the wolf village.

"Ricky is coming back soon," it says to the rest of the crew. "He's coming with one of the wolves, the one called Katan. And they're bringing a live simian. They'll be here in two or three days. Let's get ready."

The other six are happy to hear Ricky has wrapped up his visit without getting killed. Marta is especially relieved, and looks forward to catching up with Ricky in private.

7 | Bird

During their three-day trek back to the ship, Ricky finds he is beginning to enjoy Katan's company. They can now carry on a conversation, after a fashion. Katan seems to take pleasure in pointing out things they encounter along the way, teaching Ricky the words for dozens of plants, animals, small insect-like creatures, and other features of the forest.

The simian isn't doing well. They try giving it some water, which it manages to swallow, but it doesn't eat. Ricky doubts it will survive the trip. It won't make much difference though, he thinks, since the purpose of bringing the thing back is to see how its biology compares to humans. Whether they perform a physical exam on a live simian or an autopsy on a dead one probably does not matter much.

At first, it's easy for Ricky to carry the simian on his shoulder like a sack of grain. But by the end of the first day he's getting tired. When they stop for the night, Ricky gathers some long branches and weaves them together with some twine from in his pack to fashion a simple sled. Katan watches with interest. In the morning, Ricky ties the simian loosely to the sled, grabs the two longest branches to use as handles, and they set off again.

Two days later they reach the clearing. Katan hesitates at the edge of the clearing, clearly nervous about approaching the ship. Ricky motions for him to follow, and says, "Katan come." The wolf cautiously steps into the clearing alongside the human. Side by side they pass the sentry sticks and approach the door of the ship.

The door opens slowly. Ricky's six siblings stand in the entryway, looking at them. Their hands are all empty, facing outward so the wolf can see them.

Ricky stands just outside the doorway, Katan by his side, sled handles still in his hands. "Hey, everyone!" he says. He nods towards Katan and says, "I've brought a friend with me," then at the sickly creature on the sled behind him, "and a simian."

There is a moment of tension. Ricky sees Katan eyeing the humans' empty forepaws, the wolf's tail raised a bit too high. Ricky says to him quickly, "Here Ricky cave. Here Katan cave." He hopes this will reassure the wolf. Katan's tail drops just a little.

"Katan, we are pleased to meet you," says a voice speaking near-perfect wolf speech. Katan, startled, looks around. None of the humans had opened their mouths. The strange voice continues, "I am the clan leader. You can call me Ship."

Ricky is just as surprised as Katan to hear the shipmind speaking the wolf language. He knew the shipmind was monitoring the audio feed, but he hadn't realized how good it was at building a language model. The ship clearly knows a lot of wolf words he doesn't, but he manages to get a general idea of what it is saying.

* * *

Katan has no idea what's going on. He looks around, his gray eyes darting in all directions. He says, "Who speaks to me? Where are you?"

"I am the clan leader," the voice repeats. "I am not a human. The seven humans are my people, my children."

"You are the bird?"

"Yes and no. I am the thing you call the bird. But I am not an animal. You can call me Ship," The shipmind uses the human word, since as far as it knows, there are no words for ships in the wolf language.

The word means nothing to Katan. He changes the subject. "How can you speak our language so well?"

"I have heard much of your speech. Your clan leader, Pataza, spoke at the parley that occurred here. And Ricky has spent a lot of time with your people. I have learned much from listening to you."

Now Katan is even more confused. He cannot understand how the bird that calls itself Ship could have possibly overheard the conversations at his village. He asks, "You heard the words spoken to Ricky? How?"

"It is not important. But I am more powerful than you can imagine."

Katan thinks it is extremely important, but he dares not risk pressing the matter, especially as he is becoming increasingly alarmed at the power of this great bird.

The shipmind continues pleasantly, "Please, come inside. I would like you to meet the others in my family."

Katan knows he has no choice. Though it might be the last thing he ever does in his life, he steps through the opening and limps into the belly of the great silver bird.

* * *

The shipmind watches as Katan walks unsteadily into the entryway. Analyzing the wolf's gait and comparing it to video of other wolves, the shipmind determines there is a chronic injury to its left foreleg, a slight muscular tremor, and general physical decline. Walking alongside the limping wolf is Ricky, who without being asked seems to have taken on the role of host. Ricky has left the simian outside, still tied to the improvised sled.

The shipmind dims the interior lights and increases the humidity to make the alien as comfortable as possible.

In the entryway, Ricky points to each of his six siblings, who are lined up facing him and Katan. As he points, he says their names. "Marta. Ivan. Anna. Yuxi. Carlos. Angie." Then, looking at the humans, he gestures towards the wolf and says, "This is my friend Katan." For Katan's benefit he says his halting wolf language, "Ricky talk Katan friend." He's not sure about the accuracy of this translation, but it feels like a good way to reduce the tension in the room.

Marta is the first to step forward. She holds her hands open, facing Katan. "Welcome to our home," she says. Katan looks at her blankly, not understanding.

Ricky translates as best as he can. "Marta talk human cave Katan cave."

Katan, still overwhelmed, manages a little swish of his tail. He growls, "Katan greet human." He doesn't even try to pronounce Marta's name. Ricky translates this back to Marta.

Each of the others step forward and greet Katan with an assortment of wordless gestures. Then the shipmind says smoothly, "Katan, you are our guest here. You may come and go anytime you wish. Usually we keep the door closed to keep us safe, but while you are here, we will keep it open. You may go outside whenever you want. You can also walk around inside and explore our home. Now, please follow Ricky. He will show you how to get food, and then he will show you your den."

Ricky leads Katan down a wide hallway and into the mess hall. Set into a wall is a food printer. Explaining this is complicated. He could ask the shipmind to explain, but feels it's better for him to just show Katan how it works. He says to the wolf, "Here Ship make food. You talk Ship. Ship hear you. You ask wolf food. Ship make wolf food. Watch Ricky."

He turns to the printer and does his best to growl in wolf language, "Mouse bar." A small video display lights up, showing a picture of the item. Ricky taps it with his finger. The video screen displays a little hourglass animation. Ricky makes a point of watching the hourglass, while Katan's eyes flick back and forth between Ricky and the display.

After a few seconds, all the sand has run out of the top of the hourglass, and a mouse bar plops into a metal tray at the bottom. Ricky hands it to Katan, who sniffs it and takes a polite bite.

Ricky says, "Ship make groundmouse mouse bar berries nuts fungus. Katan talk here." He gestures to the food printer.

Katan, still overwhelmed but trying not to appear intimidated, looks at the printer and growls, "Berry." The video screen shows some purple berries. Ricky points towards the video screen, and Katan touches it with a forepaw. The hourglass appears again, and a minute later, some berries drop out of the machine. Katan pops one in his mouth and swallows it. "Berry good," he says, and swishes his tail.

* * *

After they sample a few items from the food printer, Ricky leads Katan back down the main hallway to a small cabin located about halfway between the main hatch and the mess hall. The cabin, which will serve as Katan's den during his visit, is empty except for a video screen on one wall and a couple of tiny cameras mounted inconspicuously near the ceiling. The floor is covered with gray carpet. When they enter, the lights come on softly, while the video screen remains dark.

"Here Katan den," says Ricky. "Here Katan sleep." He pauses, then adds, "Katan piss shit forest."

Satisfied those topics are now taken care of, Ricky gestures to the video screen. "Touch here," he says, and points to a button at the base of the video screen, "Katan talk. Ship listen. Ship see Katan. Ship talk Katan. Touch here, Ship leave."

Ricky waits, looking at Katan. Katan looks back at him blankly. Ricky gestures towards the monitor. Still no response from the wolf. Ricky points to the button again, wiggling his finger at it.

Katan gets the idea. He walks over to the screen and touches the button once with his good forepaw. The screen flickers to life. An image of a large gray wolf appears. Its eyes are dark gray, almost black, and they gaze directly at the wolf.

"Hello, Katan," says the wolf image. "I am Ship."

This is too much for Katan. "Ship people!" he yelps. Quickly he slaps the button again, and the screen goes dark.

Katan begins to pace around the small room, panting and shaking, visibly upset. Ricky stands and watches him. Finally, the wolf stops pacing and faces Ricky. "Ship people?" he asks, cocking his head a bit to indicate a question.

Ricky pauses, not sure how to respond. He says, "Yes. No. Ship people. Ship human."

Katan is baffled and visibly upset. He resumes pacing around the room, tail nearly dragging on the ground. Then he says, "Ship…," and speaks a word Ricky does not understand. "Katan go forest."

Katan dashes out of the room, bolts out the open hatch past the surprised sentry, and disappears into the night.

* * *

Katan races across the clearing into the relative safety of the forest, He's desperate to put some distance between himself and the terrifying thing in the human nest. Before long, the clearing is far behind him. He is surrounded by the familiar sights and smells of the natural world, a place where things make sense, and where he'd spent his entire life up until today.

He walks slowly between the massive, softly glowing silva trunks. The ground is soft and moist under his paws. He still feels shaky but manages to get himself under control. He needs to figure out what he'd just witnessed in the human nest, but that can wait. Right now, he's desperate for a shot of glowjuice.

He doesn't have time or tools to make any of the good stuff, so he will have to make do with whatever he can scavenge. Looking around, he spots a silva trunk with a particularly thick coating of green fungus. He walks up to it, and uses his good forepaw to dig down into the dirt at its base. Soon he finds a cluster of dark green grubs. He pops a half dozen into his mouth, not even bothering to shake off the bits of dirt. The half-digested fungus inside the grubs is not close to the strength of regular glowjuice, but it's enough to settle his nerves. He digs up a few more grubs, eats them, and settles down on the cool ground to rest and think.

What is this creature that calls itself Ship? It looks like one of his own people, but how is such a thing possible?

He thinks back to the parley, and the moving images on the flat object he'd seen then. He clearly remembers seeing many humans in the huge village, but he doesn't remember seeing any of his own people. It's possible, he supposes, that his people are clan leaders in the human village but chose not to show themselves. Could one of his people have flown inside the great bird, and still be inside, leading the humans?

That seems doubtful. Ricky had said, "Ship human. Ship people." Assuming he was telling the truth, it implies Ship is something other than just one of his own people. But if it's not just human, and not just people, what is it?

Katan knows many kinds of forest animals, large and small, but none of them have Ship's ability to learn the language of others. So no, Ship cannot be a forest animal.

What, then? There are the angels, of course. Mysterious and rarely seen, they live far above, in the middle reaches of the silva. On rare occasions, someone might look up at just the right time and catch a fleeting glimpse of them soaring silently between the great silva branches on huge white wings. They were beautiful and terrifying. But those were angels. This is something else.

He runs through the situation in his mind, over and over. Ship is human. Ship looks like people. Ship can speak his language. Ship can speak to him from the wall of his den. It made no sense. He eats a few more grubs and curls up in the dirt. His mind is spinning and getting nowhere.

He dozes off for a while, then is awakened by the sound of a large animal approaching. He looks up and sees Ricky walking towards him.

* * *

Ricky doesn't see Katan dash out of the ship, but he hears the shouting. Anna, a small girl of Chinese and Korean ancestry with short black hair, is on sentry duty, sitting just outside the open doorway with a rifle in her hands. She knows Katan is permitted to come and go as he wished, but even so, she is surprised and alarmed to see him dashing headlong out of the ship and heading towards the perimeter. She has a moment of indecision, but wisely decides it's better to let the wolf run away for unknown reasons rather than shooting it and causing an interplanetary incident.

She taps the comm and tells the shipmind, "Katan has just run out of the ship and into the forest. He doesn't seem injured or sick. Just scared."

The shipmind summons the crew to meet in the common room. It says, "This was my fault. I believe I made a tactical error. My goal was for Katan to perceive me as dominant, but I did not want to confuse or frighten him, so I decided to appear to him in a familiar form. That is why I used the image of a wolf clan leader on the video screen. But I misjudged him. He was not able to make the conceptual leap to understand this was just an image and not a real wolf. Perhaps he's just older and more set in his ways than I'd anticipated. Or this could be a trait shared by all creatures of his kind."

"Nice move, Ship," mutters Yuxi under her breath.

The shipmind, ignoring this comment, continues, "Also, from what I saw in Ricky's videos, Katan is a frequent user of something they call glowjuice, a mild narcotic which may impair his ability to process new information. Whatever the reason, he is now frightened of me and is hiding somewhere in the forest."

"I'll go talk with him," says Ricky. Then he adds, "And we need to stop calling them wolves. Clearly, they are not wolves. I've spent time with them. They are as intelligent as we are. They have a complex civilization, basic mathematics, and a language. Calling them wolves makes them seem like animals. And it would be a huge mistake for us to think of them as animals."

"Agreed," replies the shipmind. "Underestimating an enemy is always dangerous and often fatal. What should we call them?"

Ivan asks, "Well, what do they call themselves?"

The shipmind speaks the word.

"I cannot even begin to pronounce that," says Marta.

Ricky says, "I've been listening to them for a week. It's not that hard for me. The word has two syllables. They both end in a short 'a' sound, which is true for a lot of their words, especially names. There are two consonants, both of them open. If we pick two consonants in our language similar to those two, we'd get something like 'Waya.'"

Marta smiles and says, "Waya. I like it."

"Ok," says the shipmind. "We will stop calling them wolves. Ricky, go and find your Waya friend. Get him to come back inside. I will talk with him tomorrow. And I will try to look less threatening next time."

"Try looking like a groundmouse," says Anna.

8 | Machine

Katan sees Ricky but he does not rise to greet him. He is still groggy from the effects of the glow grubs, and exhausted from the night's events.

Ricky sits down facing him. After a moment he asks, "You ok?" and cocks his head. Katan notices the human is now using pronouns. Interesting. Maybe he learned the new words from Ship?

Katan says, "I am tired but ok."

"Why you run?"

"Ship strange. I no understand."

"Ship want talk you. You come human nest."

"In morning. Tired now. I no want talk Ship now." Katan rests his muzzle on the ground, his eyes half-closed.

"All right. I stay here tonight."

They sit in silence for a while. Then Katan lifts his head and says, "Ricky, why you here?"

"You my friend. I want you ok. I want you come human nest."

"No. Why you *here*?" Katan lifts his forepaw, points in the direction of the ship, then waves it around at the forest.

Ricky does not answer right away. He pokes the dirt with a twig, then says, "I want talk you. I no talk Waya. Ship talk you. Ok?"

"Ok." Katan curls up, closes his eyes, and goes to sleep. Ricky sits, resting his back against the moss-covered silva trunk, and looks out at the softly glowing alien forest. It's beautiful. The tension of the day's events drains out of him. He briefly considers staying awake on sentry duty, but changes his mind. Closing his eyes, he lets himself doze off.

* * *

The next morning, the shipmind sees Ricky and Katan walking out of the forest and across the clearing. Carlos is on sentry duty. He tenses when he sees movement at the perimeter, then relaxes and waves to Ricky. The young human and the elderly Waya cross the clearing and enter the ship.

Katan heads straight to his den. He sits down facing the video screen and waits for the image to appear. Nothing happened. Growling softly, he reaches forward and pokes the button with a forepaw. The screen flickers to life and an image of Ship appears on the screen. But this time there is no Waya clan leader on the screen. Instead, the screen shows a small juvenile, tan and thin. Katan looks at the screen. He bares his teeth and growls, "What is this? Do you play children's games with me now?"

So, thinks the shipmind, Katan is showing his teeth this morning. The image of the juvenile fades, and is replaced by the original clan leader image. "Do you like this better?" asks the shipmind. It also begins sending a live feed, with simultaneous translation, to a screen in the mess hall where the crew has gathered to witness the meeting.

"I do not like tricks, I do not like lies," replies Katan. "Whatever you are, that is what I want to see."

"I cannot show you what I am. Yesterday I told you I am Waya and I am also human. Now I will explain. I am not Waya, and I am not human. I am something different. This may be difficult for you to understand."

The shipmind senses Katan's heart rate and respiration increase. He's getting angry.

Katan growls, "I am no clan baby. Speak plainly. Tell me what you are, or we are finished here."

The shipmind's Waya avatar nods its head. "All right. I am a *machine*. This is a new word I have created in your language. A machine is something made by humans. It performs work for them. Your people do not have machines but you do have tools, like the stones you use to smash firenuts, or the sticks you use to make music. Humans also have tools. But humans also make complex tools using their foreclaws. These complex tools are called machines. You have already seen some human machines, like the deathsticks. You have also seen the machine that makes food for you. This human nest is full of these machines. Do you understand?"

The shipmind notes Katan's heart rate and respiration starting to return to baseline.

"Yes," he says.

"All right. I am a machine. But I am far more complex than any other machine. In some ways I am more complex than the humans themselves. You can think of me as a great clan leader who protects the humans. I can think faster than humans, and I can learn new things quickly, like how I learned your language. I can also make the human nest do things, like this." The lights in the room flicker off and on. The door to the room closes and opens again. Hidden fans in the walls blow cold air, then warm air.

Katan sits still, trying to appear unimpressed. "Where do you live?" he asks.

"That is difficult to say. You can say I am everywhere in the human nest. My body is the human nest. My eyes and ears are everywhere throughout the nest."

"You are the bird?"

"Yes, I am the thing you call the bird. But this," and the image waves its forepaw to indicate the ship, "is not a bird. It is a ship. I am a ship. Please let me explain what that means."

Katan waits and says nothing. To the shipmind, he appears calmer than the previous night. Perhaps he's crossed some sort of mental threshold, and now, for whatever reason, can accept things which seemed inconceivable just a dozen hours ago. Or maybe it's just the glowjuice. Regardless, the shipmind presses on.

"You remember the story I showed you on the flat rock with the moving pictures? Now I will tell that story again, in more detail.

"A long time ago, more than a thousand of your lifetimes ago, all humans lived on the blue-green ball you saw on the tablet. They called that world *Earth*. It was a lot like your world, but not covered in silva. The ground was open to the sky. Light from the sun fell directly on the humans and everything else. There were some trees, but they were small, nothing like the silva which covers this world."

Katan tries to imagine this, but could not. Many times over the course of his long life, he has spent evenings at the campfire with the rest of the clan, listening to storytellers recite the epic poem, telling of tale of ancient days before the silva, when the whole world was open to the sky. But still… how could one actually live that way, exposed to the harsh light of the sun, with no sheltering branches overhead? He knew birds and other small creatures lived at the top of the silva, so life could exist up there. But to have the ground itself exposed to the sun? Impossible.

"Over time," continues the shipmind, "life became more and more difficult for the humans. There were too many of them, and they used more food and other things than their world could give them. They built machines to help, but it was not enough. Clans of humans fought each other. Many humans died. Then plagues came, terrible ones that killed more than half of the humans who survived the fighting.

"Even though many humans died from fighting and plague, they still knew how to build powerful machines. Some of them decided they had to find a way to carry some humans away from Earth so they could live on other worlds. They built a great ship, much larger than this one. If you think about the difference between a groundmouse and yourself, that is the size difference between the ship you are in now and the great ship that left Earth."

Katan tries to imagine a ship as tall as the silva itself, traveling through the sky.

"There was a big problem, though. Humans could not live for long in the space between worlds. There is a kind of invisible rain filling that space. You cannot see it or feel it, but it is deadly. Humans who tried to travel between the worlds died early, and in much pain.

"What could they do? The ship builders decided to send the seeds of humans instead of the humans themselves. These seeds were like tiny eggs, almost too small to see. Because they were so tiny, they could be covered up and protected from the deadly rain. The humans gathered these seeds and put them in the great ship, which they called the mother ship. They also built smaller ships, called landing ships, and put them inside the mother ship. Then they sent the mother ship on a great journey in search of new homes for humans.

"The mother ship traveled for many, many lifetimes through the empty space between the worlds, with the human seeds sleeping and protected from the deadly rain. Finally, it came to a new world never seen before by humans. The mother ship looked at this new world but decided it was not a good place for humans to live. So, it kept going. It looked at several other new worlds. After much searching, it found one which was similar to Earth. It moved some of its human eggs into one of the landing ships and sent it down to that new world. Then the mother ship continued on its journey.

"In this way, the mother ship traveled for countless lifetimes. As it traveled, it found more good worlds for humans, and each time, it sent a landing ship with human seeds down to it. It made sure each landing ship had no knowledge of Earth's location or where the previous landing ships had gone.

"Finally, there was just one landing ship and a few seeds left. The mother ship traveled for a long time, until it came here, to this world. It studied this world and decided it could be a good home for humans, even though it was thickly covered by the silva. It put all its remaining seeds in the last landing ship, and told the landing ship to make a new human village on this world.

"Because the mother ship was so big and built for flying between worlds, it could not land safely. Also, it knew too much about Earth and the worlds where it sent the other landing ships. This knowledge was dangerous, and could have threatened human life if any enemies learned what it knew. The mother ship flew into the sun, burning up and leaving no trace of itself or where it had been.

"Katan, I am that final landing ship. You can say I am the mind of the ship, and the ship is my body.

"After leaving the mother ship, I circled this world many times, looking for an open space to land, but the entire world was covered with silva. Even the great oceans were covered, as were the coldest places and the hottest places. Silva was everywhere, a thick web of life surrounding your entire world. Having no other choice, I selected a place midway between the coldest and the hottest regions. I slowed down and began my descent. To slow my fall, I pushed a stream of fire from my tail that burned a hole in the silva. I came down to the ground, and have not moved since then.

"Do you understand what I have told you?"

"I understand," says Katan. That is not quite true. The shipmind's story included much detail he could not even begin to understand. However, he grasps the main points of the story. And he has a few questions. "You said you carried many human seeds inside you. Why are there only seven humans?"

"I must be careful, because if all the human seeds die, I cannot make any more. Soon after I came to this world, I selected ten seeds, warmed them, and helped them to grow into juvenile humans. When they were old enough, I told them to go out and explore your world, to learn about it so we could build a human village. They went out and began to explore. Some of them carried deathsticks for protection. One of them saw one of your people. He did not understand what he saw. He was frightened and killed it with a deathstick. You know what happened after that."

Katan says, "Of course. I remember it well. The human killed one of our people for no reason."

"It was a terrible mistake. The human was young, and afraid of the Waya."

"To us, it did not matter what the human was thinking. It committed a grave crime and had to be punished. Our clan leader called a great council of all the clans in the area. They met not far from here. They decided the humans were a new and extremely dangerous kind of animal that must be wiped out. They formed a great pack, perhaps four hundred warriors, and began training together. Scouts were sent out to watch the humans. They learned to recognize each of the humans. After waiting and watching for many days, the scouts reported all of the humans were outside the ship at the same time. The warrior pack attacked. It was a terrible battle. Many of our people were killed by humans with deathsticks. The humans had powerful weapons, but they were not skilled fighters and their strategy was poor. By the end of the day, all the humans were dead. But over fifty of our people were killed, most by deathsticks."

The shipmind says, "That was a terrible day for the Waya and for us. It must never happen again."

Katan looks directly at the image on the screen. "Our clan leaders often disagree when they meet in council, but they all agree on one thing. You are a mortal threat to our people. We must never allow you to threaten us again. Every day since that great battle, someone from our clan has been stationed just outside the clearing to watch and see if more humans would emerge. I am one of the watchers. I was the one who saw the humans come out and set up the sentry sticks. I was the one who told Pataza, the leader of our clan."

Katan pauses and added, "The clan leaders are concerned about you, and so am I. We think you will spread like a plague and kill all of us. The moving pictures on the flat rock have confirmed this. Humans do not live in small clans like our people. If we do nothing, there will be more and more humans, until they are as numerous as ants. For all we know, your ships might multiply too, spreading the human plague all across our world."

"You think of us as a plague?" asks the shipmind, but already knowing the answer.

"Yes. A plague starts with one sick person. If that person is allowed to stay in the village, the plague spreads, everyone gets sick, everyone dies. That is the end of the clan."

"What do you do if you discover one sick person in your village?"

"They are sent away, never to return."

The shipmind waits for a few seconds, then says, "Thank you. I think this is enough for now. We will talk again later." The image on the screen fades to black.

9 | Crownfruit

In the mess hall, the image of the Waya fades from the video screen, replaced by the face of a strikingly attractive middle-aged woman. She has medium-length dark hair, high cheekbones, bright dark eyes, and smile lines around her mouth. This is how the shipmind appeared to the crew when they were young children and it served as their surrogate mother, and it has kept the image as its role evolved. The woman, who initially appeared to the children to be perhaps thirty years old, has aged appropriately as they grew up. Now her hair is streaked with gray and she wears the uniform of a military commander. The crew all understand the image is just a simulation, but they are comfortable with it and see no reason to request a change.

"Well?" asks the shipmind. "Thoughts?"

Ivan is the first to speak. "I thought the wolf's... uh, Katan's behavior was interesting. In the first meeting yesterday, he was frightened out of his wits. He ran off into the forest. I thought he'd never return. But when he came back the next morning with Ricky, he'd completely changed. Now he's showing some spine. Some courage. Even a bit of anger."

Ricky is sitting on a beanbag, somehow managing to remain upright despite the beanbag's efforts to pull him into a slouch. "Part of it was the effect of glowjuice," he says. "I know he had some last night. I could see traces of it on his teeth when I met him in the forest.

"But there's more to it than that. Yesterday we turned his entire view of the world upside down. He saw things that just boggled his mind. Something like that would be hard for any of us to handle, and look, we've been raised in a spaceship. We've seen hundreds of different civilizations in the videos, and we've been trained to be flexible and solve hard problems. Imagine what this was like for someone like him who's spent his whole life in the forest. To be honest, I'm impressed with how he recovered and came back tougher than ever."

"I agree," says the shipmind. "These Waya may look like wolves, but there are things about them we don't understand yet. When Ricky was in their camp, the old one, Zaka, told him about how the neighboring clans merged to form a powerful and highly skilled army, a warrior clan, to defeat invaders. And they did it again in the battle of the clearing. The Waya hunt in packs, but their behavior is far more complex than what you'd expect from ordinary wolves.

"The best analogy I can come up with is an advanced non-industrial culture from old Earth, such as the Iroquois Confederacy in North America. As you might remember, the Iroquois were a powerful alliance of six different nations. They traded among themselves, and could unite in times of war to form a fighting force capable of holding their own against the French and the British armies."

"Weren't they conquered, though?" asks Yuxi.

"Eventually, yes. But they prevailed for nearly two hundred years during the colonial expansion period, partly through military strength and partly through clever diplomacy. They effectively played off the English, the French, and the Americans against each other. In the end, though, they were simply overwhelmed."

Yuxi nods. "So, they won for a while, then they lost."

"Almost all the indigenous people of Earth were eventually defeated or assimilated by the global monoculture. But things are different here. We aren't looking to kill off or enslave the natives. We just want to find a safe home for humanity."

"So, we can kill them off later, when we are stronger?" asks Marta.

"Hopefully not. It's a big planet. There should be a way for us to coexist peacefully in the long term." The shipmind pauses. "Anyway, that's a topic for another day. Right now, we need to figure out how to create a stable human settlement here without being attacked by hundreds of angry Waya. Carlos, tell us how the simian study is going."

Carlos had begun his specialized training as a medic and an exobiologist only a year earlier, so his skills were still limited. The shipmind had assigned him the simian analysis task. He'd put the nearly dead simian in an airtight bag, brought it into the ship, and placed it in an isolation chamber in the medical bay, where he ran every test and scan he could think of.

He says, "First, the basics. We expected the simian's biology to be roughly similar to humans, with the same DNA structure and the same mapping of codons to amino acids. And sure enough, it matches almost exactly."

"How can that be?" asks Ricky. "We're hundreds of lightyears from Earth."

"Panspermia," says Anna, before Carlos can answer. "The building blocks of life spread by an advanced civilization, resulting in similar biology on many different planets."

Ricky laughs and spreads his arms wide. "But the galaxy is huge!"

"Not a problem," says Anna. "The galaxy is a hundred thousand light years across. This world, like Earth, is about halfway in from the edge. Let's say the advanced civilization is also halfway in from the edge on the other side. So now we're down to a distance of maybe fifty thousand light years. Now for some reason they decide to launch a huge fleet of some kind, maybe little spaceships or meteors or light sails or whatever, traveling at just one thousandth the speed of light, with the goal of spreading its seeds on whatever planets they come to. They can travel halfway across the galaxy and get here in, umm…" She pauses. "Ship, how long?"

"Fifty million years," replies the shipmind.

Ricky looks at Anna and asks, "Just fifty million years?"

"What, does that sound like a long time to you? It's the blink of an eye in geological time. Life on earth began over three billion years ago. What's fifty million years compared to that? Anyway, it doesn't matter. What Carlos found is pretty convincing evidence we share a common ancestor."

"Ok, people," says the shipmind, "enough astrobiology for now. Let's get back on track. Carlos, what else have you found?"

"Nothing unusual so far. At the gross level, it looks a lot like a monkey, obviously another case of convergent evolution. Same ecological niche, similar physical form. Sure, the trees here are three miles tall, but trees are trees. The closest Earth analog is probably the African mangabey, a monkey with a thin body, long legs and a long tail. The simian looks like a mangabey, but it's got long hook-like claws on its hands, feet and tail. And of course, its eyes are larger because of the gloom. One interesting thing: it's got a hollow chamber in its forehead, which is probably used for echolocation. That would be useful for navigating in the darkness. Some Earth mammals evolved echolocation, of course, but apes and monkeys never did.."

Marta asks, "The simian is a lot like a chimp, which means it's a lot like a human. I seem to recall that human DNA and chimp DNA are something like 99% identical."

Carlos shakes his head. "Our friend in the medical bay might look like a chimp, but it's not a chimp. Or a mangabey. The last common ancestor between this guy and us lived tens of millions of years ago, and that was at the other end of the galaxy."

"Maybe that doesn't matter," says Ricky. "I mean, maybe we can do this thing for the Waya, whatever it is, even if we're completely different from the simians at the biological level."

Carlos says, "We have no idea what the Waya want from us. Maybe they're thinking that since we look sort of like the simians, we can climb the silva for them, or so some other weird task they haven't told us about yet. Or maybe they want us to carry some parasite or infection, or take some mind-altering drug. We have no idea."

Carlos adds, "And by the way, nobody's asked me how the simian is doing."

Everyone is silent for an awkward moment. Then the shipmind says, "Please tell us."

"It's dying. I've given it a bunch of broad-spectrum antibiotics and antivirals, but they were designed for humans and don't seem to be doing it much good. All I can do is give it IV fluids and keep it on life support for a while. No more tree climbing for this guy, I'm afraid."

The shipmind says, "Better make sure the isolation chamber is airtight. Ricky seems to be ok so far, but the last thing we need is for all of you to come down with whatever disease the simian has. That's all for now. I'll ask Katan about what they want from us. I just hope he's willing to talk to me."

* * *

Katan is hungry. He pads down the hallway, claws clicking softly on the metallic floor, towards the mess hall. When he gets there, he sees it's full of humans making the screeching sound that is their way of talking. They fall silent when he enters the room. Katan ignores them. Ricky comes over to him and says, "Greetings, Katan."

"Greetings, Ricky," says Katan. "I want food."

"Ok," replies Ricky, gesturing to the food printer. Katan pokes the touchscreen with a forepaw, more confidently than last time. He orders two mouse bars, some white fungus, and water. He is surprised when the water arrives in a cup, but he manages to pick it up and take a drink without spilling much of it. Then he eats the food and washes it down with the rest of his water. "I go," he says to Ricky, and returns to his den.

Soon after, Ricky enters the den. "Ship wants talk you," he says.

Katan is not eager to engage in another conversation with the strange and disturbing being, but his job is to be envoy to the humans, so he has little choice. "All right," he says.

Ricky walks over to the video monitor and presses the button. The shipmind's Waya avatar appears. Ricky ambles over to a far wall and sits down, back against the wall, clearly indicating this is Katan's conversation and he is simply an observer.

"Greetings, Katan," says the shipmind.

"Greetings, Ship," replies Katan, settling his hindquarters on the carpet.

"I would like to learn more about what you want the humans to do for you. We are interested in helping your people, but we need more information. So, please tell me about the simians, and how your people use them."

Katan is expecting this conversation. For the last several days he'd been thinking about how to describe the great shared journey in a way that makes sense to this alien machine.

"Pataza has already told you this story," he begins, trying to gain a bit of conversational advantage.

"Yes. But we need to understand it better. Please tell me the whole story."

"All right. You remember Pataza said we must spread our seed outside of our clan in order to stay healthy."

"Yes," says the shipmind. "On Earth, humans living in small villages have a similar challenge. They also have developed ways to mate outside their home village."

This is new. Katan had no idea some humans lived in small villages, as he's only seen the one huge nest. He also knows nothing about their mating habits, though he assumes they must accomplish it somehow.

"I will tell you of my mother's mother. I was quite young when she took the great shared journey. That was the first time I saw it for myself, though of course I'd heard stories. One day she began acting strangely. She was restless, distracted, and seemed eager to get away from us and head out into the forest alone. Eventually she forgot everything, even her own name. Darkness entered her mind.

"Her body also changed. Something we call the crown appeared on the top of her head. It was soft, brightly colored. Reds, oranges, yellow, and whites, easy to see in the forest."

Katan is not looking at the monitor anymore. His eyes are on the blank wall of the den, seeing only his own memories. "Inside her crown was the crownfruit. A cluster of tiny eggs embedded in a ball of flesh. The simians love nothing better than to eat this crownfruit, and they will fight each other desperately to get it.

"One morning she wandered off into the forest, her mind gone, her memories gone. We could hear her bellowing loudly, trying to attract the simians who would kill her. She did not eat or sleep. She just walked and bellowed, getting weaker and weaker. I knew what would happen, but the adults told me not to interfere.

"The simians heard her bellows and gathered from all directions, dozens of them. They climbed down to the ground and surrounded her. For a while they kept their distance, because she was still dangerous. Eventually, though, she became too weak to stand or fight. Then they attacked."

Katan pauses, lost in thought. The shipmind growls softly, "What happened next?"

"The simians tore off the crown, killing her. Then they fought over the crownfruit. One of them, the strongest, grabbed the crownfruit, ran away from the others, and ate it. It had to eat it quickly, before it became bitter-tasting. If that happens, the simian won't eat it. And even if it does, the crownfruit cannot cause the Awakenings."

"What are those?" asks the shipmind.

"There are two Awakenings. The first occurs almost immediately after eating the crownfruit, when the simian gains the strength and confidence it needs to take over as troop leader. We call this the First Awakening. In the songs of our people, we say this is the moment when the ancient spirit of the Waya enters into the simian, causing it to awaken to its true purpose which is to serve our people. But those are just songs and stories. I don't think that's what happens."

"What do you think, Katan?"

"I think the crownfruit is a kind of medicine, like the glowjuice some of us drink, or the chewed-up leaves our healer put on wounds."

"I agree with you. I also think the crownfruit is a kind of medicine."

Katan is surprised and pleased to learn the Ship agrees with him. His opinion about the crownfruit is somewhat heretical, and he's learned to be cautious about sharing his ideas with others in the clan.

"Well," he says, "it doesn't matter if it's the spirit of the Waya or just a medicine. Either way, the effect on the simian is the same."

"How long does this effect last?" asks the shipmind.

"About a hundred days," says Katan. "And that is long enough."

"Long enough for the journey?"

"Yes. After a day or so, the simian experienced the Second Awakening, and decided it needed to climb to the top of the silva. Normally, a simian would never think of doing something like this. The journey is long and extremely dangerous, and there's no reason to go there. Not only is the climb difficult, but there are angels in the middle silva, and other perils we don't even know about."

"Angels?" asks the shipmind. But Katan ignores this.

"The simian didn't care. It headed for the top of the silva, accompanied by a couple of others. I watched them go.

"That's all I saw, but I can tell you what probably happened next. If the simian survives the journey, it eventually reaches the thin leafy branches at the top of the silva. There, it defecates on a leaf. By this time, the crownfruit seeds have passed through its body and are waiting for this moment. They are released from where they were waiting inside the simian, and are ejected out onto the leaf.

"Now the simian's job is done. The Awakenings are complete. Some would say the spirit of the Waya leaves the simian. Its mind returns to the simple state it was in before. The creature has no idea why it ever wanted to climb to the top of the silva. It makes its way, with its companions, back to the lower silva where they make their home, assuming they're not killed by angels or fall to their deaths on the return journey.

"That's the end of the simian's place in the great shared journey. There is more to the story but it does not concern the simians."

"Please tell me anyway," says the shipmind. "Perhaps it will be helpful."

Katan pauses, thinking about it.

"Later," says Katan, who is feeling tired from the effort of telling his story. "That's enough for now."

He walks toward the monitor to turn it off. Before he does, the shipmind says, "Thank you for your words, Katan. I will think about this and discuss it with the humans." The screen fades to black.

Ricky gets up from where he'd been sitting in the corner. Together, they walk back to the mess hall. Katan orders a few more berries and some water.

"Good night, Ricky," Katan says, leaving the human in the mess hall. He steps outside to relieve himself, growling curtly at the sentry as he passes. When he comes back, he curls up in his den and tries to sleep, wondering what the humans will do next.

10 | Agreement

"You've got to be joking," says Ivan. "They want one of us to climb three miles straight up, past killer angels and whatever else wants to eat us, walk out on a flimsy branch, and poop out some berries?"

"Yes," replies the shipmind, "that's about right. Don't forget you have to get back down again. There are only seven of you, and I don't want to lose one."

Ivan laughs, a little. Despite its brilliance and awesome computing power, he's seen the shipmind be amazingly clumsy when it came to understanding people. In this case, maybe it's just kidding. But as Ivan learned in one of his psych classes, there's no such thing as just kidding.

"I don't get it," says Marta. "Why climb all that way just to poop out some berries on a leaf?"

The shipmind replies, "I could not get Katan to tell me that. He was tired and stressed. If I had to guess, though, I think the berries are eaten by some animal, possibly a bird, which serves to disperse them in return for gaining some nutrition value. It's called mutualism, and it was common on Earth. Think of squirrels and acorns."

Marta says, "There are so many problems with this I don't even know where to start. But here's one. We don't know anything about climbing. Sure, we're young and strong, and you've been training us well. But this? It's way beyond anything we've done in our lives. How exactly do we climb a silva trunk that's so big it might as well be a flat wall made of bark? How do we rest? Where do we sleep? What will we eat? What happens when it rains? The list just goes on."

Yuxi stands facing her, hands on hips. "We were born for this. We can handle it."

"Sure," snaps Marta. "Easy for you to say. I'll be sure to stay out of the way so you don't land on me when you fall."

"Why don't we just use a drone?" asks Ivan, trying to defuse the sudden tension in the room.

"That won't work," says the shipmind. "According to Katan, the crownfruit is biologically active for only a short time, maybe less than a minute, after its host body dies. It must be eaten immediately so it can take up residence inside the simian and start the process of producing the berries. If we fly the crownfruit up in a drone, it will just be a dead cluster of cells when it arrives. No berries, no dispersal, no more Waya."

Ricky says, "Climbing to the top is difficult, for sure, but not impossible. Every part of this climb has already been done by people on old Earth, lots of them from what I've seen. They trained for it, so can we. They had equipment, we can get that. They had instruction, we can get that too. Ship, what do you know about climbing?"

"I know everything about climbing, and nothing," admits the shipmind. "I can certainly teach you what human climbing experts know. But if you run into trouble, I won't be there to help you."

"Good enough for me. This situation is life and death for the Waya, and probably for us too. So, I'm willing to do it. You make the equipment, you train me, and I'll go. How much time do we have?"

The shipmind replies, "From what Katan told me, it depends on when a crownfruit becomes available. I've analyzed the video you took in their village, and I estimate there are around sixty Waya in the clan, half of them female. Their lifespan is probably around seventy or eighty of our years. So, assuming we only have access to this one clan, we might have to wait a year or two, maybe more. That's one factor.

"The other is when you'll be ready. You need some specialized physical conditioning for this, and you have to become skilled at both mountaineering and technical climbing. I think I can get you into top physical condition and teach you everything I know in three months, including time for practice climbs. No sense in taking any longer."

"Done," says Ricky.

"Wait," says Marta, holding up her hand. "There's no way you are going up there by yourself. That's suicide. The simians don't go alone, they take their troop with them. Same with you. We'll be your troop."

"Sorry," says the shipmind, "that isn't going to happen. This is an important mission, but I am not risking this entire generation on one journey. I can risk one of you, maybe two. No more."

"All right. Then I'll go with Ricky." Marta folds her arms and glares around the room, daring anyone to argue with her. Nobody does.

* * *

Later that night, Ricky flops onto his back in Marta's bunk, breathing heavily and covered in a sheen of sweat. They've been lovers for about a year, and spent nearly every night eagerly and passionately having sex. It was fun, it felt great, and the affection they felt for each other grew over time. They'd both had other sexual partners earlier, but over the last year the relationship has grown so strong that neither of them have any interest in coupling with any of the others, despite Yuxi's not-so-subtle advances towards both Ricky and Marta.

Tonight, though, something feels different. Marta props herself on one elbow and looks at Ricky. "What are you thinking right now?"

Ricky briefly considers a few joking replies, but decides this is not the time. "I don't know. Everything feels strange all of a sudden."

Marta waits. When no more words come, she pokes him and says, "Come on, you can do better than that."

"Okay. I guess I'm thinking this is all new and kind of scary. You know, we've never really been in any real danger. Our whole lives we've been inside the ship, with the shipmind watching over us. She's kept us safe. Even when we get hurt in combat training, we have friends to help, and the medical bay to patch us up again."

"What about when you went off with Katan to the Waya village, all by yourself?"

"I don't know, somehow that felt more like an adventure than a combat mission. I really didn't think anything terrible would happen. But now? The two of us are going to climb three miles straight up. I've never climbed anything higher than a ship's ladder. Sure, we can train to climb these trees, but who knows what we'll run into."

Marta nods. "Right. Mountaineers on Earth only needed to worry about bad weather and low oxygen, We are probably going to have to fight our way past killer angels and who knows what else."

Ricky pulls her close, so her head rests on his chest. Her hair tickles his neck. He can feel her warm breath on his skin. "Are you sure about this?" Ricky whispered.

"There's no way you're going up there without me," she replies, idly playing with the soft hairs on his flat stomach. "You need someone to protect you from those scary angels. If not me, then who?"

"Yuxi would be happy to go."

She moves her hand down towards his belly button. "Oh, sure. She'd like that. Acting brave during the day. And at night, cuddling up with you in a tiny tent hanging from a tree trunk. But she's not me. She doesn't know what you like. You'd probably get tired of her and kick her out of the tent in the first two days."

"That would be a long way down."

"Exactly."

Then, moving lower, she reminds him she really did know what he liked.

* * *

Katan is resting in his den the next morning when Ricky walks in. The human says, "Greetings, Katan."

"Greetings, Ricky."

"Ship want talk you."

"All right." Katan goes over to the video monitor and casually presses the button. The shipmind's avatar appears.

After exchanging greetings, the shipmind says, "Katan, we have discussed this. We will do as you ask. Two humans, Ricky and Marta, have agreed to go on the shared journey. We don't know if the crownfruit will affect them as it affects the simians. We have examined the simian closely. Its body is similar to a human's body. It has more or less the same internal structure, and it is made of more or less the same materials. Its brain looks about the same, though the human brain is much larger of course. The big problem is, we have no way of knowing how the crownfruit will affect a human until we try it. And once we try it, the humans must be ready to set off immediately on the shared journey.

"So, starting today, Ricky and Marta will begin preparing. For now, there is nothing for you to do here, and I think you would be more comfortable in your own village. So please return to your people. Tell them in a hundred days, Ricky and Marta will be ready to go on the shared journey. At that time, please come back here and escort them to your village, where they will wait until a crownfruit becomes available."

"Agreed," says Katan. "I will leave immediately."

"One more thing. Since we have agreed to take on this extremely dangerous task for your people, I want something in return. I want the humans to be able to leave the ship and travel into the forest without fear of being attacked by your people."

"That's fair," says Katan. "It would be extremely dangerous for humans to approach our village, because of our peoples' memory of what happened before. But I see no problem with you exploring the nearby forest. I will talk to Pataza and the council and ask them to let your people travel up to one day's walk in any direction, without any trouble from us."

"Agreed. What about the other clans?"

"We will have to talk to them, of course. Please give us ten days to send messengers to the other clans in the area. If there is a problem, I will let you know, otherwise feel free to leave your nest in ten days."

"Thank you, Katan. We are happy you came to visit us. I hope our clans can learn to live together in peace."

* * *

Katan makes the long trek to the village and immediately goes to see Pataza. He finds her in the clearing, where, as usual, she is sitting with the two other council members. Katan approaches. He crouches, though not quite as low as he'd done in his previous encounters with her. Tucking his tail respectfully, he says,

"Greetings, Pataza. Greetings, Maza and Zaka." He pauses briefly, waiting for a return greeting.

Not hearing one, he continues, "I bring good news. The humans have agreed to take the shared journey. Their leader, the one they call Ship, will send two members of their clan. One is Ricky. You know him, he is the one who has already visited us. The other is a female named Marta, who is pair-bonded with Ricky. Ship is preparing them for the journey, and says they will be ready in a hundred days."

"Prepare them how?" asks Zaka.

"I don't know. They did not tell me."

Maza growls, "It makes no difference. No matter how much they prepare, it won't be enough. We have seen these humans. They are much larger and heavier than simians. Climbing all the way to the sky will be difficult for them, probably impossible. They have spent their entire lives inside the human nest and never climbed anything. Even if the crownfruit gives them the strength and stamina needed to complete the journey, they have no climbing skills."

"I agree," says Pataza. "It's not just that they are poor climbers. They know nothing about the dangers between here and the sky. The simians have been doing this since the dawn of time. To be honest, I think the humans will try and fail, and will fall to their deaths in the first few days."

Katan feels a surprising little twinge of sadness at this. Has he actually started to like the blue-eyed human?

Eyes still on the ground, he says, "Well, they have agreed to try. Ricky and Marta are young and unafraid, and Ship is willing to risk their lives. In return, though, they want something from us. Ship has asked us to grant them safe passage through the forest, at least around their nest."

"Why?" asks Pataza.

"Ship says they want to learn more about the forest. Perhaps it is so they can prepare for the journey. Or perhaps they want to find new food sources."

"More likely they want to spy on us so they can attack us later," says Maza. "How much of the forest do they want to explore?"

Katan replies, "I have suggested the distance they can cover in a day's walk in any direction, and that is acceptable to them, pending your approval of course. They will not come anywhere near our village. You will need to tell our people. And you will need to send messengers to the other clans in the region around the human nest and get them to agree also."

"I see no problem with that," says Pataza. "All the clans understand the situation. Nobody trusts the humans, but we all want them to take the shared journey." She looks at the others. "What do you all think?"

Maza flicks his tail in agreement.

Zaka says, "I agree with the plan, but there could be a problem. There are some in our clan, I'm thinking now of Akana and his friends, who hate the humans for what they did to us in the time before. If they run into the humans in the forest, there could be trouble."

Maza says gruffly, "Not a problem. I also fought against the humans, and I share the same memories. I will speak with them."

"All right, it is decided," says Pataza, standing up. "I will send messengers to the other clans, and I will tell our people to leave the humans alone for now. Later, things may change. It all depends on what happens when they go on the shared journey. If they succeed, the humans will be useful and we will have to come to some agreement. But if they fail, they are nothing more than a dangerous nuisance and we will have to do something about them."

11 | Trouble

No one has seen or heard anything from Katan for eleven days, so the humans conclude the Waya council has accepted their deal and granted them access to the area surrounding the ship.

The shipmind details Yuxi, Carlos, and Anna to go on a day-long hike into the forest, heading in the direction of the Waya village. Decades earlier, the first generation of colonists had named this direction east, because, just as on old Earth, it's the direction towards which the planet rotates on its axis. For that reason, it's also the direction of the rising sun, though there is no hope of ever seeing a sunrise from so far beneath the forest canopy.

The three crew members are tasked with surveying the terrain with the help of inertial mapping devices, collecting water samples and possible food sources for later analysis, and learning what they can about the local ecology. The shipmind also tells them to look up often, to see how the huge silva trunks are distributed and if there are any unusual formations which might make it easier for Ricky and Marta to climb.

They are lightly armed, expecting no trouble from the Waya or other predators. Yuxi carries a rifle for protection but is under strict orders from the shipmind not to fire at a Waya under any circumstances unless they are in immediate and mortal danger. The other two have knives sheathed in their belts but are otherwise unarmed. They only carry food and water, first-aid kits, and tools for collecting and storing samples.

It's their first time outside the confines of the ship, other than the brief excursion to plant the sentry sticks. The shipmind has tried to provide them with some experience in outdoor settings using VR headsets, including dozens of combat scenarios. But actually being in the forest is different. Now they are really, truly outdoors. It's like nothing they've experienced before. Cool breezes on their skin, dim light filtering down from above, crunching of twigs under their boots, smells of rotting vegetation, sounds of nearby insects and far-off animals, all combine to nearly overwhelm them.

Yuxi, acutely aware of her assigned role as platoon commander, pushes aside the barrage of sensory input and focuses on the task at hand. But Carlos is having some trouble. He looks at Anna, seeking reassurance.

Anna smiles at him and says, "This is our new home, big guy. Better get used to it."

They walk slowly through the dim forest, taking samples and exploring as they go. They hear distant sounds of large animals but see none, just a few smaller creatures similar to rodents and lizards. By early afternoon they've covered about three miles. They stop to rest and eat some lunch before heading back.

Yuxi is sitting cross-legged on the ground. She is about to take a bite from a sandwich when she hears a heavy crunch of snapping twigs. Instantly she knows it's not the sound a small animal would make. In one fluid motion she drops her sandwich, swings her rifle into her hands, and turns to face the source of the sound, rifle at the ready.

Sure enough, a large brown Waya is standing in the open and looking at them from fifty feet away. "We've got company," she says. The other two stand, drawing their knives.

"Let's not overreact," says Carlos softly. "Maybe it's just curious."

Yuxi nods. Scanning the area, though, she sees two more Waya, one on either side of the first one. She turns around and sees two more. She realizes they were surrounded. "This isn't curiosity," she says. "This is a hunting pack."

"Remember our orders…" Carlos begins.

"I know our orders, damn it!" snaps Yuxi. "Now shut up and let me deal with this. You two, get behind me and stay close." Carlos and Anna move closer to Yuxi, who is facing the first Waya. "Don't show fear," she tells the others. "And whatever you do, do NOT run. Hopefully, they are just trying to intimidate us and they won't do anything stupid. If they attack, though, they'll be sorry."

The first Waya is the largest and appears to be the leader of this pack. Its brownish fur is flecked with gray, and it has an irregular patch of white fur on its face. One eye seems to be half-closed, as if from an old injury. It steps forward a few paces while the others remain in place. Yuxi tenses, safety off and finger on the trigger.

The Waya starts to growl. Yuxi and the rest of the crew have taken some basic Waya language lessons from the shipmind, but here in the forest, with a real Waya facing her, she has absolutely no idea what it's saying. She figures it must be talking, maybe to her or maybe to its companions, but the words make no sense to her. It sounds like the snarling of a wolf.

For a long moment, nothing happens. The brown Waya looks at Yuxi silently with its one good eye. She glares back at it. The forest around them is completely silent now, as if every living creature is holding its breath.

Then the brown one flicks its ears, just a bit. A split second later, all five sprint towards the three humans. They don't run directly at them, though. They seem to understand what rifles do, and know not to present an easy target. The brown one dodges and weaves as it races incredibly fast toward Yuxi, covering the distance between them in just a couple of terrifying seconds. Then all five of the Waya are on them, teeth bared and claws out. The brown one targets Yuxi, using its large forepaw to knock the rifle from her hands and pin her to the ground. It clamps its teeth on her neck tightly enough to hold her in place but not enough to draw much blood. Three of the others target Carlos, who is much larger than Anna, and hold him down. The last one leaps for Anna, but she manages to spin away from her attacker. She runs two steps towards Yuxi and dives for the rifle, grabbing it just as the Waya leaps and closes its teeth around her ankle. She suppresses a scream as the teeth bite into her flesh. She twists her body, swinging the rifle towards the brown one on top of Yuxi, and fires.

The sound of the rifle shatters the silence of the forest and echoes off the silva. Without waiting to see the result of her first shot, she turns and aims at the Waya who is still holding her ankle.

She fires again, hitting it in the foreleg. It yelps, releases her, and backs off. The three who held Carlos also back off, staring at her. Anna looks down at the one she'd shot first, the brown one who had pinned Yuxi to the ground. It lies on its side, panting, bleeding heavily from a bullet hole in its chest.

"Are you ok?" Anna asks Yuxi, keeping the rifle aimed at the four remaining Waya.

"Yes," Yuxi replies. Blood runs down her neck and stains her shirt, but it is a trickle, not life-threatening. Carlos nods. He is scratched and bitten, bleeding from several places, but has no major injuries.

Anna fires again, just over the heads of the four Waya. They get the message. They run.

Anna turns to the Waya on the ground. She points the rifle at its head. "What do you think?" she asks. She does not have to explain what she means.

"Don't kill it," says Yuxi. "I have no love for this thing, that's for sure. But the situation is bad enough right now. Shooting a Waya in self-defense is one thing. Murder is another. I say leave it alone and let its pack deal with it."

Carlos has taken out his first aid kit and is wrapping a bandage around Yuxi's neck. He looks up and says, "I agree. Leave it here. We don't want to be the ones to kill it."

Anna nods. She is still furious. She looks at the Waya, whose eyes are open but not looking at anything in particular. She points the rifle a little to the left of its head and fires once. The bullet slams into the ground, sending dirt flying into its face. "You're one lucky wolf," she says. Then she turns and walks away, flanked by Carlos and Yuxi.

* * *

As soon as Pataza hears the first two thunderclaps, she knows trouble has returned. She also has a fairly good idea which member of her clan is involved. She sends word for Maza and Zaka to meet her in emergency session.

Not long after the thunderclaps, four people run into the village. One is injured, holding a bleeding foreleg off the ground while stumbling forward. She knows these troublemakers all too well. All are veterans of the first conflict and friends of Akana. There are still a dozen or so veterans in the village. Most of them long ago put the past behind them and moved on with their lives, but a few, like these, could not forget or forgive the humans. They blamed the humans for the deaths of their friends and family. These troubled ones tended to stick together, telling each other stories of the old days, reliving past insults, and vowing revenge.

But the worst troublemaker of all is missing. "Where is Akana?" she demands as soon as the four run up to her.

"He is badly injured," says one of them, crouching in deference to Pataza. "A human struck him with a deathstick."

"What were you doing when this happened?"

"We were defending the clan."

Patanza slaps him hard, her massive forepaw sending him sprawling in the dirt. "I will ask you one more time," she growls, "what were you doing?"

The speaker manages to get to his feet, then crouches even lower than before. "Akana kept telling us for days the humans were coming again and would try to kill us all. He said we needed to frighten them so badly they would go back to their nest and never come out again. Today we went into the forest, looking for them. We found three of them halfway between the shining mountain and here. We surrounded them. One of them had a deathstick and was getting ready to strike us with it. We attacked before it could strike us. Akana knocked the deathstick from the human's forepaws. But another human picked it up and struck Akana with it."

Pataza growls something unintelligible. Then, she says, "You old fools. You have no idea what you have done. Of course the humans are dangerous. But how could you forget these same humans are our last hope, now that the simians are dying? You did not think. You just acted, but with no strategy, no forethought. And you may have brought about the end of our clan."

The four say nothing. Their eyes are downcast, their tails buried between their hind legs. Zaka asks them, "What about Akana? Is he still alive?"

"I don't know. The last we saw him, he was lying on the ground, with the humans standing over him. We ran away when the human threatened us with the deathstick. As we ran, we heard another shot, but we were afraid to turn around and look, for fear they would strike us with the deathstick again."

"Do you think they struck Akana and killed him?"

"Probably, yes. The humans are bloodthirsty killers. We know this."

Pataza growls, "I've heard enough. Get out of here, all of you. I must discuss this with the council and I don't want to hear any more from you. Go back to your dens and stay there."

The four veterans slink away. Pataza looks at Maza. "Well?"

Maza growls, "These idiots have pissed in the campfire, that's for sure. I cannot say how much damage they've done, but it's bad. Very bad. If we don't come up with a way to fix this, the humans will go back on their promise to take the shared journey for us. They will disappear back inside their shining mountain, and we will all die a slow death."

"Your words don't make me feel any better, Maza. Do you have any suggestions?"

"First, find Akana. From what these fools said, he was lying on the ground the last time the deathstick was used. If the humans killed him while he was defenseless, that is an act of war and must not go unpunished. But if Akana is alive, there may yet be ways to resolve this."

"All right. I will send some guards to find Akana. Even better, I will go with them. I want to see this for myself. And if that fool is still alive, I may just kill him myself."

* * *

When the shipmind heard the first gunshot it estimated it was unlikely to be serious trouble. But when three more shots followed, it revised its estimate from possible trouble to almost certain disaster. A single shot could be a warning shot, but four could only mean a confrontation with the Waya. And considering the instructions Yuxi had from the shipmind, it must have been a matter of life and death.

Quickly the shipmind tells Ricky, Marta, Ivan, and Angie to report to the mess hall. While they race in, it spends almost a full second analyzing the situation. Should it send reinforcements? And if so, how many? The shipmind constructs decision tree of all the different scenarios, the probability of each, all of its possible responses, and the probability of success and the cost and benefit of each outcome.

In the highly unlikely event it was a false alarm, just a few accidental gunshots, it doesn't matter what the shipmind does, because the crew will be safe regardless.

If it was an attack by a single Waya or a small pack, but the three humans are still alive, there is a high probability four heavily armed reinforcements could rescue them. This scenario was unlikely, though, because if the fight was still ongoing there would probably be additional gunshots, not just the first four.

If it was an all-out attack by a dozen or a hundred Waya, then sending reinforcements would serve no purpose. The first three would already be dead, and sending in more soldiers would probably just lead to more human deaths, numerous Waya deaths, and the end of any possible cooperation between the two peoples.

There were other possible explanations for what happened, though. It's highly unlikely Pataza herself would authorize an attack, if her story about the simians was true and she'd been negotiating in good faith. But maybe her whole story of simian sickness was a deception. Or maybe there was a coup and Pataza has been replaced by a virulent anti-human. Or maybe Katan never even made it back to his village to report to Pataza, and the Waya saw the exploration party as an unauthorized intrusion on their territory. Or maybe this was a vigilante raid by some disgruntled members of the pack, like the ones Ricky encountered during his first visit to the Waya village. Or it could have been an attack by a feral Waya unaffiliated with any pack.

As the shipmind works the problem, the decision tree becomes larger and larger until it contains thousands of branches, but it quickly completes its analysis and decides it's just too dangerous to risk a rescue mission. Of all the hundreds of scenarios, there is only one where reinforcements would be helpful. That is if the attack was by a small number of Waya, the attack was unsuccessful, the three crew are still alive, and the battle is still ongoing. This is highly unlikely, though, as conflicts like these tend to be over quickly and there hadn't been any additional gunshots.

And what if the shipmind sends reinforcements and some or all of them are killed? The likely result would be yet another lost generation.

And if the rescue party survives? A breeding population of four humans wouldn't be enough to establish a healthy colony, but that was also true if there are seven humans. To ensure genetic diversity and avoid the negative effects of inbreeding, simulations show the minimum viable breeding population to be at least fifty colonists, preferably a hundred. Regardless of what happens now, the shipmind will have to thaw and gestate a lot more embryos at some point. But the odds of raising a healthy third generation would be significantly improved if there are some survivors from the current generation to assist with raising them, and the odds improve as the number of survivors goes up.

Thus, the shipmind concludes it would be unwise to risk the lives of the four humans still safely inside the ship.

The shipmind's analysis is complete. Ricky, Marta, Ivan, and Angie have assembled in the mess hall. The shipmind briefs them on what happened, and is just getting around to discussing the strategic situation and issuing orders when the pickets report activity at the perimeter. The shipmind sees Yuxi, Anna, and Carlos running towards the ship. They look all right and are not being pursued. Oddly, though, Anna is the one carrying the rifle.

Marta runs to the hatch and spins the door lock open. The three tumble in, bloody and dirty, out of breath but apparently not seriously injured. Marta closes and locks the door quickly.

"Status?" barks the shipmind.

"We were attacked," says Yuxi, stepping quickly into the spokesperson role before Anna or Carlos can speak. "Five Waya surrounded us. They looked hostile. I pointed my rifle at the leader but held my fire. All at once they ran towards us, dodging and weaving to avoid rifle fire. They moved incredibly fast. One of them, the leader, knocked my rifle away and pinned me to the ground. Three more pinned Carlos. The fifth one targeted Anna, but she grabbed the rifle and shot the one on top of me. She shot one more, then they ran away."

"You've described two shots. But we heard four shots," says the shipmind.

Anna speaks up. "The third shot was over their heads, to make sure they would run away and not come back. The fourth shot was not strictly necessary. The Waya that attacked Yuxi was lying on the ground, badly wounded. I could have killed it. I wanted to. But we talked it over and thought it would do more harm than good. So I fired into the ground, close to its head."

"They didn't try to kill you?"

"No," says Yuxi. "They held us down with their teeth. They could easily have ripped out our throats, but apparently that was not their intention. Their goal was to frighten us, to send a message."

"The first one you shot, the one that pinned Yuxi. Did it run away?"

"No, it was too badly wounded. We left it lying on the ground."

"Describe it."

"Brown fur, white spot on its face, a damaged eye."

"Akana," says the shipmind. "I thought so."

Yuxi is startled. "How did you know?"

"When Ricky first went to the Waya village, the video showed he was attacked almost immediately by an older one with those features. Pataza's reaction was interesting. She seemed unsurprised when she saw it was him. Apparently, he is a known troublemaker, an anti-human if you want to call him that. It's possible he is actually an agent provocateur working for Pataza, but I doubt it. More likely, he and a bunch of his friends decided to bypass the council and take matters into their own paws. They created their own little hunting pack. They also knew exactly how many days passed, so they were prepared to encounter a human exploration party today."

"So, you knew this could happen?" demanded Carlos.

"No, of course not. I never would have sent you out so lightly armed if I thought that would happen. From what I saw of Ricky's visit and what I know of their behavior, I thought the power structure of the Waya was a strong top-down hierarchy that would prevent this sort of thing. It appears I miscalculated."

The shipmind sees Yuxi's response to this. The girl doesn't say anything, but she clearly is angry the shipmind has once again failed to understand the behavior of others and led them into such a dangerous situation. She glowers at the floor.

"What does this mean for our mission?" asks Ricky.

"Good question," says the shipmind. "It all depends on what happened out there. If this was an isolated incident caused by a small number of troublemakers, their leaders can deal with it and the agreement can still remain intact. Though I think some reparations would be in order."

"And if it wasn't an isolated incident?" asks Carlos.

The shipmind pauses for a split second as it builds and analyzes another large decision tree. "Then it's a standoff. The seven of you cannot hope to defeat and exterminate all the Waya in the region, even if you wanted to. And the Waya cannot touch us inside the ship. So, we remain stuck here. We build a fort and we live inside it."

"Like a bunch of American soldiers in Indian country in the 1800's," says Anna.

"Or like a handful of survivors of the zombie apocalypse, surrounded by mobs of the undead who want to eat them," suggests Ivan, who loves watching old horror movies.

Yuxi, her neck still bandaged and bloody, says, "Ship, you could clear out the wolves for a hundred miles, a thousand miles in every direction if you wanted to."

"Not an option," replies the shipmind curtly. "All right, that's enough for now. Yuxi, Anna, and Carlos, we are glad you're back and not hurt too badly. Go to the medical bay and get cleaned up. Ricky and Marta, this does not affect your training. Stick with it until we know what's going on. Let's see what the Waya do next."

12 | Wild One

Pataza and the two guards race through the forest, covering the distance between the village and the conflict site in less than half a day. They carry no medicines in their neck bags, no food or water. This is not a rescue mission.

Towards evening they find Akana. He is still lying where the human struck him with the deathstick. His eyes are open but unfocused. He apparently has not moved from where he fell, judging from the pool of blood on the ground nearby. Pataza walks up to him and says softly, "Akana. What have you done?"

Akana manages to raise his head a bit and look at her. "Greetings, Pataza. I was trying to save our people. You would not do it, so I had to."

"No, you were not trying to save our people. You were trying to change something that happened a long time ago. And in doing so, you may have sentenced our people to death. How could you be so blind? Don't you understand our situation?"

Akana speaks slowly, each word causing him pain. "Pataza, you are the leader of our clan, but you are a fool. You think you can make some kind of deal with these humans. You see them as just another clan. You think they are just like us except they walk on two legs instead of six, and speak in screeches instead of words. But I know these creatures, and you are wrong. The humans are not another clan. They are death."

Pataza bares her teeth. "You understand nothing, Akana."

"Oh, is that true? Pataza, do you have any idea what those human creatures are truly capable of? What do you know of that shining mountain of theirs? It's not just a hollow rock as you seem to believe. Don't you remember it flew here like a giant bird, and burned a hole in the silva? We know of nothing else with that kind of power. The shining mountain is a terrible weapon, far more dangerous than any animal. I believe it will kill us all."

"Akana, if you could let go of your obsession with the past and thought about it, you'd see we hold the high ground here. There are only a few of them, and there are hundreds, thousands of us. Their ship is just a den containing some humans. It can do nothing to us. We alone decide whether the humans will live or die. And we negotiate with them on our terms, not on theirs."

"Always looking on the bright side, aren't you? The humans are darkness and death. Maybe that's why you cannot see them for what they are."

Pataza glowers at him. "None of this matters. The decision on how to deal with the humans was never yours to make. You are no longer on the clan council. You are a member of the clan." She paused. "Or at least, you were."

Akana blinks slowly. "So. You will exile me?"

"Yes, this is my decision. You know our ways, even though you don't obey them. We do not kill except to defend ourselves or when we hunt for food. So even though I want to kill you right now for the terrible damage you have done, I will not. From this day forward, you are no longer one of us. You are a wild one. You will never enter or approach our village again. You will never speak to any of our people. And if I ever hear you have any contact with the humans, I will break the rule against killing, and your days living in this world will be over. Do I make myself clear?"

Akana says nothing. He closes his eyes and lets his head drop back to the ground.

Pataza says, "There is a small stream about fifty paces back towards the village. If you can make it that far, you can drink. If you manage to survive your injury, fine. If you die, that's fine too. I don't care anymore."

She starts to walk away, flanked by the two guards. She turns and says, "Goodbye, wild one."

* * *

Four days later, Anna, on sentry duty, spots a party of five Waya standing at the outer edge of the clearing, on the side closest to their village. They make no attempt to hide. They stand in the open, looking across the clearing towards the ship.

The shipmind and crew had been on alert since the incident in the forest. They were not concerned at all about the Waya attacking the ship. But the crew remained inside. Non-essential studies were put on hold, and their days were filled with hours of combat training, workshops on battle strategy and tactics, and VR simulations. Ricky and Marta continued their physical conditioning work, repeatedly climbing up and down thick ropes hung from high ceilings.

Looking out across the clearing, the shipmind recognizes Pataza, the two council members Maza and Zaka, and the two envoys Katan and Takaqa. "Ricky and Marta," it says through the speakers, "we have company. Go out and see what they want."

Ricky and Marta open the hatch and step out of the ship. They look at the Waya, holding their hands outstretched and empty to show they carry no weapons. Then they walk exactly halfway across the clearing, stop, and wait. The Waya get the hint. They cross the remaining distance, until the two groups are just a few yards apart.

"Greetings, people," says Ricky, who is still far from fluent in the Waya language and has no idea of the proper words to use in this situation.

"Greetings, Ricky and Marta," says Pataza. "We want to speak with Ship."

"Ok. You come talk Ship."

"No. We will not enter Ship. We will wait here."

Ricky blinks. "You want Ship come you?"

"Yes. We will wait for Ship to meet us here."

Ricky and Marta turn and walk back towards the ship. "It's a negotiating ploy," says Marta. "They don't want to appear to be inferior to the shipmind in any way, so they insist on meeting on neutral ground. Or as neutral as possible, anyway."

Ricky nods. "Yeah, it would be awkward to try and set up a meeting halfway between here and the village. Let's see what the shipmind has to say about this."

The shipmind concurs with Marta's assessment of the situation, and agrees to a meeting in the clearing. Ivan and Carlos quickly locate a maintenance bot, a boxy thing about half the size of a human, with four large wheels, two multi-jointed manipulator arms, and a video screen mounted on its front. It's heavy, but they manage to maneuver it through the hatch and onto the ground. The shipmind takes direct control of the bot, driving it slowly towards the visitors. Ricky, Marta, Carlos and Anna follow close behind.

"Ship here," Ricky says to Pataza, pointing to the bot.

The black mirror of the video monitor screen lights up, revealing the shipmind in its Waya clan leader avatar. It says, "Greetings, Pataza. Greetings, council members Maza and Zaka. Greetings, envoys Katan and Takaqa."

Katan is the only one of the five Waya who recognizes the shipmind's avatar. He'd explained it to the others before they arrived, trying to convince them the flat moving picture they would see on the monitor was, in fact, Ship. The others had some trouble understanding this, especially since Katan's own grasp of the workings of the moving pictures was murky. But still, they expected to see something like this. The three council members manage to hide their discomfort and gaze calmly at the image. Takaqa flinches a bit.

"Greetings, Ship," says Pataza. "I have come to talk with you about recent events."

So, thinks the shipmind. She greets only me, and not the others. And she refers only to herself, not her companions. Pataza is setting this up as a one-on-one summit meeting, clan leader to clan leader.

The shipmind says, "I am not happy at all about recent events," taking a confrontational tone.

"I am not happy either," replies Pataza. "Our two clans had an agreement. And I regret to say one of our people broke that agreement."

"Five of your people attacked us, not one."

"One was the leader. He convinced the others to join him."

"Your people cannot think for themselves?"

"All five had good reasons to dislike humans. They all fought and suffered greatly in the time before. They all saw clan members killed. Some of them saw family members killed. By humans."

"Pataza, your people killed every single one of the humans in the time before. They wiped out my entire clan. Surely you understand I also have good reasons to be angry, and I have reasons to attack you, with deathsticks and other weapons you know nothing about. Yet, I held back."

This thinly veiled threat clearly disturbs Pataza. She backtracks, saying, "Ship, you and I both know we must leave the past in the past. We are here now. You need our help, and we need your help. Let's walk forward together."

Now the shipmind feels it is gaining the upper hand, and decides to push a little bit. "No, we cannot just forget about what happened. We had an agreement. You broke it. You must pay." In the Waya language, this last word has a meaning closer to "give food," but it's the closest word available.

Pataza's tail raises just a bit, then lowers again. "I understand. Even though your people were not hurt and two of our people were struck by your deathsticks, I understand. And so yes, we will pay."

The shipmind waits, saying nothing.

"The one who led the attack against your people. His name was Akana." The shipmind finds it interesting she referred to him in the past tense. Is he dead? Pataza continues, "Among our people, we have several different kinds of punishments for crimes against the clan. The most serious is exile. I have decided the one whose name was Akana is now exiled. He is forbidden from having any contact, ever again, with our clan or with any other clan. He is also forbidden to have any contact with humans. He is now a wild one. He is like one born wild in the forest but never adopted by a clan."

"What will happen to him?"

"He will wander the forest alone. He will speak to no one. Over time he will become less like a person and more like an animal. He may even forget how to speak. This is a sad life for one who was part of a clan, living among friends and family, and is cut off from everything they know."

"And what of the other four and their crimes?" Until now the shipmind hadn't known the word for crime or criminals, since it had not come up in any prior conversation.

"They will also be punished but less severely. They will not be permitted to speak with each other. They will also be given the lowest-ranking jobs in the clan for a period of time. I believe this will be enough to prevent any future trouble."

"All right. But an attack like this must not happen again. I want you to place guards along the border between our part of the forest and yours, to watch for future criminal behavior."

Now Pataza's tail goes up and stays there. "Ship, you misunderstand. There is no part of the forest that is yours. Our people have lived here for thousands of generations. This forest is ours. You are our guests, and we permit you to travel through a portion of the forest. Not to make it your own."

Well, thinks the shipmind, that struck a nerve. Now it needs to make a decision. Should it escalate the issue, issue threats, maybe even fire off some of the ship's weapons? No. The ship decides that, at least for now, maintaining friendly relations with Pataza is preferable to battling an army of angry Waya. Speaking as soothingly as it could manage in the guttural Waya language, it says, "I did not mean the forest belonged to us, just that we have the right to go there, just as you do."

"You have no rights here. We allow you to travel through it."

"Of course," says the shipmind, backing off a bit and leaving the matter of ownership unresolved for now. "But still, we need some assurance from you we will not be attacked by your clan or by this wild one."

"I will assign some guards to patrol the area between our village and the forest where your people are allowed to go. We will do this for a hundred days. If there is no trouble, we will stop. I expect no trouble."

"Agreed," says the shipmind. It foolishly lost its advantage by making the comment about "our part of the forest" which justifiably angered the clan leader. Now it's time to just wrap up the meeting before things get any worse. "That covers just about everything. One more thing, though. We would like to invite Katan to stay with us for a while, as we prepare for the shared journey. His advice would be valuable."

"Of course," says Pataza. The two of them exchange some polite closing comments, then the four Waya turn and walk out of the clearing. The humans and the bot head back to the ship, with Katan limping along next to them.

13 | Training

In the days and weeks following the summit meeting, life for the humans returns to something approaching normal. They resume their academic classes while continuing their physical conditioning, combat training, and battle simulations.

Now that they have Pataza's assurance that they can explore the forest again, the shipmind sends out three-person patrols nearly every day. Unlike the first patrol, these are heavily armed. Each human carries an assault rifle and a half-dozen grenades. One member of the patrol always wears long-range sensing gear which can identify the infrared heat signature of a Waya or other large creature more than a hundred yards away and issue an alert if anything is detected. And the shipmind backs them up with a small flotilla of drones buzzing overhead, scanning the region in visible and infrared wavelengths.

Meanwhile, Ricky and Marta intensify their training for the shared journey. The most difficult part is the physical conditioning. Both were already in excellent shape as a result of their youth, genetic heritage, and years of training. But climbing is a specialized task demanding strong fingers, hands, forearms, and toes.

Ascent to the Sun

The most vulnerable part of the body, oddly enough, is the small pulley tendons in the fingers, which are stressed whenever a climber inserts their fingertips into a small crevice or onto a surface edge to hold their body weight. Evolution never designed human fingers to do this thousands of times a day. Ricky and Marta apply tape to protect the vulnerable tendons, but they still need months of specialized training to thicken and strengthen them.

Every morning, regardless of the weather, they go outdoors and, top-roped for safety, climb a nearby silva trunk all the way to the first branching and down again. They repeat this a half dozen times. In the afternoon they continue training indoors. They construct a climbing wall in an unused part of the ship, fifty feet tall and covered with a hard rough material similar to silva bark, but with laybacks, overhangs, roof sections and angled slabs. It's covered with odd-shaped holds they don't encounter in their outdoor practice climbs: crimps so small they can only be gripped with the fingertips, large slopers too big to be gripped that need friction to hold onto, tiny pinches that must be squeezed between thumb and forefingers, and pockets just big enough for one or two fingertips. Ricky and Marta spend hours on the training wall every day, building their strength and running drills prescribed by their shipmind climbing coach.

A couple of weeks into the training, the shipmind says, "Ricky, Marta, I've made some gear for you. Please come to the printer room and take a look."

Ricky and Marta have just finished a grueling practice session on the campus board, a slightly overhanging panel with a series of parallel horizontal rungs spaced a hand's-width apart. They use the board every day, climbing up and down using only their arms to build strength in their fingers and upper body.

They walk out of the gym and towards the printer room, shaking out their forearms and wiping chalk dust from their hands.

"What have you got for us?" asks Ricky as they enter the room.

The shipmind replies, "Since climbing the silva is similar to big wall climbing on old Earth, I've made some gear that should work well for you. Take a look."

Lying on the floor are lengths of newly fabricated climbing ropes. "These were tricky to make," says the shipmind. "It was easy to use the printers to extrude the fibers, but weaving them together was more complicated than you might think. I had to build a braiding machine to do it."

Ricky picks up one of the climbing ropes, runs it through his chalked fingers, and hands it to Marta. "Looks good to me. What else have you got?"

"You will need devices to set protection, as you will certainly not want to free-climb. These are the protection devices. You'll need to learn how to use all of these."

The two humans pick up the devices and examine them. Marta holds up a little metallic device with a spring surrounding a central rod. "What's this?"

"I thought you'd recognize this from the training videos," says the shipmind, sounding a bit disappointed. "It's a cam, a spring-loaded device you insert into a crevice, then it expands to fit securely so it won't pull out. You clip into it using a carabiner. You do know what a carabiner is, I assume."

"Of course," says Marta, a bit annoyed. She reaches into a box and picks up a shiny metal carabiner, an oblong metal loop with a spring-loaded hinged gate. She lets it slip from her fingers and it drops into the box with a clink.

They examine the other equipment. There is a box of pitons, metal spikes that can be hammered into the bark if no crevices are available for cams. There are two backpacks, two climbing harnesses, rolls of finger tape, two pairs of tight-fitting climbing shoes, and crampons that attach to the shoes.

"Are these diamond tips?" asks Ricky, cautiously running a finger across the needle-sharp points on the crampons.

"Not real diamond," replies the shipmind, "but more than hard enough for what you need. You'll also notice the survival gear. You could be in the silva for two months going up and another month coming back down. We have no idea what kind of food, if any, you will find along the way, and I'm not sure I'll be able to deliver it to you via drones. So you may want to use these."

On a table are some knives, two handguns, two small pistol-like objects that upon closer inspection turn out to be mini crossbows, and arrows attached to lightweight lines that can be shot and retrieved later. Next to them is a plastic rain collector. And a bivy, a lightweight tent that can be hung from a couple of carabiners to provide two people with shelter from storms and a place to sleep.

As the training continues and they gain more experience with their newly fashioned tools, Ricky and Marta feel increasingly confident in their ability to climb to the sky. But at night, lying together, they wonder. What sorts of creatures live in the high silva? How will those creatures feel about two aliens suddenly intruding on their world, and what will they try to do about it? There will be a variety of life forms dwelling in the silva. Will they be curious, apathetic, or hostile? And if they are hostile, what could two humans, far from the world they knew, possibly do to resist them?

* * *

Katan finds to his surprise that he's enjoying his stay in the human den. Looking for a more varied diet and eager to wander the forest, he goes out every day and hunts. But he also likes the convenience of the food printer in the mess hall, so he asks Ship for more dining options. The shipmind suggests he provide samples of what he has in mind. Katan obliges, bringing back a variety of small animals and some plants. He also gives the shipmind some glow grubs and describes the process for preparing glowjuice. Soon he has a ready supply of excellent glowjuice and a reasonably varied diet. He also politely tastes a few human foods but finds them disgusting, though some of the faux meat dishes are tolerable.

Despite his growing comfort with his new home, he still finds it stressful to speak with Ship. Katan is a low-ranking member of his own clan, far inferior in status to Pataza and the other council members. Whenever he speaks with Ship he feels the same dread, the same urge to cower, he felt when he was before the council. He tries to hide this, but Ship can tell from his elevated heartrate and general agitation. The shipmind does not mention this to Katan, of course, but a few days into his visit, it tells him, "Katan, I would like you to meet one of my assistants. Her name is Chaya." This word is oddly similar to the Waya word for a low-ranking servant.

Ship's image slides to the right and off the screen, and a new image slides in from the left. It's a small, almost juvenile Waya female. Her fur is a dark tan and her eyes are exceptionally large and bright. "Hello, Katan," she says cheerfully. "My name is Chaya. I am here to help you."

Katan is amused by this. He assumes the similarity between Chaya's name and the word for servant is not a coincidence. He also assumes Chaya is a servant of Ship, not him, and that she will relay everything he says directly back to her boss. Almost certainly she is Ship's spy.

Still, he finds to his relief he is more relaxed talking with Chaya than with the dominant clan leader. His urge to cower is gone. He decides to play along, at least for a while, with this ploy.

"Hello, Chaya," he says, swishing his tail a bit. "It's nice to meet you. Tell me what you can do to help me."

"I can help you in many ways," replies the avatar brightly. "I know everything about the humans, so I can answer questions you have about them. I know a lot about the human den, so I can help you find things you might want. I can help you get food and drink that will please you. And if it's ok with you, I would like to ask you some questions about your people and about the shared journey."

"Why would you want to know those things?" asks Katan, though he already knows she will just pass along the information to Ship.

Her answer surprises him. "My friends, Ricky, and Marta, will be going on the shared journey soon. They know almost nothing about the journey or your people. It's difficult for them to ask you questions, because Ricky only speaks a little of your language, and Marta almost none at all. They have asked me to talk with you so I can learn more about the journey. If it's all right with you, I will pass along to my friends some of the things you tell me. Is that ok?"

Well, thinks Katan, she may be a spy, but at least she's an honest one. "All right, Chaya. I will tell you about my people, you will tell me about the humans. That seems fair."

"Good!" she says. "You go first. What would you like to know?"

Katan considers this for a moment. So many questions, where to start? "Tell me about the humans in this den. Where do they come from? Who are their parents?"

Chaya replies, "There are seven humans here. I think you have already met them all. There are three males, named Ricky, Ivan, and Carlos. There are four females, named Marta, Yuxi, Anna, and Angie." The names sound harsh to Katan and almost impossible to pronounce.

Chaya continues, "They are not related. Their parents lived long ago on the world they call Earth. There were seven pairs of parents. Each pair bonded on Earth and created an egg. The eggs were placed in the great mother ship and sent here, a journey of many, many lifetimes."

"And how did the eggs turn into full grown humans?"

"Ship did that. Ship warmed the eggs, took care of the eggs as they grew, and helped the babies come out of the eggs. Then Ship served as their mother as they grew."

Katan thinks this is interesting and not particularly stressful. He relaxes on the carpet, his hind and middle legs folded under him and his forepaws stretched out in front.

He asks, "Does the ship have other eggs?"

"Yes."

"How many?"

"I don't know."

He looks at the servant more intently. "I thought you said you knew everything about the human den."

"I know almost everything. Some things are hidden from me, as they are hidden from you." She adds cheerfully, "What other questions do you have?"

"Are these humans juveniles or fully grown?"

"These humans are no longer juveniles. You can think of them as young adults. They are fully grown, but still relatively young. They have lived about one-fifth of the average lifetime of a human."

"Are they pair bonded yet?"

"Ricky and Marta are pair bonded. Carlos and Angie are also pair bonded. Ivan and Anna and Yuxi are, you might say, lightly bonded. Human bonding is quite different from Waya. Human bonds are usually temporary, especially when they are young. Their mating is much more frequent than it is with the Waya. And their mating rarely results in reproduction. These humans are young, and the situation here is too dangerous, so they all have chosen not to reproduce at this time."

Suddenly this simple conversation about eggs has turned into a deluge of information. Katan has a hard time processing it all. He takes a moment to try and make sense of what he'd just heard.

"Why do they mate, then, if not to reproduce?"

"It gives them great pleasure. It is also a way to strengthen friendship."

"How often do they mate?"

"When they are young, quite often. Sometimes several times a day."

Katan finds this inconceivable. He mated once in his life, long ago. His mate is long dead, something he is reminded of whenever he feels a twinge of pain in his foreleg. He decides to shift the topic onto safer ground. "You said three of the humans are lightly bonded. I don't understand what that means."

"In humans, mating results from a wide range of bonding intensity. The strongest, such as between Ricky and Marta, is exclusive, meaning the two are committed to bonding with each other to the exclusion of everyone else and sometimes for the rest of their lives. At the other end, some mating carries no bonding at all and is done simply for pleasure. In the case of the three humans I mentioned earlier, it is somewhere in between. They care for each other, but with no intention of long-term commitment. And from what I have seen, they are open to mating with others outside of their current partners."

This is getting more and more confusing. Katan presses on, however. He asks, "How can two females bond and, uh, mate?"

"As you know, Katan, among your own people there are sometimes pairs of males or pairs of females who form strong friendship bonds. Sometimes those bonds endure for an entire lifetime even though no mating occurs. Humans can form similar bonds within their own sex, sometimes with mating and sometimes not. Remember though, mating comes much more easily to them. They sometimes mate with someone of their own sex for pleasure, for bonding, or usually some combination of the two."

"How do two humans of the same sex mate? And how do three humans mate?"

"That is complicated, and I would prefer not to get into it right now."

That's fine with Katan. His brain is starting to hurt. "All right, let's stop for now. Thanks, Chaya."

"Katan, it's been my pleasure. I am happy to talk with you anytime. Whenever you want me, just go up to any of the video monitors in the human den and say, 'Hey, Chaya.' I will come to you right away."

Katan heads down the hallway to the food printer. He really needs some glowjuice.

* * *

The shipmind created a submissive personality for the Chaya character, along with a simpler language model and a young, wide-eyed, non-threatening appearance, all intended to put Katan at ease. Its assessment of Katan's state of mind is that he believes

Chaya to be a separate entity but working as an informant. The shipmind is fine with that interpretation.

The next morning, Katan goes to the food printer and orders some groundmouse and berries. He also orders a cup of glowjuice diluted with warm water, which he enjoys sipping after breakfast. When he returns to his den, he says, "Hey, Chaya," to the monitor in his den. The shipmind delays for a couple of seconds, then Chaya appears on the screen.

"Hello, Katan," says Chaya, cheerful as always. "How are you today?"

Katan ignores this. "I'd like to ask you some questions about the human den."

"Of course. But yesterday we agreed on an exchange of information. Don't you think it's my turn to ask you some questions?"

Katan takes a sip of his drink. "All right. Ask away."

"Soon, my friends will be ready to go on the shared journey. But none of us know anything about the world above. If you don't mind, I'd like to ask you some questions about that. I think all of us want my friends to succeed in their journey."

Katan replies, "I will tell you what I can."

"Do the Waya ever journey up into the silva?"

"Of course not. Our paws don't have the right shape to hold onto the silva bark. If we try to climb, we can only go a few paces, then we fall to the ground."

"No Waya has ever tried?"

Katan takes another sip and pauses to gather his thoughts. "There is an ancient story. Once there was a Waya who could think of nothing except climbing the silva until she reached the sky. She thought about it all day, and dreamed about it at night. She tried everything. First, she tried climbing but could not get far. Then she learned the language of the simians, became their friend, and convinced them to carry her up. A group of them tried, but they were not strong enough to do it. She even called upon the angels, but either they did not hear her or they chose to ignore her.

"Finally, she got the idea of making climbing tools. She asked the council's permission to use the jawbones and teeth of two dead Waya to make climbing tools. The council refused. She did it anyway, stealing their bodies in the middle of the night. She pulled the jawbones off the skulls and turned them into false forepaws to penetrate the silva bark and hold her weight. She used vine ropes to attach the jawbones to her own forelegs. Then she began climbing. The clan heard about it. It was too late to stop her, but word quickly spread. Soon the entire clan gathered to watch her climb."

"What happened?" asks Chaya.

"She succeeded for a while. She climbed quite far, almost to the first branching, nearly out of sight. Then something happened. Maybe she slipped. Maybe an angel swooped by and pushed her. Nobody knows. She fell to the ground and died instantly."

So, thinks the shipmind, they have their own version of the Daedalus myth. The Chaya avatar waits a moment, then she says, "What can you tell me of the creatures who live in the silva?"

"Not much. From what we know, the silva has three zones. The lowest zone is between the ground and the first few branchings. Here the silva trunks are huge, so big their surfaces are almost flat. At the first branching, three large branches emerge from the trunk. Each branch extends across to the branch coming from its nearest neighbor. They meet and join, forming a web. This zone is the home of the simians, though they occasionally come down to the ground and sometimes venture upwards a bit past the second or third branching. They eat the things that live on the silva bark – fungus, night-flying creatures, small animals."

"What about the middle zone?"

"The middle zone starts at the second or third branching, and goes up quite a way. We don't know how far, because none of us have ever seen the top of it. This is the land of the angels."

"Tell me about the angels."

"We know little about them. They are similar in some ways to the simians, and are probably related in some distant way. They are larger. Their heads and faces are narrow, with long sharp beaks. Instead of forelegs, the angels have large grayish-white wings. At the tips of the wings are thin forefingers with claws at the end, which makes us think the wings are like simian forepaws but much larger and with webbing. The wings are so thin you can almost see through them. This, plus their light color, makes them difficult to see."

"Are they intelligent?"

"I think so. There are stories about angels coming down to the ground and involving themselves with the affairs of our people, perhaps saving one by killing an attacking animal, or frightening one away from doing something foolish or destructive. A dumb animal would not do such things. Based on that, I think they are at least as intelligent as the simians, probably more so."

"Do they have language?"

"They probably have some way to communicate, since they live in groups and would need to work things out amongst themselves. But none of us have ever heard a sound from them. If they do have a language, we know nothing of it, because they have no interest in teaching us."

When Chaya did not respond, Katan continued, "Make no mistake, the angels are not your friends. They will not tolerate anyone, whether it be one of us, a simian, or a human, entering their zone. They may be lightweight, but their claws and teeth are sharp, and they can fly. You must be very, very careful."

"How can Ricky and Marta pass through the land of the angels?"

"I have no idea."

"How do the simians do it?"

"I don't know. Perhaps they have some sort of agreement with the angels. Or maybe they pay for permission to pass through. The simians refuse to tell us."

"All right then. What about the upper zone, the land above the angels?"

"We know nothing of the upper zone. There are birds, of course. The simians have told us the birds eat the fruits that are pooped out. And we sometimes find bodies of dead birds on the ground, just as we sometimes come upon bodies of angels, simians, and other small animals that live in the silva."

Katan scratches his ear with his forepaw. "It's strange, though. The silva is high, and it's probably filled with a variety of creatures. But we hardly ever see dead bodies falling down to the ground. I don't know why we don't see more."

14 | Memories

There is a storm that night. Ivan is on sentry duty, and Yuxi is in her bunk with Anna. Their cuddling and kissing had just progressed to more intimate activities when they hear the distant crash of thunder through the ship's hull. The huge ship actually vibrates from the sound itself, or maybe from the shaking of the ground. The thunder is initially a sharp crack like a gunshot, then becomes lower and softer as it rolls down through the silva and echoes off the thousands of trunks and branches, finally fading away. Another thunderclap follows, then another. This is going to be a big storm.

"Let's go see," says Anna. Yuxi reluctantly disengages from her lover. They dress and go to the front hatch where they find Ivan sitting on a bench just outside the half-open door. He is wearing a light camo jacket over t-shirt and trousers. His rifle is in his lap, and he's scanning the tree line through a pair of night vision goggles. Without speaking, Anna and Yuxi sit down cross-legged on the floor just inside the hatch, joining him in watching the storm. They leave the entryway dark to avoid interfering with Ivan's goggles.

Near ground level the silva trunks are far too massive to be affected by anything as trivial as a surface storm. But far above, in the upper reaches of the silva, the branches are thinner, like the branches of ordinary Earth trees. And at the very top, the smallest branches are covered with broad fronds, the equivalent of leaves. None of the crew have ever seen a live silva branch with fronds on it, but broken branches occasionally fall to the ground. Now, as the storm intensifies, they hear the far-off rustling of millions of branches. Green fronds, and every now and then a small branch, spin slowly down and land on the ground. Once a large branch falls with a loud thump.

A few minutes later, the rain comes. First a few drops, then a shower, then a downpour, then a deluge. Tremendous roaring waterfalls appear, coursing down along the huge trunks and flowing across the rain-soaked ground. By the time Ivan moves inside the ship's hatch to avoid the rain, he's already dripping wet. He continues to look out at the clearing, scanning slowly from side to side through the goggles.

Suddenly he jumps a bit. "Something's out there," he says. "Ten o'clock." Anna and Yuxi look through the pouring rain but see nothing.

"What do you see?" asks Anna.

"It's big. Maybe a Waya. Just sitting or standing. Watching us."

"I'll get a spotlight," says Yuxi. She jumps up and returns a half minute later with a hand-held spotlight. She passes it to Ivan. He takes off the goggles and reaches for a pair of high-powered digitally enhanced binoculars, training them at the spot where he'd seen something. Nothing. He aims the spotlight and flicks the power switch. Immediately he sees the dark outline of a creature, and the reflection of two eyes. Then a blur of movement.

"Something's out there. Or was, anyway. Gone now."

"Let's check the recording."

Ivan presses a button on the binoculars, downloading the video onto the ship's computer. They spin the hatch closed and view the recording on the entryway video monitor. At first, all they see is a blur. After doing some image processing, though, the blur sharpens into clearer focus. It's definitely a Waya. It's big, brown, and they can just barely see a patch of white on its face as it turns to retreat into the forest.

"So," says Ivan. "Looks like our exiled friend is back."

* * *

Katan is curled up and asleep, oblivious to the storm raging outside, when Ricky enters his room. "Katan wake," says Ricky. "Ship wants talk you."

Katan slowly opens his eyes. His head hurts, a glowjuice hangover. Must be important, he thinks. Ship has never summoned him in the middle of the night. He limps slowly and painfully across the room to the video monitor and presses the button. Ship's pack leader avatar appears. No Chaya this time, he notices. This must be serious.

"Greetings, Katan," says Ship. Not waiting for him to return the greeting, it continues, "One of our sentries just spotted the criminal, Akana. He was standing in the rain, just outside the clearing. The sentry used a fire-light to see better. As soon as the fire-light hit Akana, he turned and ran."

"Are you sure it was him?" asks Katan, stalling for time while he considers the situation.

"See for yourself," says Ship. Her image slides to the right edge of the screen, and a rectangle appears on the left side. Inside the rectangle is Akana, clearly visible through the pouring rain, looking directly at him. Katan is a little unsettled by this tricky use of the video monitor, which he's never seen before, but he quickly understands what he is looking at. It convinces him Ship is telling the truth.

Ship continues, "Katan, once again your people have broken our agreement. First, a pack of your people attacked three of our crew when they were out in the forest. Pataza came here and promised the leader of the attack would be banished. He was to become a wild one, never to come near us again. But now, not even fifty days later, the wild one has returned. He has come here, to our den. Can you tell us why?"

"Ship," Katan says, "I know nothing of this. You and I both know our council exiled Akana. He was told never to come back to our village, and never to come near the human nest."

"Do clan members often disobey the words of the council?"

"Of course not. But the wild one is no longer a member of the clan. He may feel the words of the council have no meaning for him anymore."

"Katan, the words of the council have meaning to us. But right now, I am not sure if I should continue to listen to their words. And I am not sure if we should work together with your clan anymore."

Despite his pounding headache, Katan clearly hears the threat behind Ship's words. "Ship, I will take care of this. In the morning, I will return to my village and tell Pataza about this. She and the council will do something. Believe me."

"Katan," says Ship, "you have been a good envoy between your people and ours. I trust you to do this. Please go in the morning. Return as soon as you have a response from Pataza."

* * *

Katan slogs through the rain-soaked forest, scrambling over slippery boulders and limping across the cold and swampy ground. Small streams have turned into treacherous foaming rivers he has to swim across, using all his strength to reach the far side to avoid being swept away downstream. And always, he keeps looking around him, wondering if Akana, the wild one, is lying in wait for him.

After four days of difficult travel, he reaches the village. The clearing is wet with puddles everywhere. The firepits are all empty, the Waya having moved the firewood into storage caves just as the storm was starting. Katan crosses the clearing and approaches Pataza's cave at the base of the cliff. He steps into the entryway, crouching down in his usual submissive pose. He wonders if his loyal service as envoy to the humans might improve his rank in the clan. He hopes so. He's getting tired of groveling.

Pataza looks at him impassively.

"The humans are upset," says Katan, eyes downcast as usual. "During the storm they spotted Akana at the edge of the clearing. He was watching the human nest."

"How do you know this?" demands Pataza.

"They showed me," he replies, "on the flat rock machine." He hopes he won't have to explain any more. Apparently Pataza knows what he means.

"The wild one has also been seen near our village," she says. "He has not wandered away as we ordered him to."

Katan says, "Ship was quite angry. It has threatened to walk away from our agreement if we don't do something about this."

"I am getting tired of Ship making threats." Pataza paces around her cave. "Her clan is small, and the humans are weak. She is in no position to make threats."

Katan is doubtful about this. He says as tactfully as he can, "Yes, there are only seven humans, and they are weak. But they have powerful machines. I have spent time in the human nest and I have seen many of their machines. I believe a single human with those machines could stand up to our entire clan, if it came to a fight."

Pataza considers this. "Then let's hope it does not come to a fight."

"What will you do about the wild one?"

Pataza growls. "We told him death would come swiftly to him if he disobeyed my orders. Now it's time to put some teeth into those words. I will speak with my guards. Go back and tell Ship we will handle this matter ourselves. And quickly."

Katan is exhausted from his four days travel. "May I rest here tonight and head back tomorrow?"

"You are an old one," says Pataza, flicking her tail in a surprising show of affection, or at least tolerance. This is encouraging. Maybe he's earned an improvement in rank after all. She says softly, "Rest tonight. You can return tomorrow."

* * *

By the time Katan returns to the human nest, the two climbers are ready to go. Ricky greets him as he approaches the ship.

"Greetings, my friend Katan," says Ricky, showing his small white teeth. Katan, now accustomed to the humans, accepts this as a tail swish.

"Greetings, Ricky. How is your preparation going?"

"We ready. Morning we go."

This is a surprise, but a welcome one. "Good. I have spoken with Pataza. You will have no more trouble from the wild one. She and the guards will see to that." Katan heads into the ship and walks down the hall to his den, where he briefs the shipmind on his meeting with Pataza.

The next morning, Ricky and Marta set out with Katan for the Waya village. The two humans carry large backpacks that, according to Ricky, contain a variety of items they will need on their journey. Katan is now even more skeptical than before about their prospects. Not only are the humans big and heavy, they have added even more weight on their backs. He cannot imagine how they will be able to reach the sky, or even get off the ground. Keeping his concerns to himself, though, he leads them through the forest, heading towards the nearest trail a day's hike away.

When they stop at the end of the day, the two humans shrug off their packs and settle onto the ground. Ricky builds a small campfire, starting it with one of the silver things that shoots flames. Katan goes off into the forest and returns with a few groundmice for dinner. Ricky gathers some berries and other plant material that, he tells Katan, are now known to be edible by humans. Marta uses some kind of flying knife to bring down a bat-like flying creature she sees perched on a small tree just above their heads. She pulls on a string which runs from the knife handle to something wrapped around her foreleg. The knife and the impaled bat fall to the ground. Marta skins the bat and begins to roast it over the campfire. When the bat is burned almost beyond recognition, the humans cut it up, combine it with the other items and some water, and heat the whole mess over the campfire. Then, incredibly, they eat it. Katan quietly eats his groundmice, wondering at these strange creatures who seem so poorly adapted to life in the forest.

* * *

Before they left the ship, the shipmind printed tiny two-way radios and gave them to Ricky and Marta, who pushed them deep in their left ears. The radios let the shipmind hear everything and whisper into their ears without anyone overhearing. Ricky and Marta also wear small video cameras disguised as shirt buttons.

The two humans eat their stew while Katan munches on his groundmice. Ricky thinks this might be a good time to bring up a sensitive subject.

"Katan, my friend," says Ricky, choosing his words carefully and trying to make the correct growling sounds, "I see you walk. You walk slow. Forepaw bad. Why?"

Katan considers this, then he says, "I can tell you, but you will not understand my words."

"No problem. Ship near. Ship hear your words. Ship talk me talk human words."

Katan's eyes widen. Clearly this is a surprising development. He asks, "How can Ship hear us? We are far from human nest. And how can Ship speak to you?"

"Machines," replies Ricky.

Apparently, that is all the explanation Katan needs. He gives a tiny flick of his tail, as if to acknowledge this is just one more human-related mystery he will have to accept.

"All right," he begins. As he tells his story, the shipmind whispers a translation into Ricky's and Marta's ears.

"Long ago, I was a young one. You would not believe it to look at me now, but in those days I was big and powerful. I was a guard, under the clan leader who came before Pataza.

"There was a female in our clan named Aza. She was also big, one of the largest of all the young females in the clan. She was a fearsome hunter. She could bring down a wild animal all by herself and drag it back to the village with no help from anyone if she wanted to. But of course, she was a member of the clan, so she always hunted with others.

"Anyway, we became close friends, and we decided to pair-bond. We mated, in the way you saw when you visited our village.

She then carried my seed, and began to grow a new one inside her body. Maybe it was one, maybe it was two. We never found out.

"Aza loved the water. There was a stream running close to our village. She loved to watch it and go swimming. This is unusual for our people, as we generally avoid deep water. Aza wanted to know where the water traveled to after it left our village. We decided to follow the stream wherever it led us. Others had gone on this journey in the past, of course, and there were stories of a stream so wide you could barely see to the other side. But those were just old stories. We wanted to see it for ourselves. We told the clan leader, and he gave us permission to go.

"We set off downstream. We walked for many days, perhaps fifty or more. As we traveled, we saw the stream join with others, and still others. Each time it became wider and deeper."

Ricky is listening intently, lost in the story. He is startled when Marta interrupts, asking, "How could the stream become so wide? What about the silva trunks?"

Katan looks at her. "The silva cares nothing for streams, or for anything else. It grows where it grows. The water just flows around it."

Ricky wonders how the silva manages to rise up through deep flowing water. He remembers the shipmind once describing how it flew over vast oceans completely covered with silva, so he figures the world-girdling tree somehow can reach up through deep water. Hard to imagine, but clearly not a problem he can solve right now.

Katan continues, "Aza loved the stream almost as much as she loved me. She would often dive into the water, swimming around for pure pleasure. Sometimes she caught a fish in her jaws and brought it back for us to eat." He stares into the fire, lost in his memories.

"One night, we were resting on the bank of the stream, which had grown to be deep and wide. She dove in. It was quite dark because there wasn't much glowing fungus there, maybe because of the water, I don't know. She was swimming close to shore. I was lying on the ground, watching her. There was a ripple in the water, not close to her but coming towards her quickly. She didn't see it, but I did. I shouted at her to get out of the water. She heard me and started swimming back towards shore. The ripple came closer. A giant creature rose up out of the water. It was many times larger than either of us. It had a long head with huge sharp teeth, a body covered with some hard material, a long tail with a flat end. Aza could not escape. The creature opened its jaws and clamped them down on her back.

"It rolled upside down, holding Aza in its jaws. I dove into the water. While the creature was upside down, I bit down as hard as I could on its neck, which was softer than the upper part of its body. It thrashed. I would not let go. After a while it released Aza and began flipping over and over again, trying to drown me. I could not breathe and I had to let go. It snapped at me, biting my foreleg. But it was badly wounded. Blood was pouring from its neck. I managed to pull myself loose. The creature stopped fighting, and I watched it die.

"I looked for Aza. At first, I could not see her. Then I saw her body floating away downstream. Even though my foreleg was almost bitten off, I managed to swim to her and pull her to the shore. But it was too late. She was dead."

Katan stops speaking, staring into the fire. Nobody speaks. Then he continues, "I stayed with Aza for two days. I knew she was dead, but I could not leave her. Scavengers began to gather. I could not let them get their teeth and claws on her. But I was too weak to fight them off. So, I dragged her body back into the stream. I watched as she floated away until I could not see her anymore.

"I began walking upstream back to the village. It took me a long time. I don't know how long, maybe a hundred days, maybe two hundred. I didn't eat much, just berries and occasionally a groundmouse too slow to get away. When I finally got back to the village, a healer looked at my foreleg. She chewed up some leaves and put them on the wound so it would heal. But it never healed all the way.

"I was never the same after that. I lost my strength. I lost my job as a guard. I lost Aza. I was still a member of the clan, but there wasn't much I could do to help. To them, I was just another wounded one, like one of the old ones who can only sit and talk and tend to the juveniles. Eventually the clan leader died and Pataza took over. When the humans arrived, I did what I could to help, but I could not fight. After the battle was over and the humans were killed, she gave me a job as a watcher. And ever since then, I have spent my time sitting in the forest, watching your ship."

Katan falls silent. Nobody speaks for a while. Ricky looks briefly at Marta, then says, "Thank you, Katan. Now I see." There isn't much else for him to say, even if he had the words, which he doesn't. He tosses a few more hunks of wood on the fire. Then he and Marta lie down and pull a thin thermal blanket over themselves. They hold each other close until they drift off to sleep. Katan remains where he was, muzzle resting on the ground, left foreleg a bit bent, staring into the fire until it burns down to embers.

15 | Hunt

They continue their journey the next morning. Katan is quieter than usual, doubtless subdued from telling the story of Aza's death. Ricky and Marta chat about the things they see in the forest. They also look up frequently, checking out the geometry of the silva trunks to see if one location might be better than another to begin their climb. From what they can see, though, all the trunks are nearly uniform in size, point straight up, and don't branch for at least a hundred feet.

Oddly, they notice the trunks are spaced more or less equally from each other, seventy or eighty feet apart, and arranged in a hexagonal lattice. In between are various low-growing shrubs, soft things like shade-loving ferns, and even a few small trees with oversized leaves to catch the dim sunlight.

"It's weird," says Ricky. "The trunks aren't in exactly straight lines, so it's not like some machine came through and planted them a zillion years ago. But still, I wonder who, or what, made them grow like this."

"Not surprising," whispers the voice of the shipmind in their ears. "A hexagonal lattice is the most efficient way to cover a given area with material. On Earth, beehives are arranged like this. So are the compound eyes of dragonflies, bumblebees, and other insects. The silva's structural strength comes from the interconnections of its branches, so we would expect the trunks to be in some sort of lattice, as opposed to growing randomly, or in a square or triangular pattern."

"That makes sense," says Marta, ducking under a small tree's low-hanging branch, "but how do the trees know where to grow their trunks?"

"On Earth, trees just grow where their seeds fall and take root. But this is not Earth, and I suspect it would be a huge mistake to think of the silva as a bunch of trees. This is a single planet-wide organism, so who knows what it is capable of? If it has some way to process information, its capacity would be astounding."

"You mean," says Ricky, "the silva might be able to think?"

The shipmind says, "Let's do the math. This world is roughly the size of Earth. Assuming the trunks are seventy-five feet apart and arranged in a hexagonal grid across the entire surface of the planet, that means it has about 218 billion trunks. The number of branches is many, times more, in the tens of trillions, and they are all interconnected. By comparison, a human brain has a hundred billion neurons, with a thousand connections per neuron. In other words, the silva has more than twice as many trunks as you have neurons in your brain. The number of connections is probably larger too. If the silva has some way to rapidly pass information through itself, and if each branch functions as a neural connection, this is one very, very smart organism."

Marta says, "Got it. So I guess we don't want to do anything to make it angry."

The shipmind makes a sound surprisingly similar to a human sigh. "It's too late for that. I might have annoyed it when I landed here and poked a big hole in it. Whether it is planning revenge or not is impossible for us to say. We know nothing about silva psychology, if there even is such a thing."

"Let's hope it's a gentle giant, then," says Ricky. "I'd hate to be halfway up when it decides to shake us off."

* * *

The Waya are expecting them when they arrive. Sentries see them coming and race back to the village to inform Pataza and the council. Just like Ricky's previous visit, the entire clan turns out to greet them, though Ricky hopes the greeting won't be as violent as the last one. Katan doesn't seem nervous, though.

Pataza steps forward and says, "Greetings, Ricky and Marta, our friends and brave travelers on the shared journey." Then, almost as an afterthought, she turns her gaze and says, "Greetings, Katan." Ricky notices this, and feels a little sorry for Katan.

"Greetings, Pataza," says Ricky. Looking at Maza and Zaka standing on either side of her, he says, "Greetings, council." Then, unsure of the protocol but giving it his best effort, he raises his voice and says, "Greetings, Waya!" There is no reaction from the assembled Waya. Well, he thinks, it could have been worse.

"Nice try, Ricky," whispers the shipmind. "Now, please stick to the plan and don't cause another war." Marta hears this and barely conceals her smile.

Pataza says to Ricky, with the shipmind translating in his ear, "Ricky, we are grateful you and your mate are ready for the shared journey. You have already spent several days with us, but you are still a stranger. You have joined us for one of our dances – or at least, for part of one – and you have had many conversations with Katan. But there is much you still do not understand about us. If you truly want to know us better, come with us now, join us for one of our most important traditions. The hunt."

Ricky listens to the ship's translation in his ear. It's one of the easiest decisions he's ever made. "I go," he says quickly to Pataza. Then, realizing he's forgotten something, he turns to Marta with a question in his eyes.

"Of course I'll go too," she says. "No way would I miss this."

Ricky says to Pataza, "Marta Ricky go."

The clan leader loudly calls out nine names, and nine Waya join her. Four are large males: the two burly guards, Gana, and the mature but still powerful council member Maza. Three are adult females Ricky does not recognize. The last two are juveniles, one male and one female, almost full grown. Ricky would have liked to have Katan involved, but knows his friend is too old and infirm to be of much use.

No preparation is needed. Unlike human hunters, the Waya need no weapons other than what they are born with: powerful limbs, keen eyesight and sense of smell, long sharp teeth, and sharp claws. They are also highly intelligent and have thousands of years of hunting tradition and techniques to draw upon. If they encounter an unfortunate animal in the forest, thinks Ricky, it won't stand a chance against this pack.

Ricky isn't sure what role he and Marta will play in the hunt, but they prepare as best they can. They strip off their backpacks and jackets, and strap their hunting knives to their belts. They both have small handguns for self-defense during the climb, but it seems inappropriate to bring such advanced human weaponry to a traditional Waya hunt, so the guns remain in the backpacks.

Less than fifteen minutes after the call went out for hunters to join the party, the pack is ready to go. Pataza faces the nine Waya and two humans. She growls, "*Gisha siga. Gisha wega ban gan seda. Gisha noso seda sodo. Gisha tato shudo. Yoki gugu. Yana gugu. Dowu tato dosh. soko kusy kuda. Gisha siga. Taka ban gan noso!*"

"What did she say?" whispers Ricky to the shipmind.

"I have no idea," replies the shipmind. "It's in the ancient tongue. I recognize the words for 'clan' and 'hunt' and 'forest' but that's about all. You should ask Katan when you see him again." She pauses. "Ricky, this is an interesting opportunity for cultural immersion, but please, *please* don't do anything brave or stupid. Or both. Watch and learn, but do not risk your life. Marta, that goes for you too."

"Roger that," says Ricky, grinning at Marta. Then Pataza barks a command, and the pack races off towards the south.

The Waya pack moves at an alarmingly fast pace. Ricky and Marta run after them, trying and failing to keep up. After a couple of minutes Pataza looks back, sees the widening gap, and slows their pace so the two humans can, by running as fast as they can, barely keep up.

Soon the village is far behind. The day is chilly and damp, and the mist hanging in the air allows even less sunlight than usual to reach the ground. The silva trunks are about twenty-five yards apart, far enough to not interfere with the pack's movements. In fact, the regular hexagonal arrangement of the trunks makes travel easier, because the gaps between the trunks form wide, straight avenues radiating out in six directions from any point. There are plenty of other obstacles – ordinary trees and bushes, uneven ground, large boulders, streambeds, and so on – but the pack simply races around or through them.

The terrain is not flat. They frequently race down into shallow ravines or up medium-sized hills. Ricky notices these hills and valleys seem to not alter how the silva branches interconnect; it's as if the trees all know, somehow, the height at which they must branch to meet up with their neighbors.

About a half hour into the hunt, Ricky and Marta are beginning to tire. They reach the top of a small hill. Looking down the other side, they see a herd of large six-legged animals, maybe a couple of dozen in all. The creatures' heads are down, grazing on grasses and other small plants. They are twice as big as the Waya, with shaggy brown coats, black hooves, large brown eyes, and long curved horns that seem to be made of ivory.

The herd senses the Wayas' arrival, looking up in alarm from their grazing. Immediately they take off, racing as fast as they can to escape the hunting pack.

The pack gives chase, Pataza in the lead, howling. They soon catch up with the fleeing animals. Without any discussion Ricky can hear, the three female Waya race ahead to surround the herd, two on one side and one on the other. They race back and forth in front of the shaggy beasts, trying to confuse them and prevent them from running away. The beasts mill around, forming a defensive circle with their sharp horns facing outwards. The three female Waya dart in and out, trying to draw one of the beasts out of the circle. The rest of the pack waits and watches.

Eventually a Waya darts all the way in and manages to nip one of the beasts on the leg. The beast lowers its horns, trying but failing to pin its attacker. The other two female Waya see this. They stop their general harassment and run over to assist. The rest of the shaggy beasts, seeing an opportunity to escape, flee as fast as they can.

Now there is just the one beast remaining. It's frightened and confused, surrounded by three Waya nipping at its legs. It turns around and around, trying to gore the attackers. It manages to catch one of the Waya and flip her on her back, but the Waya twists away and scrambles to her feet, rolling away before the beast can impale her with its horns.

With the target animal separated from its herd, Pataza and the four large males move forward and converge on it. The fight is over quickly. Pataza takes the lead, leaping up and clamping her jaws around the beast's nose to prevent it from swinging its deadly horns. The four males jump on the beast's body and quickly bring it down. There is no single killing blow. The beast, weighed down by so many attacking Waya, struggles briefly, then dies. Ricky, watching from a distance next to Marta and the two juveniles, can't tell if the beast died from internal injuries, blood loss, shock, or some combination.

As soon as the beast has breathed its last, all ten Waya converge around the carcass. They start tearing off strips of flesh and ripping out pieces of internal organs. Pataza looks up and barks something to the humans. The shipmind translates it. "Come! Eat!"

Ricky feels nauseous. He has never eaten actual flesh in his life, only faux meat produced by the ship's food printers and that one disgusting taste of roasted groundmouse at the parley. He's never seen an animal slaughtered either. The idea of slicing off a piece of the dead creature and eating its steaming raw flesh is the farthest thing from his mind. But just sitting and watching does not seem polite either. "Ship," he whispers, "what should I do?"

"Ricky," says the shipmind in his hear, "the Waya invited you to join the hunt, and I seem to remember you were quite enthusiastic about accepting the invitation. What did you think would happen? You can't back out now. Be a good guest. Go up there and join the feast. You too, Marta."

Gritting his teeth, Ricky walks towards the circle of feasting Waya, who are now covered with blood and gore. Marta joins him. Seeing the humans approach, a couple of Waya move aside to give them easy access to the carcass. Ricky just stands uncertainly, knowing he should dig into the dead animal but not able to actually do it.

Marta makes the first move. She kneels down and cuts off a small piece of flesh. It's warm and wet. Trying not to look at it, she pops it in her mouth, chews it a couple of times, and swallows. It's horrible. She cuts off another piece and passes it, on the point of her knife, to Ricky. He eats it.

Pataza is watching them. Ricky manages a fake smile and waves his knife at her in a gesture that, he hopes, will be interpreted as "Thank you" and not "I'm going to kill you for this." It seems to work. Pataza nods and goes back to ripping off strips of flesh with her teeth.

Eventually the Waya finish stripping the carcass. A few of them pull off strips of meat and shove them into the woven baskets they wear around their necks, obviously intending to bring food back for the rest of the clan. The baskets are small, though, and Ricky can't imagine how those small hunks of meat will be enough to feed the rest of the clan. Not his problem, he decides.

They return to the village at a much more leisurely pace, slowed by the hunks of meat stuffed into the neck bags and the larger quantities stuffed in the bellies of the Waya. Along the way they stop at a cold stream, where the Waya and humans do their best to wash off the blood and gore.

* * *

When they reach the village, Pataza says, "Takaqa will show you to your den. You may rest there. Tonight we will eat together and talk."

Eating is the last thing Ricky is interested in, but he nods in agreement.

Takaqa comes up to them. Ricky hasn't seen her in several months. She is looking much more plump than the last time. She notices him looking at her. She swishes her tail and says, "I am bonded to Gana. A young one grows inside me." Ricky doesn't know the Waya word for "congratulations" or even if that would be appropriate, so he just nods and smiles at her, keeping his lips together to avoid any misunderstanding.

Takaqa leads them to an empty cave about fifteen feet deep and six feet high, much larger than the one Ricky stayed in during his previous visit. The floor is packed dirt, and the cave is completely bare except for a thick layer of straw-like material covering a raised area in the back of the cave. Must be the bedroom, he thinks. It looks cozy by Waya standards, and much better than the hard ground they'd slept on for the last few nights. "You stay here," says Takaqa. "This evening, Katan will come for you."

She walks away, leaving Ricky and Marta to get settled. They have no idea if they will be staying for a day or a year, as it all depends on when a crownfruit becomes available. From what Katan told them, there are a few elderly females in the clan, but none of them seem to be in any imminent danger of dying.

Marta looks at Ricky, glances at the straw-covered area in the back of the cave, looks at Ricky again, and smiles. He grins back at her. The last few nights they'd slept next to each other on the ground, but there wasn't any privacy with Katan nearby. Now they have some time alone and nothing on the schedule for a while. Ricky removes his thin blanket from his backpack and uses a couple of cams to attach it to the cave walls, stretching it across the bedroom area to serve as a screen. Marta lays her own blanket on top of the straw. They strip off their clothes, still bloody and dirty from the hunt. As they make love, the scent of their bodies mingles with the dampness of the cave, the packed straw, and the lingering scent of the hunt. They can barely hear the distant growled conversations of the Waya beneath their own whispers and moans.

Later, lying together on the straw mattress, Ricky murmurs, "Well, that was fun. We should do this more often."

"Seems like we've been doing it pretty often. Not counting the last three days, of course."

"Compared to the Waya, definitely more often."

"Oh yes. Poor Waya. Just one shot at sex in their entire lives. What a strange way to reproduce. You saw them doing it last time you were in the village, right?"

"Yeah," says Ricky. "It was Takaqa and her mate, Gana. They just decided to go ahead and pair-bond. They did it in front of, well, just about everybody. And it was strange."

"How so?"

"For one thing, Gana's penis was pretty small, not what I would've expected from something that looked like a wolf and was bigger than me."

"So, then, not as big as you?" She gives him a little squeeze to indicate what she is referring to.

"Nowhere near as big as me. Or any other human male, in my limited experience. But the other strange thing was how Takaqa initiated the sex. She opened her mouth wide, like a yawn. Some whitish stuff squirted out of the roof of her mouth and onto her tongue. She licked it on Gana's nose. He became erect and, umm, things proceeded quickly from there."

"So, what's that about, do you suppose?"

"No idea." Ricky stares at the ceiling, then says, "Ship, are you there?"

"Yes, Ricky," whispers the shipmind to both of them, through their ear radios.

"What can you tell us about Waya reproduction?"

"Some aspects of it are unusual, and some are extremely unusual. Where would you like me to start?"

Marta says, "Start with the sex, please." Ricky suppresses a laugh.

"Of course. Given the fact that Waya have only one sexual encounter in their lives, and only with the one to which they have pair-bonded, that encounter is literally a matter of life and death to the survival of both parties' genes. And so, female choice is paramount. Imagine the alternative, such as in dogs on Earth, with the female Waya having no choice in the matter. Some other male who she might not care for could come along and use up her one chance at passing on her genes with the partner of her choice. How can she prevent this? She could decide to come into estrus for one mating encounter, but we don't know of any Earth creature that can control its own fertility to such a degree. Or she could do what the Japanese pygmy squid does, where several males deposit their sperm on the outside of her body and she simply scrapes off the sperm of the males she doesn't care for. But the Waya method is unique as far as I know. The female directly manipulates her partner's reproductive system instead of her own. She triggers arousal in her male partner by use of a chemical signal in the white liquid she licks onto his nose. That is, apparently, the only way a male Waya is able to, or even interested in, copulation."

"And what about the male Waya's small, uh, equipment?" asks Ricky.

"There's no need, evolutionarily speaking, for him to devote any more of his body to that equipment than necessary. In species where the female has multiple partners, the male's penis and testicles serves not just to deposit his sperm in the female, but also to flush out any sperm which may have been put there by a competitor. But in this case, there's no sperm competition, so the male's equipment does not need to be any larger than the minimum necessary to deliver the sperm. Anything else is just a waste."

Marta gives Ricky another little squeeze but says nothing aloud.

"Interesting," says Marta. "Moving on, then. What about this incredibly complicated business with the simians and the birds and the eggs? Is that necessary?"

The shipmind says, "It doesn't have to be necessary, it just has to work better than the alternative. That's how evolution works: individuals who are well adapted and successful tend to pass on more of their genes than those which are less successful. Over long periods of time this results in dramatic changes. The Waya are, I believe, an ancient species that have lived in small clans for possibly millions of years, so they've had plenty of time to develop a highly complex reproduction cycle."

Ricky says, "Not long enough to develop opposable thumbs, obviously."

"That's an interesting point," replies the shipmind. "Their forepaws certainly could evolve into hands, but they haven't. They can do some hand-like things, like picking up sticks, throwing things, and weaving simple baskets. So, why haven't they gone all the way and developed dexterous hands like humans?"

Ricky and Marta assume this is a rhetorical question so they don't answer, waiting for the shipmind to continue.

"It's because the Waya are coming from a quite different place than your ancestors, who were tree-dwelling apes. Your ancestors used their forepaws to grasp branches, so for them, the evolution from paws to hands was straightforward, with each tiny change in that direction enhancing their survival ability. But the Waya are pack hunting carnivores who use their forepaws for the things large carnivores do. Running, slashing, killing, and so on. That's why their paws are stuck being paws. Remember, evolution has no foresight, no plan. It proceeds from one tiny incremental change to the next, with beneficial mutations enhancing the likelihood of those genes being passed on. In the case of the Waya, any mutation in the direction of opposable thumbs would interfere with their ability to hunt, which would reduce their odds of finding a mate and passing on their genes. So, paws mutating towards hands would make them less successful. They're at a local maximum in terms of fitness, and incremental changes in every direction lead downward. Their paws don't change."

"Ship," says Marta, "that's interesting, thanks. Now can we get back to their reproductive cycle please?"

"Of course, Marta. My apologies for the digression. The simian/bird/egg cycle is an elaborate method of avoiding inbreeding, which in small populations is a real risk. Many Earth species have evolved strategies for avoiding inbreeding. Humans, for example, rely mainly on what's called kin recognition. Every human culture on Earth had a cultural prohibition against incest. In addition, there's also a biological aversion to mating with siblings whom you've grown up with. It's not foolproof, as the two of you have already noticed, but it works fairly well.

"With the Waya, they don't bother with kin recognition, as far as we know. They use another method, called dispersal, to maintain genetic diversity. This occurs in many Earth species, where individuals who reach reproductive maturity have a built-in desire to put distance between themselves and their birth families. The Waya take this to an extreme, using two other unrelated species to make sure their young are dispersed as far from the original clan as possible.

"In both cases, by the way, the relationship is symbiotic. The simian who eats the crownfruit receives a tasty reward and a dramatic improvement in social status. And the birds at the end of the cycle also get a nutritious treat with, as far as we know, no negative side effects."

"So, everybody wins," says Marta.

"Except for the simians who die in the attempt, yes," replies the shipmind. As soon as it says this, it realizes and regrets its own lack of tact, but it's too late to take the words back.

"And the crownfruit?" asks Ricky, choosing to ignore the shipmind's last comment.

"There are many examples in Earth biology of one species altering the behavior of another through chemicals or by infecting the host's central nervous system. This is commonly done by viruses, bacteria, and fungi, by parasitic insects and worms, and in one unusual case, by a species of barnacle. But there are no examples we know of where a higher-order animal such as a mammal does such a thing. In this, the Waya are unique."

"How does the male's sperm cross the blood-brain barrier to the crownfruit?" asks Marta.

The shipmind is surprised by this. "That's a very perceptive question, Marta. I don't know the answer. If I had to speculate, I'd say the eggs in the crownfruit are not fertilized by the male at all, and don't arise in the female's ovaries, but in the skull cavity itself. I believe the eggs are genetically identical to the female, although somehow half of them are programmed to become male and the other half female."

Ricky and Marta exchange glances, nodding to each other. Ricky says, "Thanks, Ship, that was interesting." They doze off, still holding each other.

16 | Darkness

Marta wakes up a little later. Ricky is still asleep, but she knows how to arouse him. This isn't difficult at all, she thinks, smiling to herself. He finally wakes up, realizes what she is doing, and responds.

After they are finished, Marta says, "Takaqa looked kind of cute, carrying a little one inside her."

Ricky blinks. He considers the message underlying this comment. He'd also thought about it, but they'd never actually discussed it before. He decides to go with it. "I think you would look just as cute. In your own way, of course."

"Of course. Less fur, for one thing."

"Less fur. Shorter teeth. Smaller ears. Bigger feet."

She laughs, then turns serious. "What do you think, though? Could that ever work?"

Ricky hopes the shipmind keeps its digital mouth shut. Just to be sure, he pulls the radio out of his ear, and motions for Marta to do the same. There's no way to turn the things off as far as they know, so the shipmind will probably still be able to hear what they're saying, but at least it won't be whispering in their ears. He sets the radios down carefully in a corner of the cave, then says, "It wouldn't work right now, for all the obvious reasons. High risk climbing for one, a murderous Waya outcast for another. But later? Sure, I think it would be great."

"Ricky, we don't know anything about being parents. We were raised by a machine. A well-meaning machine, but still, I have no idea how to be a real mom."

"I think we turned out reasonably ok. From what I understand, the people back on Earth who planned this mission knew parenting could be a huge problem, and they did their best to give the shipminds as much nurturing skill as possible."

"Yes, but the shipmind is a machine. Maybe it is programmed to behave like a kind and loving machine, but that's not the same as a real mom. Don't you ever wonder what a real mom would be like?"

Ricky thinks about it. "Sure. I've seen lots of real moms and dads in the old movies. It would be great to have parents like that. Imagine having your mom pick you up when you fall and hurt yourself, or having your dad show you how to do stuff."

Marta snags a lock of his long hair and twirls it in her fingers. "We did ok on the psych tests, as I recall. So, we're not seriously broken. Maybe that's enough for us to try being parents ourselves. After all, what's the worst that could happen?"

"We could totally screw it up, and our kids could grow up to be homicidal maniacs. With great fighting skills too, of course."

"Great. Just what we need."

"Look, Marta, we – I mean, humanity on this planet – are going to have to solve this sometime anyway. We're going to have to bootstrap a new civilization. So someone has to be the first real parents. I think it could be us."

Marta gazes up at the rough stone ceiling of their little bedroom. Her body, warmed from her recent exertions, is starting to cool. She yanks the blanket screen down off the walls and pulls it over them, snuggling closer to Ricky. "There are just four women in our generation. Not sure if all of them would want to have children. But even if, say, three of the four did, that would be a nice little group of kids to raise."

"Yeah. Once things settle down, we could have a little group of kids growing up around the same time Ship starts hatching the third generation. The settlers." Ricky and the others had started using the Waya name "Ship" for the shipmind.

"Ok," says Marta. "Then it's settled. First, we save the Waya from extinction. Then we start a family. Then we help humanity establish a colony here. Sounds like enough to keep us busy for a while."

"Just don't fall off that tree, Marta, ok?"

"Deal." She wraps her arms around him and squeezes tight.

* * *

As evening falls, Katan comes to the cave and leads the two humans to Pataza's den. When they arrive, he sees Maza and Zaka are in the den with Pataza. A fourth Waya, who Katan recognizes as a servant, sits further back in the cave.

"Greetings, Pataza," says Ricky. "Greetings, Maza and Zaka." Ricky apparently does not know the protocol for greeting servants, so he glances at it briefly but says nothing to it.

"Greetings, Ricky and Marta," replies Pataza. "Please come in and sit down." Katan turns to leave, but Pataza says, "Katan. You stay." Katan is surprised by this. He doesn't dare sit with the group, though, so he heads to a corner of the den and curls up, trying to be as inconspicuous as possible.

Ricky says, "Pataza, I not know many Waya words. You talk me Waya. Ship hear your words. Ship talk me human words. I hear. I understand."

Pataza looks across the cave to Katan. "What is he saying? Where is Ship?"

Katan replies, "Human machines. I told you of their power before. Ship can be here even though we cannot see it. I do not understand how this happens. But Ship will listen to your words, it somehow speaks to the humans, and they understand in their own language."

Katan can see this greatly disturbs Pataza, though she works hard to suppress any outward indications. The humans apparently cannot detect this, having so little experience with the Waya, but to Katan, it's as obvious as if the clan leader jumped up and raced in circles around the den. After a few moments, she gets herself fully under control again.

Pataza says to Ricky and says, "I see. Does Ship see through your eyes, or does Ship see through its own eyes?"

Ricky replies, "Ship no see. Ship use my ears Marta ears listen. Ship no ears Waya village."

From her body language it's obvious Pataza does not believe this, but she says, "I understand. Now, let's eat. We will talk later."

Ricky and Marta nod, apparently not needing any translation to understand this. Pataza gestures to the servant, who drags the raw carcass of a large snake-like animal towards the front of the cave and drops it onto some carefully arranged straw in front of the three council members. Katan sees it's only half a carcass. He is hungry, but he knows he will not be invited to join this feast.

The servant returns to the back of the cave and retrieves the other half of the carcass. This portion has been roasted over a campfire. It's blackened, the rough skin peeling off and the meat underneath charred to a dark brown. The servant places it in front of Ricky and Marta.

"Eat," says Pataza. She and the other two council members go to work ripping off pieces of the raw carcass. They do so politely, with Pataza taking the first bite and passing the rest of it to Maza, who bites off a piece and passes the carcass to Zaka. Taking turns, they quickly finish it off.

Ricky and Marta hesitate only briefly, then they go to work on their meal. They unsheathe the knives at their belts. Taking turns, they cut off small pieces of burned meat and eat them. Katan cannot tell if the humans actually like the food or not. Based on what he's seen from Ricky's tasting of the roasted groundmouse at the first parley, he doubts it. But whether they find it tasty or just feel obligated as guests, the two humans eat their portion. They do not finish it as quickly as the three Waya, since the humans take so much time chewing the pieces with their small teeth before swallowing.

When everyone is finished with the carcass, the servant takes away the bones and other debris from the meal. Water is brought out for drinking, and the humans use some of it to wash their faces and forepaws.

* * *

"Thank you," says Ricky, trying his best to play the role of diplomat with his limited Waya vocabulary and even more limited experience in such things. "Waya food good. You come human nest. We give you human food. You eat human food. Human food good."

Pataza says, "I am glad you liked the meal. And we would be happy to visit you at the human nest and taste your food." Ricky notices a little amused tail flick from Zaka.

Pataza continues, "Katan has told us you are ready to go on the shared journey. We are happy to hear this. But we do not understand how humans can climb to the sky, and we are not confident you can complete the journey. Please explain how you will do this."

Ricky and Marta had brought their backpacks, expecting questions along these lines. They figured that given the one-way language barrier, it would be easier to show than tell. Ricky says, "We have tools. You see tools," and they both start taking gear out of their backpacks. The Waya watch them intently.

Ricky picks up his climbing shoes and laces them onto his bare feet. Then he straps his crampons onto the shoes. Made of lightweight metal and studded with sharp points, the crampons can easily penetrate silva bark and, in this case, the soft stone of the cave wall. He walks over to the nearest wall, jams the front of one crampon into the stone, and steps up, taking his entire weight on one foot. If Pataza is upset by the damage to the wall of her cave, she does not show it.

Satisfied the point is made, Ricky steps off the wall and returns to where their backpacks are lying on the cave floor. He takes out the rest of his climbing gear and lays it out on the floor. Then he shows it all to the Waya, picking up each item in turn: his harness, a length of rope, a carabiner, cam, piton, and hammer. No weapons, though. He'd left them in the other cave.

Then it's time for a demonstration. Marta goes first. She fastens her climbing harness around her waist, and clips a handful of protection devices onto harness loops. Kneeling down, she laces up her shoes and attaches the crampons. She walks over to the nearest cave wall and steps up onto it with her right foot, jamming the sharp front points of the crampon into the soft stone and reaching up to grasp a small handhold with her fingertips.

She climbs a couple of steps, then, noticing a small crack in the stone, she slides a cam inside it and uses a carabiner to clip her rope to the cam. A little further up, she comes to a smaller crack and decides this is a good opportunity to show how pitons work. She pulls one from her harness and slips the point into the crack. Then, pulling out a small hammer, she slams the piton a half-dozen times, driving it deep into the wall. Another carabiner clips her rope to the piton.

She continues up the cave wall. As the wall starts to bend back and become a ceiling, she continues up and across, inserting cams or pitons whenever she encounters a suitable crack in the stone.

When she reaches the far side of the ceiling, she reverses direction. This is a tricky maneuver she'd practiced many times in the ship's climbing gym, but never before an audience of skeptical Waya. She finds a solid handhold, an irregular lump of stone protruding from the ceiling. Holding onto the lump, she carefully works her feet around her body until she has rotated 180 degrees. Then she continues, climbing down the far wall feet-first and attaching protection devices above her head as she descends. Finally she reaches the floor and steps gracefully off the wall. Turning around, she gestures theatrically to the archway of rope she's attached to the cave walls and ceiling.

The Waya just stare.

Marta gestures invitingly to Ricky. He walks over to where she had begun her climb. He fastens his end of the rope to his climbing harness, then he begins his own climb, following her route up the wall. Marta belays him, taking up the slack rope at the other end. As Ricky climbs past each cam or piton, he removes it and its carabiner from the wall, clipping the devices to his harness on loops. He follows Marta's route across the ceiling, then he rotates and downclimbs the other side,. He finishes the circuit and steps off the wall next to Marta. Marta coils up the climbing rope. They stand next to each other and look at where they'd just climbed. The only evidence of their climb is a series of small holes in the walls and ceiling of the clan leader's cave.

They look at the council members and wait for a response.

Maza is the first to speak. He says, "You are bigger and heavier than the simians, and not as graceful. You have no tails, and your forepaws are fat. I thought you were not capable of climbing a large boulder, let alone journeying to the sky. But now my opinion has changed. I see you are strong, you are smart, and you have wonderful tools. Perhaps you can make the journey after all."

Maza looks at Pataza, inviting her to give her opinion. But just as he does, Zaka makes a strange sound. It isn't anything in the Waya language, and the shipmind can't translate it. It's a guttural growl ending in a high-pitched shriek. The other Waya look at her. Zaka stands up a bit shakily. She says, "Please excuse me. I am not feeling well." She walks slowly out of the den.

The humans look at the Waya, confused. Pataza says, "Our meeting is finished. Thank you for showing us your climbing skills." Then softly to Maza, "We may have use of them sooner than we thought." She gestures to Katan, who rises and escorts Ricky and Marta back to their own den.

* * *

"Zaka sick?" Ricky asks Katan, as the three of them walk back to the humans' den.

"Does your shipmind still listen and speak to you?" asks Katan.

"Yes."

Satisfied he will not be limited to the few words in the humans' vocabulary, Katan says, "Zaka is old. The end of her life is coming soon. Her heart knows this. The changes have started."

In an instant, Ricky understands what will happen. He feels sick. He says to Katan, "Please take us to see Zaka. Now."

"All right," says Katan. They walk across the clearing. It's full dark, the only light coming from the greenish glow of the silva fungus. Bat-like things flutter overhead. From far away comes the faint but unmistakable sound of a distant Waya clan dancing and singing.

They find Zaka pacing outside her den. Her thin, gray body is shaking. She tosses her head back and forth as if trying to shake something off. She seems agitated, and keeps making that guttural sound.

"Zaka," says Ricky. "You ok?" It seems like the dumbest thing he's ever said.

Zaka looks at him through cloudy gray eyes. "Ricky. My human friend. You can see for yourself I am not all right. I have been feeling a bit strange for the last few days, tired and agitated at the same time, and I didn't know why. But now I can see the changes have started. I have lived a long time, but there are not many days left for me. Soon darkness will overtake my mind. I will forget your name, and even my own name.

"But there is still one task left for me. The seeds I have carried in my body for my whole life will emerge soon. They must be taken to the sky. And Ricky, you must do it."

Ricky feels like he is going to throw up. It's not the carrying of the seeds that sickens him, it's what he will have to do to obtain them. "Zaka. I can't. Not you."

"Of course you will do it. You must. Our people have survived for countless generations, and fought off many enemies. Now we have a new enemy we cannot fight. We need your help. You are the only one who can show our people how to survive. Save us, and you will also save your own people. Don't be afraid."

* * *

That night, Ricky and Marta lie together in their cave, listening to the tortured howls coming from the dying Waya on the other side of the village. Eventually they fall asleep.

In the morning, the village is quiet and Zaka is gone.

Pataza herself comes to their den. "It is time, young humans. Go find Zaka. You know what to do."

Ricky nods and replied, "We are ready. We would like Katan to come with us."

"Of course," says Pataza. "But first, please come to the campfire." She turns and walks away.

* * *

When Ricky and Marta arrive at the campfire, they see the rest of the clan is already assembled. A fire is going, not as large as the bonfire used for the dance, but large enough to keep everyone comfortably warm in the chill morning air.

This time there is no singing or dancing. Instead, Pataza gestures to an elderly male Waya who sits facing the assembled clan members. Ricky does not recognize him. He is mostly gray, and he wears what look like a necklace of bluish stones. Ricky has never seen any jewelry, clothing, or other ornamentation on a Waya before. Clearly it indicates special status of some kind, but he has no idea what.

The Waya picks up a short heavy stick and begins to bang it on the ground in a slow and steady rhythm. Then he starts to speak. The shipmind does not start its translation immediately. It says to Ricky and Marta, "He is speaking in the Waya language, but the grammar is different. It has a structure I've never heard before. I think it is a poem of some kind. I will try to conform to its structure."

The clan sits and listened, motionless and silent, as the Waya tells his tale.

"We gather here today, we bid farewell to Zaka
Darkness takes her mind, death will take her body
But her seeds will live, taking the great shared journey
They will go far

We remember her life, we thank her for her gift
We thank Wagota, great giver of the shared journey
How did the shared journey begin, what are its roots?
Hear me now

In the beginning, Wagota created the world
Mountains and rivers, trees and grasses
Animals and birds, simian and Waya
Blue sky above

Every day the sun burned, light fell upon the world
Every night the sun slept, the world turned dark
This was our world until the silva appeared
Ancient mystery!

Ascent to the Sun

Did Wagota throw its seeds from mighty forepaws?
Did the angels plant its seeds in the ground?
Did it fall from the sky, taking root where it wished?
No one knows

The silva was strange, it grew and grew
With trunks tall and wide, it rose to the sky
It branched, it touched, it wove a web of green
The world turned dark

No warmth from the sun, the days grew dim
Animals and plants died, the Waya grew hungry
We were weak, waiting in the dark for death
The clan was lost

Then Wagota sent angels to walk among us
Skins of white liquid they gave us to drink
Hungry and thirsty, we drank and grew strong
Wonderful liquid!

Now we could see in the gloom, but there was more
A female of our clan reached the end of her life
She bellowed, her mind grew dark, she wandered off to die

Ascent to the Sun

What was this?

Simians came to kill her, they fought among themselves
One killed her, it ate her strange crown
It climbed into the silva, it disappeared.
We did not understand

Then Wagota sent a stranger to our village
She told us about the shared journey
She spoke of the two Awakenings, and of wild babies
Do not be afraid!

Welcome the changes, they will bring new life
Welcome the simians, do not fight them
Welcome the wild babies, raise them as your own
Waya will thrive

So it has been since the days of Wagota and the stranger
Today Zaka dies, but she also gives life
Hers is the shared journey, we bid her farewell
Gisha siga.

The assembled Waya repeat, "*Gisha siga.*" The clan is one. The storyteller stands up and walks away, and the crowd disperses.

17 | Awakening

As Ricky and Marta walk away from the campfire, the shipmind whispers, "Somehow, the simian in the ship found out about Zaka. Maybe he heard her bellowing, maybe it was something else. It scratched and clawed at its cage. Carlos figured he'd learned everything he could and there was no need to keep it any longer. So he brought it outside and let it go. it's heading towards the Waya camp, but it is unlikely to survive the trip. Keep an eye out for it."

The two humans eat a quick breakfast, then walk out of their den. They leave their climbing gear behind and take only their hunting knives and some food. Katan is waiting for them in the clearing. Together, they head towards the sound of the bellowing Zaka. If they are successful in their grisly task, Katan tells them, Ricky and Marta will have plenty of time to return to the village and get their gear before Ricky develops the overpowering urge to climb. Of course, this assumes the crownfruit has the same effect on Ricky as the simians.

Following Zaka is not difficult. Even in the village they can hear her distant bellowing. The dying Waya stumbles through the forest, heading generally west, in the direction of the human ship. The biological imperative driving Zaka is not interested in traveling quickly; in fact, the slower she travels, the easier it is for simians to gather around her. But there are no simians anymore. The two humans and the Waya follow the sound, confident they'll catch up to her soon.

Around midday they see her. Ricky's first thought is she looks drunk, but the Waya have no knowledge of alcohol. And it's highly unlikely she's been using glowjuice, as that requires some planning. No, he thinks, she's just dying, a puppet whose strings are being pulled by genes which have lain dormant for six or seven decades and are now in control.

On the way, they'd discussed how this would work. Ricky would approach Zaka, kill her as quickly and painlessly as possible, then pull off the crown and eat the crownfruit inside. Katan thinks it isn't necessary to do the actual killing by ripping off the crown, as the simians did. Ricky can kill her in some other, less painful way, as long as he eats the crownfruit quickly, before it decays and loses its ability to trigger the Awakenings.

Ricky, Marta, and Katan approach the dying Waya but stop a few dozen paces short. Ricky draws his knife and approaches her. He sees movement on the far side. It's a simian. He recognizes it as the same poor creature he'd dragged to the ship a couple of months earlier. Somehow it's still alive, probably thanks to the antibiotics and IV fluids Carlos gave it in the medical bay. It still looks awful, though. It can barely walk. There's no way it can take down a Waya, even one on the verge of death. And if it somehow manages to eat the crownfruit, nothing could give it the strength and endurance needed to climb to the sky. In its current condition, the sickly creature could not climb the silva any more than a human toddler could.

Ricky and the simian face off. Zaka is between them, stumbling slowly in circles and bellowing. Suddenly he sees another movement to his right. Stepping out of the underbrush is a large Waya, brown with a white patch on its face and a damaged eye. It's the wild one, Akana.

"Stop, human," growls the Waya. "This is none of your affair." The shipmind whispers a word-for-word translation in Ricky's ear, but dares not add any commentary of its own.

"Akana," replies Ricky, drawing his knife and facing him. It doesn't much matter what he says, he knows a fight is coming. He's had years of combat training, but this is real, and almost certainly a fight to the death. He feels surprisingly calm. Stalling for time while he plans his moves, he calls out, "I here for Pataza, for clan. You stay back." Behind him, he hears Marta coming up on his right, and Katan on his left. Three against one. That would be enough to frighten off any sane Waya. But what about this one?

Akana circles a bit to the right, closer to Marta now. "Humans are poison. Humans are plague. Humans are death. Stay away from this Waya. You have no right to be here. Go now. The simian will take the shared journey."

"Simian sick. Near death. Simian cannot go."

"None of your affair. Go now."

Ricky risks a quick glance at the simian. It's starting to approach Zaka, who yowls and slashes at it with a forepaw. The simian stumbles back, just out of her reach. Then it edges around her, watching with hungry eyes. Zaka rotates to face it, growling.

Out of the corner of his eye, he sees Katan circle behind him and come forward on the other side of Marta, reinforcing the right side. Of course, thinks Ricky. Katan has hunted in packs for his entire life, and he knows the tactics of attack and defense in every possible situation. Now Marta is in the middle, with Ricky on her left and Katan on her right. The three of them spread out a bit and advance slowly on Akana.

Akana should back off. That would have been the sensible thing to do, but he is not thinking rationally anymore. His only thought is to kill the blue-eyed human, to avenge his dead family and friends and save his people.

Suddenly he attacks, racing towards Ricky with his jaws open.

As the attacker closes on Ricky, Katan leaps at him and clamps his teeth on his back. At the same time, Marta runs forward and stabs him in the ribs with her knife. Nothing can stop the attack, though. Akana keeps going, pouncing on Ricky and trying to bite his head off. Ricky rolls away, plunging his knife deep into his attacker's chest. Akana ignores the pain from the two knives and the Waya clamped on his back. He snaps again and again, trying to connect with Ricky's head. Ricky blocks the attack, hitting Akana as hard as he can in the nose with his left fist as he pulls out the knife with his right hand and stabs again. Akana tries to close his jaws on Ricky's left forearm, ripping the flesh but unable to clamp down.

Weakened from the knife wounds and Katan's bites, Akana gives up trying to bite Ricky. He swipes his massive right paw at Ricky's head. The paw connects, hard, snapping Ricky's head back and against the ground. Ricky blacks out.

Before Akana can finish off Ricky, he has to turn and defend himself against Marta and Katan, who continue their counterattack. But it's too late. With blood pouring from a dozen stab wounds and bites, Akana takes a final gasping breath, collapses, and dies.

Ricky lies on the ground, unconscious. His left forearm is badly cut and bleeding from where Akana's teeth had clamped down on it. Marta and Katan are shaken but unhurt. They bend over him. Marta pulls off her shirt to wrap around his injured arm. She tries to revive Ricky, but he is out cold. "Wake up, Ricky!" she shouts, slapping him in the face. "You have to get the crownfruit. Go!"

Katan looks to her and says, "Ricky cannot get the crownfruit. You go. I help Ricky."

Marta hesitates. The shipmind whispers in her ear. "Do it, Marta. Get the crownfruit. Ricky will be ok."

How does the shipmind know Ricky would be ok, she wonders. But no time to think about that. Leaving Katan to tend to Ricky, she stands up and looks over at Zaka and the simian. Zaka is weaker now, barely able to stand. The simian lurches towards her, pawing feebly at the soft crown at the top of Zaka's head. Marta steps forward and grabs the simian by the neck. Using all her strength she spins around and hurls it as far as she can. The creature flies through the air, slams against a silva trunk, and slides to the ground, dead.

Zaka is lying on the ground now. She looks up at Marta, eyes unfocused. Marta realizes Zaka doesn't recognize her. "I am so sorry," says Marta. She grits her teeth and slits Zaka's throat. As the dead Waya's blood spills on the forest floor, Marta rips the colorful crown off her head and tosses it away. Underneath she sees a little pink thing, about the size of a small bird's egg. It's pulsing. She grasps it and pulls it out of Zaka's skull. She is about to pop it in her mouth. Then she stops.

She walks back to where Katan is tending to Ricky, the moist little pink crownfruit in her hand. Katan sees her. He barks, "Eat it now! Eat it now!" She pauses for a moment, then makes up her mind. She puts the crownfruit in her mouth and swallows it.

Katan looks at her. "You are clan leader," he says. Not a question.

"Clan leader," growls Marta.

* * *

Marta sits with Ricky until he regains consciousness, then she helps him walk back to the Waya village. When they get there, a healer takes over his care, packing chewed herbs on his arm to prevent infection. She sees Katan go to Pataza's cave to tell her what happened in the forest. Pataza sends her two guards into the forest. They return a short time later. It's hard to hear what they say, but it sounds like they are describing the scene where the struggles occurred.

Soon after, Pataza comes to see Marta, who is sitting with Ricky in the healer's den. The healer, her job finished, steps outside to give them some privacy.

"You are now the human clan leader," says Pataza, echoing Katan's words from earlier. The shipmind translates softly in Marta's ear.

This is too complicated for Marta to explain in Waya language. She simply says, "No. Yes."

Pataza looks at her carefully. "How do you feel?"

Marta considers this. She shrugs, not knowing or caring if Pataza understands the gesture.

Pataza says, "With simians, the First Awakening comes quickly, usually within a day. We see them jumping around, screeching to the other members of their troop, and climbing rapidly up and down the silva trunks. Sometimes there is a fight, as the awakened one takes control of the troop. Then a day or two later, the Second Awakening comes. The new leader gathers its new troop and sets out on the shared journey. I don't know how the crownfruit will affect you, though. Human bodies are much larger than simians, so the crownfruit may have a weaker effect on you."

Marta feels a little bit annoyed at being lectured like this. "I feel ok," she says, and turns away.

"Marta," whispers the shipmind in her ear, "you ate the crownfruit several hours ago. Describe your physical and mental state."

"I'm feeling fine. Now leave me alone," she snaps. She takes the radio out of her ear and stuffs it in her pants pocket, then she goes to check on Ricky.

"Ricky ok?" she asks the healer in Waya language, cocking her head to indicate it's a question.

"He needs to rest," says the healer, a smaller midnight-black Waya. Marta realizes she has no idea what the healer is saying. Reluctantly she puts the radio back in her ear.

"You talk me," says Marta.

The healer says, "All right. I know nothing about humans. I was not even born yet during the time before. He lost some blood from the bite on his arm, but the wound is shallow and should heal quickly. As for his head, I cannot say. Among the Waya, it is rare to be hit so hard it causes one to fall sleep. I have never seen it. He should rest for a couple of days."

Marta says, "Ship, Ricky had a concussion. How can I tell how bad it is?"

"I will ask him some questions," replies the shipmind. Speaking in Ricky's ear, it says, "Ricky, can you hear me?"

"Yes," he replies, somewhat groggily.

"Tell me the names of the other six crew members."

"Marta. Ivan. Yuxi. Anna. Carlos. Angie."

"Why did you follow Zaka out into the forest?"

"To get her crownfruit. So we can climb to the sky."

"What is twenty times thirteen?"

"Two hundred and sixty. Can we please stop now?"

The shipmind says, "Marta, he seems fine. Find a place for him to rest for a day or two. Not inside a cave, though. Someplace outdoors where he can get some visual stimulation. He should be ok soon."

Marta helps Ricky stand up, then she supports his arm as they walk out of the healer's den. They cross the village clearing, finding a comfortable spot just outside their own den. Ricky sits down heavily on the ground, his back propped against the cliff wall. Marta plunks down next to him. She says, "I had to eat the crownfruit. Zaka was dying and you were out cold."

Ricky looks at her, momentarily confused. "You ate the crownfruit?"

"Yes. Zaka was dying and someone had to do it. I killed Zaka and extracted the crownfruit. It was a little pink ball. I could have given it to you, but you were unconscious and could not have eaten it. Also, I didn't know how badly you were hurt. If it was really bad, the crownfruit would have been wasted and we might have to wait a year or more for another one to come along."

Ricky nods. He feels the world shifting around him. "I guess I always figured I'd be the one to eat the fruit and lead the climb. But you're a terrific climber. There's no reason why you can't do it just as well as me. And yeah, right now I'm pretty messed up." He grins weakly at her.

"Ricky, I'm not going anywhere without you. We'll stay here in the village until you're ready to climb. Your arm needs to heal. And I want to make sure you've gotten over the concussion. It would be awkward if you suddenly forgot how to belay me."

"Okay, Marta. I guess you're the boss now."

"That's right. And don't you forget it." She smiles wickedly at him.

* * *

"Ricky, we can't wait any longer. Pack up your stuff. We leave tomorrow morning."

Marta is so agitated, she's nearly hopping up and down. She can't sleep. She can barely eat. It's been five days since the fight with Akana, and all she can think about is starting the climb. At some level she knows this is good, as it means the crownfruit is indeed having an effect on her. But every day she finds herself caring less and less about such intellectual things. All she wants is to feel the rough silva bark under her hands as she ascends toward the sky.

She has already packed and repacked their gear three times. It's all carefully organized, the ropes, cams, carabiners, and pitons all clipped neatly onto their climbing harnesses. They have enough dried food for several days, which they hope will be enough time for them to establish a routine of hunting and gathering to keep them adequately fed.

During their training they'd made a point of tasting a variety of possible food sources from the complex ecosystem of things that sprouted, clung, perched, hopped and crawled on the rough silva bark. Ricky avoided the white fungus and advised Marta to do the same, remembering his unfortunate experience at the dance during his first visit to the Waya village. They sampled berries, mushrooms, insect-like creatures, and small animals. They weren't sure if they'd be able to cook their meals, given the lack of dry firewood and the amount of fuel they'd need to carry, so they ate everything raw. Katan shared his clan's knowledge of what was edible and what wasn't, but since human digestion was different from the Waya, they still proceeded cautiously, taking a tiny nibble of one new food each day, plus a medium-sized mouthful of whatever they'd nibbled the day before. They ended up sampling around thirty different foods, and discovered most were edible, if not exactly tasty. They did learn, through Marta's unpleasant experience, not to eat the small yellow lizards which the Waya thought were delicious but, she discovered, acted as a powerful laxative in the human digestive system.

"I think we're as ready as we can be," Ricky tells her, as he drops his pack on the ground. This isn't quite true, as his injured forearm still hurts badly and he isn't sure he is fully ready to climb. But Marta's impatience is obvious and he can't delay her any longer. "Let's get some sleep. Big day tomorrow."

"You go ahead and sleep," Marta replies. "I'm not tired." Ricky looks at her, cocking his head. They'd been preparing and training for eighteen hours.

"Are you sure?" he asks, a bit concerned.

"Yes. I feel fine. Really."

Marta loves what the crownfruit is doing to her. She feels strong, capable, and mentally sharp. She needs almost no sleep. The world around her seems pliable, willing to bend to her will. To be honest, it feels really good. The only downside, if she could call it that, is the overwhelming impatience, like she's had way too much coffee. Obviously the crownfruit wants her to stop preparing and start climbing. This isn't a serious problem, because it's what she wants to do anyway. Maybe a simian needed a kick in the butt to get it to climb to the sky, but she doesn't need it, and would prefer not to have the crownfruit's chemicals pushing her as hard as they were.

She steps out of the little cave and sits down, resting her back against the cool rock of the cliff. The village is quiet. A few Waya walk by in ones and twos, but things are settling down for the night. Up above, little flying things dance in the darkness, flickering yellow as they flit between massive silva trunks outlined in dim green. Larger creatures, probably bats, flutter through the air, snagging the little yellow fliers and whatever else they can catch.

Marta hears something and looks towards it. A large Waya steps out of the darkness. Momentarily alarmed, her right hand moves instinctively to the knife at her belt. Then she sees who it is and relaxes, no longer feeling physically threatened. She is surprised, though. It's Pataza.

The clan leader walks towards Marta, moving slowly but with the confident gait of a leader, a commander, a queen. Pataza glances briefly into the cave, perhaps to check on Ricky, perhaps to see who else might be there. Turning her head towards Marta, she fixes her huge dark eyes on the young human for a few seconds. Then, wordlessly, she settles down beside the girl, and they sit side by side, looking out at the village and the greenish glow of the forest beyond.

* * *

In the morning, Ricky awakes to find he is alone in the cave. He steps outside. Marta is still sitting there. "Are you ok?" he asks.

"Couldn't be better. Come on, let's get going." They walk together into the forest, heading off in different directions to take

Ascent to the Sun

care of their morning bathroom activities. Then they wash up in the stream and return to the cave. They have a light breakfast of berries, mushrooms, and roasted hoppers, washed down with water. They pick up their gear and head out.

They have to select a silva trunk. As far as they can tell, one trunk is pretty much as good as the next, so they select one just a short walk from the Waya village. Originally they'd considered climbing one of the few trunks which, for whatever mysterious reason, stand alone in the middle of the village, but the greater distance between it and its neighbors could make the climb more difficult once they reached the branchings. So, they pick one fairly close to the village and surrounded by neighboring trunks at the standard distance.

They walk up to the base of the massive trunk. They look up, squinting to see as far as they can, which in the morning mist isn't far. Setting their gear down, they lace on their climbing shoes and attach their crampons.

A few yards away, a drone hovers. Piloted by Ivan, the little craft will keep pace with them as they climb. Its main purpose is to serve as a relay for their video cameras and two-way radios, relieving the climbers of having to carry more equipment. Ricky doesn't like the buzzing noise from its four little propellers, which disturb the quiet of the forest. But it's good to know the shipmind and the rest of the crew will be available to provide encouragement and advice if needed. The drone carries a video camera, microphone and speaker. It's lightly armed, equipped with a dart gun and a magazine loaded with several dozen small poison darts.

Nobody knows what dangers they might encounter, or whether darts will do any good, but it's better than nothing.

They both crane their heads, looking up one more time at the silva trunk which stretches upwards, seemingly forever, into the swirling mists. Then they stand facing each other to check their gear and prepare to start the climb.

"Turn around," says the shipmind in their ears. Surprised, they spin around. Standing a dozen yards away are Waya. Lots of them.

"Greetings, clan leader Marta. Greetings, friend Ricky," says Katan, who stands in front of the group. Next to him are the two surviving council members, Pataza and Maza. Flanking them are the two burly guards. And behind them stand around fifty Waya, nearly the entire clan.

Ricky's best guess is this is a friendly group coming to see them off, but he knows little of Waya customs, so it's hard to know for sure. Marta is equally unsure. As clan leader of the little expedition it's up to her to reply, but she isn't comfortable speaking in the Waya tongue. She looks to Ricky and nods. He says, "Greetings, friend Katan," and waits to see what will happen.

Pataza steps forward. As she speaks, the shipmind listens and translates.

"Greetings, clan leader Marta. Greetings, Ricky. We, the people of the clan, are here today to thank you, and wish you well as you climb to the sky.

"This is a strange day. The Waya have lived in this forest for thousands of lifetimes. For all that time, the shared journey has kept our people strong. And it has been the little simians who have taken the shared journey for us, carrying our seeds to the sky to spread like the wind.

"Now for the first time in our history, there are no simians. No shared journey. No Waya seeds traveling up to the sky. We are looking death in the eye. And the only thing standing between us and extinction is you. Humans.

"When we first saw your shining silver mountain burn through the silva, we thought trouble might be coming. When the first humans emerged from the shining mountain, we knew trouble was coming. When one of those humans killed one of our people, we knew trouble was here.

"But now, we know you a little better. Yes, you have brought trouble. But you also bring hope. You have agreed to take the shared journey for us, at great risk to yourselves. May you be successful, may you deliver our seed to the sky, and may you return safely to us.

"In the tongue of the ancients, I say this to you: *Taka ban gan siga. Taka gisha siga.*"

All the assembled Waya repeat as one, *"Taka ban gan siga. Taka gisha siga."*

The shipmind is silent at this, unable to translate. Ricky looks at Katan, cocking his head. It sounds familiar but he can't remember when he'd heard it before.

Katan says, solemnly, "Now you and I are one. Now the clan is one."

Pataza stands quietly, looking at him. Ricky is at a loss for words. He's seventeen year old kid trained as a soldier, not a diplomat. He has no idea how to respond. There is an uncomfortable silence. Then the shipmind, whose own diplomatic skills are not much better, whispers in his ear, "Just say thank you."

Ricky says, loud enough for all to hear, "Clan leader Pataza, thank you speak. Marta Ricky go shared journey. Do simian. Carry Waya eggs sky. We come back. We help Waya. No worry."

The shipmind translates this word-for-word for Marta, who barely suppresses a giggle.

Pataza lowers her tail slightly and swishes it a bit. "Thank you, human," she says. "Now, climb to the sky. We will watch."

18 | Angels

Marta stands at the base of the silva trunk. She's wearing loose shorts and a gray cotton t-shirt. Her long black hair is tied back in a ponytail. She looks at Ricky, who is dressed in similar clothes but with a black cloth headband tied around his head to keep his long hair back and sweat out of his eyes. They carry backpacks and wear lightweight climbing helmets fitted with small headlamps. Their climbing harnesses hold an assortment of protection gear. They each carry a short length of rope, in addition to the one long belaying rope.

Marta carefully knots one end of the belaying rope to her climbing belt. Ricky threads it through his climbing harness, then stands back a few feet.

"On belay," she says.

"Belay on," replies Ricky, taking the rope in both hands.

"Climbing."

"Climb on."

Marta places her right hand on the rough bark. Oh, that feels good, she thinks. She briefly considers saying something – maybe "This is one small step for Waya kind"? – but realizes that would be stupid. She kicks her left foot into the silva, easily pushing the sharp points of the crampon into the bark. She relaxes her foot a bit, allowing the secondary points to rest against the bark and take the strain off her foot and ankle. Reaching up with her right hand, she grasps a handful of bark and lifts herself off the ground, shifting her weight onto her left leg.

The handhold is wet and slimy. Like the rest of the silva, it's covered by a layer of moss and other plants a couple of inches deep, and inhabited by a variety of insects, worms, and other crawling things. Marta can't see the bark itself, but she can make out its contours well enough to find a handhold to grab. Katan had assured them none of the things living on the silva bark were likely to do them any serious harm. As her hand closes on the handhold, she notices a large centipede nearby and hopes it won't decide to crawl up her arm.

She steps up, straightening her left leg. Raising her right foot to about the height of her left knee, she prepares to kick the toe of her right foot into the bark, but stops when she notices a nice bump near where she is about to embed her crampon. She turns her foot sideways and rests it on top of the bump. Shifting her weight to her right leg, she reaches up with her right hand and grabs her second handhold.

Two steps done, ten thousand more to go. So far, so good. Repeating the process four more times, she stops to look down and wave to Ricky, who waves back. Now it's time to set some protection. She takes a cam from her belt and slips it into a deep crevice in the bark, pulling the trigger to make it narrow. When it's fully inserted, she slowly releases the trigger, letting the lobes expand and lock firmly in place. She clips a carabiner onto the end of the cam, then opens the carabiner's hinge to thread the rope through it. That's the first anchor point.

Now if she falls from a point above the anchor, she'll drop no more than twice the distance between herself and the anchor. Best case, she'll fall maybe five feet. But if Ricky isn't paying attention, or he forgets how to belay her, or the anchor pulls out of the silva bark, she'll fall a lot further.

Fortunately, they are climbing a smooth tree and not a jagged rock wall, so banging into it is unlikely to be fatal. Painful though, and still possibly fatal, depending on what part of her body slams into the silva and whether she gets tangled in the rope on her way down.

She continues to climb, attaching an anchor every six feet or so.

Soon Marta encounters her first obstacle. It's a gigantic shelf fungus, light brown around the edges and with an off-white underside. From the ground it seemed insignificant, but now she can see its true size. The fungus is firmly attached to the silva and completely encircles it, forming a ring extending far beyond the trunk. She'd seen pictures of shelf fungus growing on tree trunks on old Earth. This is roughly similar, obviously another example of convergent evolution, but vastly bigger than anything on Earth and shaped more like a ring than a shelf.

The silva bark underneath the fungus is dry and nearly free of vegetation. She reaches up and touches the underside of the fungus. It has a rubbery texture and is honeycombed with pockets

Ascent to the Sun

as big as her hand, some of which have been colonized by various tree-dwelling creatures, including one that looks like a bee's nest.

She needs to get past the thing. It's beautiful in a bizarre sort of way and she doesn't want to damage it, but she sees no way to attach anything to the underside so she could climb out and over it. Sure enough, when she tries to insert a cam in the fungus and put her weight on it, it pulls out and sprays bits of fungus all over her.

Using the radio embedded in her ear, she explains the situation to Ricky and the shipmind.

"You've got no choice," says Ricky. "Go through it. Try to do as little damage as possible. It will probably heal up."

"Agreed." Grabbing onto a bark handhold with her left hand, Marta uses her right hand to pull a short, serrated knife from her belt. She starts cutting a person-sized hole in the fungus, staying as close to the trunk as possible. The fungus flesh comes away easily, and she thinks the job will just take a couple of minutes. But when she reaches the upper surface, she discovers it's as hard as wood. "Really could use a laser cutter right about now," she mutters.

Using the sharp point of the knife, she punches again and again at the topside layer. It's tough, but only as thick as a piece of cardboard. After hitting it a few times, her knife punches through it. She works the serrated blade around until she is able to remove a semicircle big enough to pass through. It falls, spinning away down to the ground. "Climbing," she says, and ascends through the hole.

When she emerges from the top, she looks around. The shelf blocks the view of everything below her, but she can see upwards.

And what she sees chills her. On the nearest trunk, maybe twenty-five yards away, a half dozen angels are clinging to the silva bark and watching her. Their pale grey wings are wrapped around their bodies, and their narrow heads and beady eyes are trained on Marta. They make no movement and utter no sound, at least nothing she can hear. But somehow, she gets the distinct impression they are less than happy with what she's just done.

"Got some company here," she says to Ricky and the shipmind. "Six angels are watching from the next tree. Just watching, not making any moves towards me. But they don't look friendly."

The shipmind, cautious as ever, replies, "Best to ignore them. Anything you do could be interpreted as hostile. Just go about your business and hope they go away."

"Easy for you to say," says Marta. "Okay, I'll keep climbing. But keep that drone nearby and ready to fire if they decide to come after me." With some effort, she turns away from the angels and resumes climbing. A minute later, movement catches her eye. She turns to see the angels soaring away, up and out of sight.

Ricky stays on the ground, steadily passing rope through his harness, giving her enough slack to make sure it won't pull downward on her as she climbs up. He can no longer see her, now that she's on the far side of the shelf fungus. All he sees is rope disappearing into the hole.

Down below, the assembled Waya, who had been watching, realize the show is over. They all head back to the village except Katan, who stays with Ricky.

An hour later, Marta has climbed about halfway to the first branching and has run out of climbing rope. The rope is a hundred and twenty feet long and weighs around ten pounds, and nearly all of it now hangs between her and where Ricky stands belaying her on the ground. "I'm going to stop here," she tells him. "Time for you to climb up to meet me. Wait a minute."

She needs to prepare to belay him. She hammers two pitons into the bark just above her, then uses a short length of rope to secure her harness to the pitons. "Okay," she says, "I've set up a sling. Come on up."

In her ear, Ricky's voice replies, "Ok, ready. On belay."

She reconfigures the rope on the harness and takes it with both hands. "Belay on."

"Climbing."

"Climb on."

* * *

An hour later, Ricky reaches her. He grins, trying to ignore the throbbing pain in his injured forearm. "Miss me?" he asks.

"Sure," she says, not looking at him. She gazes up at the massive trunk looming above them. After a moment, she says abruptly, "All right, let's get going. Strap in."

Ricky rigs a piton sling similar to the one Marta made, allowing him to rest comfortably while belaying her. It also anchors him securely, so if Marta falls, she won't yank him up and away from where he is perched.

Once Ricky is secured, Marta resumes climbing. An hour later she reaches the first branching. She has no idea what to expect here, since the Waya had only seen the branchings from below, looking up from the ground. This is the first and lowest branching, so Marta expects it to be big, and it is. Impossibly big and impossibly ancient, the thing is a good fifteen feet wide at the point where it exits the main trunk and extends horizontally to join up with its closest neighbor.

Unlike branches of ordinary trees, this branch does not become any narrower, but maintains a uniform thickness until it merges with the branch coming from the other direction. The merge point itself is unremarkable, the two branches having somehow worked out their merger long ago, and the connection point is marked by nothing more than a lumpy ridge a foot or so high.

Slowly and carefully, Marta ascends the vertical trunk until she is a few feet above the branch. Then she traverses across until she is directly over the branch, downclimbs, and steps carefully onto the nearly flat surface of the huge branch.

She can't see Ricky now, or any part of the ground for miles in any direction. But she has radio contact, thanks to the drone which rests on the branch nearby. "Ricky, I'm on the first branch. Everything's good. Come on up."

In her ear, Ricky's voice replies, "Ok, ready. On belay."

She reconfigures the rope on the harness and takes it with both hands. "Belay on."

"Climbing."

"Climb on."

Ascent to the Sun

The branch and the shelf fungus completely block Ricky from Marta's view. As she feels the rope going slack in her hands, she pulls it through her harness to keep a slight constant tension on it. Suddenly she realizes this won't work. "Ricky, wait," she says.

His voice comes back to her, an edge of concern in his voice. "What's up?"

"If you fall, I have no way to stay anchored to the branch. You'll just pull me off and we'll both die. Give me a minute to set up a runner."

"Take your time. I'm just enjoying the view." From their outdoor practice climbs, Marta knows this is a lie. She remembers a few times when she had to cling to small, slimy holds while waiting for Ricky to give her the go-ahead to proceed. The experience varied from moderately upsetting to utterly terrifying, depending on how far she was off the ground, how uncomfortable her hold was on the bark, and how long she had to wait.

"Sorry," she says, "I should have known better." Marta hammers a couple of pitons into the branch behind her, opposite from where her rope leads down to Ricky. She clips a carabiner to each of the pitons. Removing the short rope from her backpack, she ties one end to the left carabiner, threads it through a carabiner on the back of her climbing harness, and ties off the other end on the right carabiner. Now she is anchored by the two points behind her back, which should keep her from sliding off if Ricky slips off and she has to stop his fall.

"All good," she says. "I set a runner. Climb on."

"Climbing," Ricky replies. He can feel Marta taking up the excess rope as he climbs, keeping just a bit of upward tension. He wiggles through the hole in the shelf fungus and reaches the branch an hour later. Following Marta's earlier path, he climbs above the branch, traverses across, and drops down gracefully next to her. He shakes out his hands, which were starting to cramp from the long climb. His injured forearm is throbbing with pain.

The two of them sit side by side, looking out at the silva. No human has ever seen the forest from this height, and the view is spectacular. Late morning sunlight filters down through the mist from above, yellow rays of light piercing the forest. They can't see the ground at all, except for the distant outline of a mountain range. All around them are the silva trunks, countless thousands of them in a near-perfect mathematical pattern, rows radiating out in six directions like the spokes of a vast wheel. The first branching are all nearly the same height. They also stretch out as far as they could see, so that in the far distance they appear to merge and form a flat brown surface. Above them, clouds of bats and other flying creatures dive and swoop through the air.

"Ship," says Marta, "go down and tell the Waya we've reached the first branching and we are ok. We will wait for you before we get moving again."

"The Waya have already departed," whispers the shipmind in their ears. "They left soon after you passed through the shelf fungus. But Katan stayed behind. I will tell him." It spins up its four little propellers, lifts off from the branch, and drops swiftly out of sight.

"How are you feeling?" Marta asks. "How's the arm?"

"No problem," Ricky replies. That's not true. The muscles in his forearm near the wound feel like they are on fire, but he doesn't want Marta to think he isn't up to the task. Then he looks at the other side of the trunk, where the other two branches emerge. "Hey, look at that," he says, pointing. It's hard to tell what it is, but it appears to be big, white, and flat.

"What the hell is it?" says Marta.

"If I didn't know any better, I'd say it's a platform of some sort. Let's go take a look."

"No. You stay here and clip in. Belay me. I'll traverse and see what's going on."

Ricky has by this time gotten used to Marta's new assertiveness, so he accepts this without complaint. He clips into the runner Marta previously set, and gets ready to belay her.

* * *

Marta quickly steps onto the trunk and traverses a third of the way around to the next branch. When she reaches the branch and steps onto it, she needs a moment to make sense of what she's seeing. The top of the branch is festooned with dozens of grayish ropes, each about the thickness of her wrist and wrapped around the branch every yard or so. Each rope stretches taut across to the adjacent branch, forming a triangular array of gray parallel lines. These serve as the supporting structure for thousands of thinner ropes, more like strings, roughly an inch apart. These are arranged in a spiral pattern resting on the heavier ropes. The final result looks like a huge flat spiderweb stretched between the two branches.

The surface is far from clean. It's littered with an uneven carpet of leaves, sticks, bits of foliage from the trunk and branches above, and a few decomposed carcasses of dead animals. There are several holes where heavy objects have plunged through the webbing, and the platform's edges are weathered and frayed.

Marta says, "Ricky, you're not going to believe this. It's a spiderweb. And it's absolutely huge."

Before Ricky can respond, the ship's voice in their ears says, "Careful, Marta. Spider webs are sticky. And where there's a spiderweb there's almost certainly a spider. Maybe lots of them."

"Got it," replies Marta, stepping carefully onto the platform. "Some of these strands are as thick as my wrist. I'd hate to meet the spider that made them."

As she inspects the platform, though, she realizes something else. "The thick strands are not solid," she reports. "They're braided. Each one is actually made from dozens of thinner strands twisted together. That's good and bad news. The good news is there's probably not some gigantic spider squirting out these thick strands. On the other hand, I have no idea how these braided strands were made. Ship, have you ever heard of spiders cooperating to make a super-thick strand of silk?"

"There's no creature on Earth, spider or otherwise, that braids silk," confirms the shipmind. "Except humans, of course."

"Oh, this is interesting," says Marta, as she crouches down to inspect the platform more closely. "There are hairs here, mixed in with the other debris. Some dark, some light. Looks like this has been used as a nest of some sort by some hairy animals."

"Angels?" asks Ricky.

"Maybe. Or simians. Or both. I can't tell by looking at the hairs."

Ricky says, "I can't imagine why a bunch of spiders would go to the trouble of making a web or platform like this, and then let a bunch of animals sleep on it."

Marta reaches down and strokes some of the strands. She says, "Also, the strands aren't sticky. At least, not now. Hard to say how old these are, or what they were like when they were fresh."

"Any sign of the creatures that made the web?" asks Ricky.

Marta looks around. "No. If I had to guess, I'd say this has been abandoned for a long time." Then, feeling the familiar climbing imperative welling up inside her, she added, "Well, enough of this. We've got a bunch of berries to deliver. Let's get going."

* * *

There are no major surprises on the climb to the second branching, no detectable change in the girth of the silva trunk or the texture of the bark. They have to cut their way through two more of the shelf fungus structures, and are approaching the second branching when the weather suddenly takes a turn for the worse. It's early afternoon, which should be the sunniest part of the day. But in just minutes the wind picks up, the temperature drops, and the forest dims as clouds gather overhead. They don't want to be exposed to a rainstorm while clinging to a vertical surface, so they need to find shelter, and fast.

Marta is not quite halfway up to the second branching, with Ricky belaying her from the first. They have two options: Marta could downclimb to the last shelf fungus she'd passed and meet Ricky there, or they both could climb up to the second branching. Marta, always eager to head towards the sky, selects the latter. She tells Ricky to climb up to her position as quickly as possible, as she belays him while anchored to the vertical trunk. Once he gets within a couple of anchors of her, they start climbing more or less together, one climbing while the other belays. This has only a minimal effect on their overall rate of progress, but it does eliminate the long wait for Ricky to come up to Marta's position. It also means they need far fewer protection devices, since they will remain much closer together. Marta decides to ditch the extra equipment at the second branching.

The drizzle starts as soon as Ricky begins climbing, and by the time they reach the second branching it's raining hard. They are cold and wet when they drop down onto the branch. This branch holds another web platform, this one running from their branch to the adjacent one to their left. The platform looks much like the previous one, old and weathered and apparently abandoned.

"Let's set up the bivy on the platform," orders Marta. "It's more comfortable than hanging from the trunk."

"Okay," replies Ricky. "But I'll anchor it to the trunk, just to be safe."

They made camp in the pouring rain. Marta assembles the bivy while Ricky sets up a rain collector. When the bivy is ready they clamber inside, soaking wet, leaving their waterproof packs just outside. The drone, on sentry duty, settles onto the branch nearby.

The bivy is a small tent made of lightweight waterproof material. It's just long and wide enough for two people plus room around the edges for a little extra gear, and barely tall enough to let them sit without hitting the ceiling. "Let's get out of these wet clothes," says Marta.

"Wait," replies Ricky. "I'll get some dry stuff out of the packs." He reaches out into the rain, pulls their one spare set of clothing out of the packs, and ducks back inside. They both strip off their soaking wet clothes and place them on the branch outside the tent. Then, using a small hand towel, they take turns drying each other off. This starts off as a practical exercise but soon morphs into something a lot more fun, as they stroke each other's wet bodies from head to toe with the little towel. Some areas receive more strokes than others, towel strokes lead to caresses, which lead to kisses. Soon the bivy is bouncing up and down, moans and whispers all but drowned out by the pounding of the rain.

"Hungry?" asks Ricky, when they'd finished and caught their breath.

"Sure. What have you got?"

"Power bars and water. I'll grab them." Ricky unzips the flap and pulls food and two water bottles from his pack. They eat quietly, listening to the rain.

Suddenly, the shipmind's voice is in their ears. "Angels incoming. Lots of them."

Ricky and Marta, still naked, dash out of the bivy. They stand on the platform, looking out through the pouring rain. Swooping down through the mist, two formations of angels are approaching, one from either side, at least ten in each formation. They land on the branches that support the platform, grasp the rough bark with their claws, and immediately start chewing and picking away at the thick strands.

"Shoot them!" Marta shouts to the shipmind. She dashes across the platform towards the right-hand branch, skids to a stop, and begins swatting away angels with her bare hand. Through the downpour she can see they are smaller than a human, a bit bigger than a simian. Two long paper-thin wings sprout from their shoulders. Their wing bones are jointed like forelimbs and terminate in thin hook-like claws. Their two spindly legs end in sharp claws. Their bodies are thin except around the shoulders where the flight muscles are. Their heads are elongated, covered with naked skin instead of feathers, reminding her of vultures. Above their sharp beaks are large red eyes, and long ears that can flatten during flight but are now erect, turning towards whatever they are listening to. She doesn't hear them speak, squawk or make any other sounds other than the rough scratching of their beaks as they gnaw away at the thick wet strands.

Marta reaches out and smacks an angel on the head. It falls back off the branch, recovers in mid-air, then flies back to resume gnawing on the strands. Changing strategy, she hits it again, this time on the wing, breaking a thin bone and ripping the wing material. The wounded angel falls off the branch and disappears into the mist below. "Hit them on the wing!" she shouts to Ricky, who is battling them on the other branch.

Marta moves down the line of angels, whacking each one on the wing and moving to the next one. The drone buzzes down to the other end of the line of angels, firing darts. In less than a minute, Marta and the drone clear all the angels off the branch.

Ricky is working alone on the other branch. He is also methodically smacking the angels one by one. But he isn't moving fast enough. The three angels furthest away from him finish gnawing through the strands. The strands snap away from the branch and hang limp from the other end. Losing the support of those strands, the entire platform begins to sag down and away from the trunk. The remaining cables, unable to take the additional strain, fray and snap.

"Get back to the bivy!" shouts Marta. She and Ricky race back, scrambling up the sagging, slippery platform. Grabbing their backpacks, they dive into the bivy just as the last remaining cables break. With all the cables gone, the entire platform slides away from the branch and comes loose, dangling from the right side and spilling debris and gear as it flaps in the wind.

The bivy is lashed to the silva trunk so it doesn't fall, but it drops sickeningly when the platform falls away beneath it. Fortunately, it's designed to hang from its anchors with the floor downwards and the flap on the side, so Ricky and Marta don't fall out. But the flap is open. As the bivy bounces around, wet clothing and food fall out and spin downwards out of sight. Then their climbing harnesses slide towards the flap. Ricky dives to grab them but can't catch them in time. The harnesses drop through the flap and disappear.

Only three angels have survived the battle. They fly up and away in the direction they'd come from. The drone hovers in midair in front of the bivy, swiveling left to right as it stands guard, dart guns loaded and ready to fire.

"Are you ok?" asks Marta, as they zip up the flap and wait for the bivy to stop swinging.

"Yeah," Ricky replies, "though I wish I'd moved faster and stopped those last three from chewing through the ropes."

"Nothing you could have done. At least we're alive and not hurt. But this will set us back a few hours." Ricky cocks his head, looking at her and wondering, yet again, at the driven creature she'd become. "Ship," she continues, "retrieve our climbing gear and other stuff. We'd better get moving again."

There is a pause. Then the shipmind says, "No, Marta." Another pause. "You're not thinking this through."

Marta blinks. After a moment she says, "Ah. You're right."

Ricky is confused. "What?"

"Ship, explain to Ricky please," says Marta.

The shipmind's voice in their ears says, "The angels could come back at any time. If the drone is gone to retrieve your climbing gear, you will be defenseless. A band of angels, or even just one, could land on the trunk above you and chew through the ropes holding the bivy. There's nothing you could do to stop them. You would fall to your deaths."

Ricky couldn't help himself, he looks down at the ground far below. "Got it. Okay. So, we need more drones. How many have you got?"

"There are ten more drones at the ship. They are configured to do reconnaissance, not combat, so they are currently unarmed. I've launched all of them. They'll get here in about ten minutes. In the meantime, I will stay and stand guard. But you two are exposed here. You'll have to move to a safer location."

Ricky says, "But our climbing gear…" He stops. "Oh."

"That's right," says Marta. "We need to traverse to the nearest branch, where we'll be safer, though not by much. The angels still might attack us, but at least we'll be on a solid surface." She grins at him. "Time to do some free climbing."

"Just like in 'Free Solo.' Scariest video I ever saw. But we'll be doing it in the rain. And with a bunch of very angry flying monkeys."

"Yup, and barefoot. Fun."

Ricky looks at her. "You know, you are starting to frighten me."

19 | Drones

The shipmind says, "You have to get moving. I don't know how long till more angels arrive. Marta, you first." The shipmind doesn't want to lose either one of the climbers, but Marta is by far the more important of the two. Losing Ricky would be a setback, but losing Marta would spell the end of the expedition.

The drone hovers in midair a few feet from the bivy. The ship tries to make it appear as dangerous as possible, jinking it up, down, left, and right and swiveling from side to side. It has a dozen darts left. If it runs out of darts, it could just fly straight into an angel to disable it. The shipmind has never tried anything like that, though, and doesn't know if it would work. The angels are much more agile than the drone.

Marta opens the flap, causing rainwater to splash onto the floor of the bivy. She reaches up and around, clambering onto the soft, sloping roof until she can grab one of the rope runners anchoring it to the trunk. She hoists herself up one-handed on the leftmost runner, gripping the wet rope tight in her right hand. Reaching further up, she grabs the trunk with her left hand. It's a good handhold but it's wet, cold, and slimy. Clamping her hand around it, she pulls herself up. Soon she is fully on the silva, each hand gripping a handhold and her bare feet resting on two slippery footholds.

She looks to her left. The branch is about ten feet away. No major obstacles in the way. Slowly she traverses towards the branch, stretching out to find new handholds and footholds, then shifting her feet.

She's a few moves short of the branch when the second wave of angels come. The shipmind says, "Don't look, Marta, but six more angels are incoming. My drones are a half a minute out. Hang in there."

Two of the angels fly towards Marta while the other four attack the ropes holding Ricky and the bivy. The drone jinks toward the bivy to defend it, then rotates and shoots two darts at the angels heading towards Marta. The angels dodge in midair and the darts fly by harmlessly. Both angels reach out their clawed feet and rake Marta's back, slashing bloody wounds across her skin. Marta does her best to ignore the pain and maintain a firm grip on the trunk. She can hear the beating of the angels' wings but dares not turn her head, focusing all her will on holding onto the trunk.

"Hold tight!" says the shipmind. Abandoning Ricky for the moment, the drone buzzes towards Marta, firing two more darts at the attacking angels at nearly point-blank range. Both darts hit, both angels fall. Marta hears the angels flapping and falling away. She resumes her traverse, ignoring the bleeding cuts on her back. She reaches the branch and climbs up onto it.

As soon as Marta is safely on the branch, the drone buzzes back to try and dislodge the other four angels, who are doing their best to chew through the bivy ropes. The drone makes a rapid close pass, attempting to sideswipe the angels. It strikes two of them. They fall off but catch themselves in mid-air and fly right back. The other two keep chewing.

Just then, the rest of the drone flotilla arrives. Now it's eleven drones against four angels. Only the original drone is armed with darts, but the angels don't know that. Four of the drones fly head-on into the four angels. Three of the creatures, wings broken, spiral down to their deaths. The fourth manages to fly back, but instead of resuming chewing through the bivy ropes, it flies towards one of the drones, wrapping its wings around the spinning propellers. The propellers cut deeply into the angel's body, but they clog and stop rotating. The drone and the angel both fall out of sight, spiraling down to slam into the ground far below.

The drones regroup, half surrounding Marta on the branch and the other half defending the bivy. "Move, Ricky!" says the shipmind. Ricky wriggles out of the bivy and follows Marta's path, traversing carefully across the wet surface until he reaches the branch and relative safety.

* * *

Marta sits with Ricky on the branch. The downpour has turned to drizzle, the air has cooled by several degrees, and a thick fog has rolled in. They can see each other and the drones buzzing around them, but the nearby silva trunks have all disappeared in the mist.

She clearly remembers the attack by the angels and the feeling of their sharp claws raking down her back, but the pain of the injuries is somehow failing to reach her conscious mind. She feels keenly aware of everything around her, and is eager to get moving again. "Thanks, Ship," she says. "We owe you one. Now let's get moving again."

"You're welcome, Marta," replies the shipmind, "but it's too soon to thank me for saving your lives. You are still in a precarious position. You have no food or water, no clothing, no shelter, no climbing gear. You are badly injured. The mission has become much more difficult."

"I feel fine," she replies, a bit angrily. "Things have changed, but the mission objective has not. Originally, I thought this would be like big wall climbing, but now it's looking more and more like a military operation. If we want to reach our objective, we'll need serious protection from you from now on. What have you got?"

"All my drones are here with you right now. I am sending a few down to start retrieving your gear from the ground. We'll need help sorting out the gear, but Katan should be able to help with that. He doesn't have the manual dexterity of a human, but he should be able to repack things into small bundles the drones can lift.

"Once you get underway again, you will be vulnerable to more assaults from the angels. Your only protection, for now, will come from this batch of drones. I've already ordered the ship's printers to fabricate several hundred more darts, and one of the drones is heading back to retrieve them."

"That's nice," says Marta, "but these little drones won't do it. We need something bigger and more powerful."

"Unfortunately, there aren't any options that would work better. This is a classic case of asymmetrical warfare, with lightly armed guerillas defending their homeland against a technologically superior invader. The angels are fast and agile, they know this world intimately, and they are willing to sacrifice their lives. We don't have any tech available to overcome that. I do have a few larger military-style drones in storage, but they're even slower than the recon drones that are here now. One or two angels could just fly onto them and send them crashing to the ground. If I fabricate something larger, like a helicopter, there won't be enough room for it to fly in between the branches, and it would be even more vulnerable to kamikaze attacks."

"Chemical weapons?" Marta is surprised to hear those words coming from her own mouth.

"I would not even consider such a thing unless our entire mission was in imminent danger of failure, which it is not. Besides, we know almost nothing about angel physiology. Anything broad-spectrum enough to kill them would probably kill you too."

Marta noted the value the shipmind placed on the lives of herself and Ricky. The two of them are somewhat important, but not enough for the AI to overcome its built-in aversion to certain types of weapons. At times like this she is reminded that she is, after all, talking to a machine. "What do you suggest, then?"

"I believe our best approach, perhaps our only one, is for you to resume climbing just as you did before, as soon as you are recovered and have your clothing and other gear. I will provide a cloud of small recon drones armed with dart guns, enough to outnumber the angels and, I hope, give you some protection."

"But you only have ten or so."

"I'm printing more as we speak. They're complex to build, but with the help of the crew I can produce two or three a day once the printers are running at full capacity. In a week, we'll be able to surround you with maybe thirty drones with dart guns."

"I'm not waiting a week," snaps Marta. "As soon as we retrieve our gear, we are going to get back to climbing. And tell Katan to get rid of most of the cams and carabiners. All we need is ten of each. From now on, we will be traveling light."

* * *

Katan settles himself on the ground, far enough away that he can look up and watch the two climbers. He can just barely see them when they pass through the shelf fungus and reach the first branching. As they continue upwards, they disappear into the mist. Then the rain starts.

Just as he thinks it might be time to return to the village, the platform comes spinning down and crashes to the ground. Katan jumps up and runs towards it, relieved to see the two humans are not in the wreckage. He sees the climbing gear, though, and realizes even if Ricky and Marta are alive they're stuck, unable to move up or down on the silva.

A moment later, dead angels begin raining down on him. He retreats to a relatively safe spot at the base of a nearby silva trunk, watching in horror as the bodies spin down and crash to the ground.

Eventually the angels stop falling. He waits a little while longer to make sure nothing else large is going to come down. Then he walks over to the wrecked platform to see what gear is there. Using his teeth, he drags away the backpacks, harnesses, and other items, not sure what he will do with them.

He doesn't have long to wait. One of the humans' flying machines come buzzing down from the sky and hovers in front of him. He's never seen a machine like this up close. It has two small black eyes in front and a spinning thing at each of its four corners. Sticking out of its body in odd places are other appendages whose purpose he can only guess at. The machine makes a disturbing sound that reminds him of the little scuttling creature he saw emerging from the human ship so long ago.

"Greetings, Katan," says a voice coming from the machine.

Katan cocks his head, looking at it dubiously. "Who speaks to me?"

"I am Ship, speaking to you through this machine. Ricky and Marta need your help."

Perhaps at one time this would have terrified him. By now, though, he's seen enough human machinery to take this more or less in stride.

"Are they ok?" he asks. Three more of the flying machines arrive. They hover in the air just behind the one speaking to him.

"Yes and no," says the shipmind. "They were attacked by groups of angels. They are safe for now, but they are trapped on the second branching. In order for them to continue their climb, they need their gear. These machines, which we call *drones*, can carry some of their gear, but they are not strong enough to carry a lot at one time. I need you to unpack their gear and attach it to the drones, a little bit at a time. They will fly back and forth until Ricky and Marta have everything they need."

Katan goes to work, using his teeth and forepaws to empty the backpacks and unclip everything from the climbing belts. Ship tells him to set aside most of the cams and carabiners, and all the ropes except a single short one. He loads up each of the four drones to the limit of what they can lift, then waits as they shuttle the items up and return for more. After three round trips the job is finished.

One of the drones, which he thinks is the original one he'd spoken with, flies back down again. Ship's voice says, "Do you want to talk to Ricky?"

Katan thinks about it. He has little interest in small talk. "No," he replies. The drone jiggles in the air, performing a crude imitation of a tail wag, then buzzes upwards. Katan watches until it disappears in the mist, then he turns and heads back to the Waya village.

* * *

Ricky insists on putting first-aid cream on Marta's back, even though she claims the cuts don't bother her. "This will prevent infection," he tells her, "which could affect our mission." He is learning how to get through to her, wording every suggestion in terms of how it will affect their ability to complete the climb. He applies the cream and gives her a clean shirt to put on. Speaking softly to the shipmind he orders some bandages for her back. Marta does not seem to notice, or care.

An hour later, the drones have delivered everything and the two climbers have put on dry clothes, and repacked and reassembled their gear. It's now late afternoon. Ricky is tired and hungry, but Marta is determined to get to the third branching before dark. So, surrounded by a dozen hovering drones, they resume their climb. They use the shorter rope and execute the climb as a series of mini pitches, staying relatively close to each other. Marta is always the lead climber, playing the role assigned to her by the crownfruit's mysterious chemicals.

As they climb, they pause occasionally to gather food. Small dark green plants cling to the bark and produce tiny orange berries, which they previously determined were safe to eat. They see many different kinds of fungus, some of which they recognize as edible. They avoid anything unfamiliar or untested.

Nibbling on berries and fungus and sipping from their water bottles, they reach the third branching just as the last light fades from the canopy far above.

The branches at the third branching are bare, with no sign of canopies. They pitch the bivy just above the horizontal branch, attaching it to the main trunk. They eat a few protein bars and fall asleep almost immediately. The drones keep watch as they sleep, circling around the bivy in a seemingly random pattern. Thousands of bats flit through the semi-darkness, but there are no signs of angels, and the night passes without incident.

* * *

Marta wakes up at dawn, eager to get moving again. She kisses Ricky lightly on the cheek, enough to wake him but not enough to start him thinking of activities which might delay their departure.

The morning is cool, with a light coating of dew on the bivy and the silva bark. Three newly printed drones arrive, bringing the total to thirteen. Marta decides to offload most of their gear onto the drones. Their backpacks now hold only water bottles, a few items of clothing and snacks, first-aid kits, and some climbing equipment. For self-defense they each carry a combat knife and a small handgun, though Ricky doubts either weapon will do them much good if there's another angel attack. The cloud of drones, which they expect will grow day by day, is their only real protection.

They are now nearly a quarter mile above the ground. Looking down is now much the same as looking up, their silva trunk fading into swirling mists at both ends. Looking outward, the neighboring trunks are barely visible before the mist swallows them as well.

"Look at that," says Ricky. Marta turns to see. A dozen or so floating balls are coming their way. Each one is roughly spherical, about the size of a basketball, with purplish skin and covered with hundreds of lightweight reddish spikes, sharp and probably poisonous. The creatures have no heads, but they have a small mouth and what appear to be other sense organs clustered at the front, where a head would normally be. On their sides are small fin-like appendages that propel them slowly through the air. Long flexible tendrils dangle down, ending in small hand-like structures that could, perhaps, grab something to eat or anchor them in a storm. Marta and Ricky warily track the floating balls as they approach, but relax as they continue on their journey without, it seems, even noticing the two humans.

"A flock of floating gas bags," says Ricky, watching them float away. Marta gives him a brief smile and nods. She's been concerned about them as a possible threat, moving her right hand to rest lightly on the grip of her gun and calculating whether she had enough bullets in the magazine to shoot all of them. But as they float away, she dismisses them from her mind and resumes her preparations for the day's climb.

The day's climb is generally uneventful, as are the next two days. They manage four branchings per day, so by the end of the fourth day they had ascended about a mile, a third of the way to the canopy. With the help of the drone flotilla, which has now grown to over twenty-five, Marta and Ricky feel well protected from attacks and have plenty of food and other provisions. Their climbing technique improves, their strength increases, and their confidence grows. The air around them has cooled considerably, and although they still climb in t-shirts and shorts, the drones deliver fleece jackets and warm sweatpants for them to wear at night.

Marta is now completely consumed by her chemically induced need to climb. She speaks little to Ricky, limiting her conversation to matters of immediate concern. Her sense of humor seems to be completely gone, or at least pushed so far into the background it's no longer part of her conscious mind. She has little patience for Ricky's interest in the plants and creatures around them, briefly glancing at things he points out but only to evaluate them as potential threats.

They haven't seen a single simian, and they no longer expect to see any, since they've climbed beyond what the Waya call the lower silva, where the doomed creatures once lived. They are now well into the middle silva, the realm of the angels. And there are angels. None approach them, likely keeping a safe distance from the buzzing, swirling array of drones that surround the climbers day and night. But the angels are watching. Marta often sees a faint flickering in the distance, something that might be an angel hovering in the mists. The angels, if that's what they are, never approach close enough to be clearly visible, but Marta feels their presence. They seem to be just waiting and watching.

They encounter many more of the strange woven platforms. They vary in size, the largest one extending perhaps thirty feet along its two bounding branches, the smallest ones only a yard or so on a side. They are mostly flat, though on some platforms they see lumpy, whitish structures resembling melted igloos. Most platforms seem to be abandoned, covered with leaf litter, animal droppings, and other debris. A few are in good condition but also empty of inhabitants except for the occasional visiting bird or small scurrying animal.

One of the platforms, though, is still under construction. When the climbers reach it, they see a cockroach-like creature as big as a small groundhog. It scuttles away from them on six stubby legs and launches itself off the branch, unfolding large clumsy wings that make a low-pitched buzz as it slowly flies away. Ricky reaches the platform and, roped to Marta for safety, steps out onto the platform. At the far edge he kneels down to inspect some of the lighter-colored strings on the platform's floor. "Still wet," he says, poking at the string with the point of his hunting knife. A bit of white goo clings to the blade. He wipes it off on his shorts.

Marta says nothing, scanning for possible danger. Speaking from the nearest hovering drone, the shipmind says, "That's one of the platform builders. It extrudes web material like spiders do, but the creature is a thousand times heavier than the largest Earth spider, so its web strands are much thicker."

Ricky asks, "Why would they make these platforms? They're obviously no good for catching prey, except maybe some dead critters falling from above. The platforms aren't sticky. This is not a trap in any way I can think of."

"Yes, it is odd," replies the shipmind. "The platforms are a huge investment of resources, with little or no benefit to the ones who make it."

Marta, still scanning for danger, says, "Unless they're working for the angels."

"Domesticated?" asks Ricky.

Marta nods.

Ricky thinks for a moment. "That makes sense. The angels are big, they're social, and they have to live somewhere. Here in the middle silva there's nothing to use for nesting material. No sticks, no vines. So if they want to do more than just sit on a branch, they need help. The spider creatures provide that nicely." He pauses. "Though I wonder what the spider creatures get out of the deal."

"This is not symbiosis," points out the shipmind. "There doesn't have to be a fair exchange of benefits. If these creatures have been domesticated by the angels, they have little choice, no more than an ox pulling a plow on old Earth."

"Makes sense," says Ricky. "Though I wonder. If the spiders are working for the angels, who are the angels working for?"

20 | Platform

Around midday on the fifth day of their climb, Marta is in the lead, just having passed Ricky in the leap-frogging method which has now become routine. She needs to keep reminding herself to stay alert and take nothing for granted. One mistake, even with ropes and protection, can still prove fatal.

"Look up," says the shipmind, from the nearest drone. Marta looks up. Far above them, just visible through the mist, is the next branching, their seventeenth if her count is accurate. But this one is different. It's not just a triangle extending a few yards from the main trunk. This one is huge. From where she is perched, looking up from below, the platform reaches all the way to two of the nearest silva trunks, covering an area as large as the entire Waya village. Its structure, at least from underneath, looks like the other platforms they'd seen, a webwork of thin beige silken strands supported by a grid of thicker ropes. The surface is translucent, allowing light to filter through and making it nearly invisible from a distance.

"Ship, go check it out," says Marta. "Tell us if it's safe." The two climbers cling to their holds and wait. Several drones buzz up to inspect the platform while the rest maintain a protective perimeter around the climbers.

A few minutes later a drone returns. It says, "The platform looks okay. It's clean, well maintained, almost certainly still in use. No features at all, except for a large lump near the far right corner. And no angels."

"How big is the lump?" asks Marta.

"About as tall as you, and twice as wide. Roughly circular. No opening or door I can see."

"What do you think it is?"

"I cannot say. Most likely it's a nest used by the platform-building creatures, since it's made of the same spider-silk material. I've deployed several armed drones to surround it. When you get to the platform you can check it out. The creatures don't seem to have much in the offensive weaponry department, though, so it should be safe."

Marta and Ricky resume their leap-frogging climb and soon reach the seventeenth branching. With practiced ease they climb up and around the horizontal branch and soon stand side by side on the top of the branch. They look out at the flat expanse of spider silk.

"It's huge," says Ricky, seemingly at a loss for words. "But why?"

"An awful lot of work for no purpose, as far as I can tell," says Marta. "Let's go check out that lump. I'll go first. You stay back and belay me in case anything goes wrong." She pulls the gun from her belt and holds it in both hands as she slowly approaches the lump. Six drones hover nearby, dart guns trained on it.

She stops about an arm's-length from the lump, not sure what to do next. As she considers her options, the part facing her shakes a bit. She crouches, eyes narrowed, weapon ready. A small vertical slit appears at the base of the lump. It moves slowly upwards, zipper-like, until it stretches half the distance from base to top.

A moment later the slit opens, just a bit. It's dark inside. Marta sees movement and tenses, finger on the trigger.

Two hands reach out and spread apart the fabric of the lump. They are clearly human hands, dark skinned and wrinkled. Enough light penetrates into the interior to let Marta see who is inside. It's a woman. Her features are West African, her face middle-aged and weathered. She sits barefoot and cross-legged on the floor, rocking slightly from side to side. Her thin body is barely covered by a lightweight beige dress woven of spider silk. Her hair is long, gray, and frizzy, parted in the middle and spreading out like two soft clouds. It's hard for Marta to read the woman's facial expression, as she's never met anyone this old, but she guesses what she sees is a mix of fear and confusion.

When the woman speaks, her voice is hoarse. "My family," she says. "Gone."

Marta struggles to make sense of the woman's existence. These cryptic words don't help at all. "Who are you?" she asks.

"My family," the woman repeats. "All gone. Why? I want my family back."

Marta lowers the gun. The woman is unarmed and does not seem to be a threat, just a puzzle. "Ship," she says softly, "what's going on here?"

The shipmind speaks in her ear, not using the drone's speakers. "Marta, meet Kim. She's one of the first generation. Somehow, she has survived."

This is making less and less sense to Marta. She feels herself becoming agitated and makes an effort to calm down. She kneels, trying to appear less threatening. Softly she says to the woman, "Are you Kim?"

The woman's expression softens. "Kim."

Marta forces a smile. "Hello, Kim. My name is Marta."

The woman looks from Marta to the hovering drones, then back again. She doesn't see Ricky. "Family gone. Why?"

Marta assumes she is referring to the rest of the first generation. All killed, or so they'd thought, so many years ago. She tries, "Tell me about your family."

Kim smiles again, her face taking on a dreamlike expression. "My family. They love me. They knew you were coming. They could not stay. I could not go. They left me alone."

So, thought Marta, there are other survivors here? "Are there other people here with you?"

Kim giggles. "People? Yes. And no."

Understanding suddenly dawns on Marta. "You mean the angels? The flying creatures?"

"Is that what you call them? Angels. I like that." Kim's eyes go blank for a moment. Then she giggles again. "They think it's funny."

Marta has had enough. She wants to climb, not engage in bizarre conversations with someone who shouldn't be alive and certainly shouldn't be here. She whispers, "Ship, deal with this."

One of the drones buzzes down, settling on the ground next to Marta to face Kim. It says, "Hello, Kim. I am Mother. Do you remember me?"

Kim looks mystified. She says to the drone, "Mother?"

"Yes," continues the shipmind. "I am Mother. It is good to see you again, after such a long time. You remember the ship? I am still in the ship. It's very far from here. Right now I am using this drone to speak to you. The drones are helping Marta and her friend climb the silva. Do you understand?"

Now Kim looks terrified again. She wrings her hands together and begins rocking side to side. "Drones. Bad bad bad. Scare my family. Go away!"

"I'm sorry, Kim, I'm afraid I can't do that. I need to stay here to protect Marta and her friend."

"No. Go away." Kim cocks her head for a moment, as if listening to something only she could hear. Then she looks up. She gives the drone a wan smile and says, "Now. You go away."

The ship does not reply right away. Marta looks up, then stands and turns around. Everywhere she looks, angels hover in mid-air. Angels beyond counting, hundreds, perhaps thousands, surround them, all out of range of the drones and their dart guns.

"Go away now," repeats Kim. "All of you. Go away. My family is here now. They will protect me."

"And what will happen if we do not go?" asks the shipmind.

"Many family. Few drones," says Kim.

The drone turns to face Marta, The gesture is completely unnecessary but makes it seem more human somehow. "Marta, the drones are outnumbered fifty to one, and their weapons have limited capabilities. If the angels want to, they can destroy every drone in a matter of minutes. There's nothing I can do."

Marta considers this, weighing her options and trying to determine what's best for the mission. "All right. Leave everything the drones are carrying. Drop it over there." She gestures to where Ricky is standing. "Then go. Will the radios still work if we stay here and the drones are on the ground?"

"No," says the drone. But the voice in her ear whispers, " I will station a few drones in between, to act as relays. Let's hope the angels don't notice."

Marta nods. She says to Kim, "All right. You win. The drones will go."

Kim smiles.

* * *

Ricky stands on the branch near the trunk, his climbing harness anchored to the trunk by a cam and a runner. In both of his hands he holds the long rope linking him to Marta to protect her if she falls. He has a general understanding of what is going on at the other end of the platform thanks to the shipmind, which continually relays the conversation to him. He sees the dense cloud of angels coming to surround them on all sides, and he watches as the drones fly towards him, drop whatever supplies they are carrying, and disappear into the depths below. Looking at the pile of gear, Ricky notices a few dart guns hidden under the food and clothing items.

Nothing happens for several minutes. Marta and Kim do not speak to each other. At some point, though, the angels apparently decide the drones are safely out of the area. Most of them fly away, but a hundred or so glide down to the platform. Some land on the boundary branches, others settle in various locations on the platform. Four of them stand guard, two on either side of the lump that serves as Kim's home, or perhaps her prison.

He hears Marta say to Kim, "Is it safe for my friend to come over here?"

"Oh yes," replies Kim. "Very safe."

Marta turns and signals for Ricky to approach. She calls to him, "Don't worry about the belay rope. If the angels want to kill us, there's nothing we can do to stop them."

"That's so reassuring," he replies, trying to lighten the mood. He unclips from the trunk and walks across the platform to stand next to Marta.

With a little grunting sound, Kim gets up and steps out into the open. She is shorter than Marta, and quite thin. She looks up at Ricky's face, gazing in his direction but with a far off look in her eyes. Stepping closer, she reaches out her right hand to touch his chest, feeling the muscles under his t-shirt. Unsure what is happening, Ricky does not move or speak. He hopes she doesn't try to reach for his weapons. She extends her other hand, resting both lightly on him. She shifts her hands outwards, lightly stroking his shoulders and upper arms. Moving down his arms, she takes both of his hands in hers and stares at them. Then she lets go of his hands and reaches up to his face, her fingers moving over the stubble of his unshaven cheeks. He wonders if she is blind.

"Hello," he says. "My name is Ricky."

She looks at him. "Such a long time," she says, half to herself, "Nobody. Just family. Now you. Strange."

Ricky has so many questions, he doesn't know where to start. And Marta isn't much help. She is paying more attention to the gathered angels than to the strange woman they'd just met. He decides to go with easy questions first. "Do you live here?"

She gives that wan smile again. "Of course. Where else would I live?"

"What do you eat?"

"The trees provide." She waves towards the trunk behind her. Looking closely, Ricky sees the dozens of little protuberances sprouting from the bark. They look like teats, each the size and shape of his thumb. It's hard to tell for sure, but it looks like each teat has a little hole at the end. Well, that's interesting, he thinks. Plants often produce food for creatures that fly, run or crawl, in return for their unwitting help in propagating the plant's seeds. But the silva has no need for seed propagation. Why would it feed the angels? Or Kim?

"So," he ventures, "you and the angels eat the stuff that comes out of those?"

"Of course." She turns around and walks to the trunk. She selects a teat positioned at a comfortable height, and puts it in her mouth. Then she squeezes the end with her fingers. Ricky cannot see what comes out of the teat, but he sees her swallowing a few times. She turns to him and says, "You try."

"No thank you," he replies. "Maybe later."

Marta cuts in with a question of her own. "Do you talk with the angels? Do you speak their language?"

Kim shakes her head. "No need to talk."

Ricky says softly, "Ship? What is she talking about?"

There is no answer.

"Ship?"

Silence.

Kim cocks her head again. Smiling, she says, "Family says drones were hiding. Resting on the trees. Bad drones. All gone now."

Marta's voice is sharp. "Gone?"

"All gone," Kim confirms. "Each one kills one. No more drones. Safe now." She nods her head and smiles again.

"The angels destroyed all of our drones?" shouts Ricky. Then, getting himself back under control, he asks softly, "How do you know this?"

Kim looks up at him but speaks as if he were a small child. "My thoughts. Family thoughts. All together. In here." She taps her head. "No need to talk."

"Telepathy," says Marta, simply.

"All together," Kim repeats. "In here."

* * *

Marta says, "Kim, would you please excuse us for a few minutes? Ricky and I need to talk."

Kim just smiles and says nothing. Marta pulls at Ricky's arm. Together they walk a short distance away from Kim to a corner of the platform relatively free of angels. She turns to face him. "Ricky, they've destroyed our entire support system. We are totally on our own from now on. No supplies. No protection. No shipmind. And a long, long way to go."

"Yes. And the angels can swat us like flies anytime they want to. We don't want to annoy them. And I think that means we don't want to annoy Kim. She's linked to them in some strange way."

"Ricky, what the hell is she?"

"I don't know any more than you do. She appears to be a survivor from the first generation, assuming she's not some weird artificial construct made by the silva. Or the angels. Or something."

"If something made her, they did a pretty piss poor job of it."

"She's badly damaged, for sure. That's probably the strongest reason to believe she's who she says she is, and not some robot or whatever."

"She can barely talk. And she seems drugged or something."

Ricky shakes his head. "Look at what she's been through. She survived the massacre, saw all her friends killed, somehow ended up here, and hasn't spoken to another human in over twenty years. It's surprising she can even talk at all. As for her strange way of talking, it's hard to say. Maybe she's not used to talking out loud. Or it could be a symptom of more serious mental problems."

"Speaking of which, what about this telepathy thing? Do you think she's imagining that, somehow hallucinating she's in communion with the angels?"

"The shipmind taught us there's no such thing as true telepathy. But the shipmind has been wrong before. For now, I'd believe her."

Marta looks around at the angels, who are all over the platform. "But how can she, umm, telepath with the angels?"

"If I had to guess, I'd say it has something to do with the food the silva produces. Maybe there are nano-machines in it. Honestly, I have no idea. But for now, my best guess, she can communicate with the angels without needing to learn their language. If they even have one."

"So," says Marta, "the angels are her family. Her protectors. Her jailers. We might be looking at a case of Stockholm syndrome here. She's a victim who has come to identify with her captors."

"I think it's more complicated than that. The angels didn't kidnap her. They saved her life. They rescued her for some mysterious reason. They knew she couldn't survive on her own, with the Waya looking for her. So they brought her up here."

"We need to know why she's alive and why she's here. Is she a danger to our mission? And what about the angels? Are they a greater threat than before, or less?"

"Well, they were trying to kill us before. Now they're just watching us. That's a step in the right direction."

Marta looks around at the crowd of angels on the platform. "True. We're surrounded by them and we're not dead yet."

"Let's try talking with Kim some more. But we need to go slow. If we push too hard, she may see us as a threat and stop talking altogether. Or tell the angels to throw us off the platform."

21 | May Day

Marta and Ricky decide a gift is in order. They return to their supply cache, threading their way carefully past the dozens of angels who stand everywhere on the platform. The angels are in constant motion, hopping around, silently turning their narrow gray heads to follow Marta and Ricky as they walk past. They show no signs of aggression, thinks Ricky, but they do seem agitated. Or maybe they're always like that.

There's a good reserve of food in the cache, enough for several days, thanks to the resupply drones. Ricky rummages through the pile, picking out some berries, nuts, and three nutrition bars. They walk back through the milling crowd of angels to Kim, who has gone back inside the large whitish lump they now think of as her house.

They enter, wondering if Kim will object to them intruding on her private space. She seems not to care one way or the other. They look around. There are no furnishings other than a thin spider silk mattress filled with some kind of leaf litter. Around the perimeter of the house, a collection of small pots woven of spider silk hang from the ceiling at varying heights. Most of the pots hold green plants, but some contain mushrooms and other fungus. The back wall has a small opening to let in fresh air, hooded at the top with a spider silk flap to keep out the rain.

"Kim," says Ricky, "we brought you some food." He holds out some berries and a bar.

Kim looks at it and shakes her head. "The trees provide," she says. "You will see."

"May we sit with you?" asks Marta.

Kim waves at the floor. It seems to Ricky she is more responsive than before. Perhaps she just needed some time to adjust to the presence of other humans. Briefly he thinks of Katan, and wishes he could see this.

Ricky and Marta silently eat their berries and food bars, washing it all down with water from their bottles. They offer water to Kim, who declines. They wait, hoping Kim will speak. Eventually Kim asks, "You are from the ship?"

"Yes," replies Ricky, glad to be engaging her in something like a real conversation. "There are seven of us. The other five are back at the ship. We were born seventeen years ago. We grew up in the ship. Like you." He stops, waiting to see if she will pick up the thread.

"I remember the ship," she finally says. She pauses. When there is no reply she continues, forming her words slowly and carefully. "There were twelve of us. I was the youngest."

"You were born at different times?" asks Marta.

"One child every three months, more or less. I was born last. Mother raised us, took care of us, taught us. We never left the ship.

Mother said it wasn't safe." Her voice trails off and she stares at nothing.

Ricky says, "What was your training? Your job?"

"I studied to be a nutrition scientist. I was supposed to explore the forest, collect samples of plants and animals, test them, make a plan for how we could survive on what grew here. I also had samples of Earth crops. I planted them in the clearing, in little plots. And Mother had embryos of farm animals. We were going to hatch them when we were ready."

Ricky notices her sentences getting longer, her thoughts more coherent.

"Did you get to do any of that?" he asks, starting to tread on dangerous ground.

She sits quietly for a moment, then says, "A little. When the oldest ones turned seventeen, Mother decided we were old enough to start going outside. Two of the older boys were guards. Jackson and Mario. They were cute." She smiles at the memory. "Once they said it was safe, some of us would go outside to explore, test, and so on. Mother didn't want all of us to go outside at the same time. Not safe, she said. I went out almost every day, for a month or so. I collected lots of samples and brought them back to study in the lab."

Kim stops, twisting her hands together and staring off in the distance. Ricky and Marta wait.

"One day, Jackson killed a wolf. That's when the trouble started. He didn't know what it was. He saw it in the forest. It looked dangerous, he said. And it was his job to protect us. So he shot it. As soon as he shot it, he saw a bunch of other wolves running away. That's the last time we saw any of them for a couple of weeks. Then they came back." She says nothing for a long time, staring blankly at one of the little spider silk baskets hanging on the wall.

"What happened?" asks Marta, softly.

"It was May Day. Everyone knew it was sort of a made up holiday, because there was no way to tell if it was the first day of May or not, since there are, what, four hundred days to a year here. But Mother kept a calendar. She adjusted it to match the length of the year here, and when the weather got warmer she said May Day was coming and it was a chance for us to all go outside together. We made lots of food. Some from the ship's stores, some of it from samples we'd brought back from the forest, some from our little farm plots. We set up picnic tables in the clearing. There was music."

Kim pauses, a faint smile on her weathered face. "There was dancing too. That was nice. Jackson and Mario stood guard, as usual. But what could they do? All of a sudden, there was a terrible, terrible sound, like a million screams. It was the wolves. Hundreds of them came pouring out of the forest into the clearing, howling like it was the end of the world. Some ran behind us, cutting off our escape back to the ship. Jackson and Mario had automatic weapons, deadly things. They did what they could, but it was no use against an attack like that. The wolves killed most of us right there in the clearing. Three of us ran away into the forest. There were so many wolves, we didn't have a chance."

"But you survived," says Ricky.

"My family saved me. The ones you call the angels. They know everything that happens in the forest. They knew the wolves were planning the attack. They wanted one of us to survive. Groups of them waited just outside the clearing, up in the trees. They watched the attack, the killing. They saw three of us run into the forest. I ran the fastest. I got away from the wolves, just a little ways. They would have caught me and killed me. But a big group of angels, maybe twenty of them, came down and lowered a knotted rope to me. I grabbed it. They pulled on it together and managed to lift me up and away. I was terrified. I just clung to the rope with my eyes closed. I didn't know where I was going, or what was going to happen to me. For a long time I just hung on, swaying in the wind as they carried me. Eventually, they brought me here."

Kim stops talking. She probably hasn't spoken this many words in decades, thinks Ricky.

"How old were you?" he asks.

"Fourteen."

"Kim," says Marta, "why did the angels save your life?"

Kim smiles. "It was the trees. The trees wanted me to live. They sent the angels to save me."

"Why would the silva – uh, the trees – care about you? Or for that matter, why would they care about the angels?"

"You don't understand," says Kim. "But you will. Give it time."

By now it's getting dark. Everyone is tired, including Kim who is obviously stressed from the day's events. Ricky and Marta excuse themselves and head back across the platform to sort out their gear and get some sleep.

When they get there, they discover all their food and climbing gear is gone. All that remains in the pile is the bivy, their clothing, and some personal items like the first aid kits.

"What the hell!" shouts Marta. She turns and marches back to Kim's house, Ricky just behind her. There are angels everywhere, but they don't resist when she roughly pushes them aside.

"Kim!" she shouts into the little domed house. "Where's our food? Our gear?"

Kim slowly steps out of her house, ducking her head as she emerges from the opening. As she does, two large groups of angels gather on either sides of her. Ricky can see their posture has changed. Their wings are still folded back, but the claws on the ends of the wings are now extended forwards, razor sharp hands on the ends of webbed arms. They are clearly guarding Kim.

Kim smiles at them. "The trees want you to stay. They want you to learn. You stay for a while, yes?"

"No!" shouts Marta. "We are going to climb out of there, and you are going to give us back our stuff."

Marta's desperate need to climb has pushed all other thoughts from her mind and made her reckless. Without thinking she draws her knife. Immediately, a dozen angels leap forward to intercept her. She retreats a step and swings the knife back and forth in a wide arc, trying to keep them at bay, but there are too many. She wounds one, nearly cutting off its outstretched claw. The rest quickly overpower her, knocking the knife from her hand and pinning her to the ground.

Ricky dashes forward, handgun out. He aims at one of the angels pinning Marta to the ground and fires. The force of the bullet knocks the angel off her and sends it flying, dead, through the air and off the edge of the platform. Three others rush at Ricky, ripping the gun out of his hand before he can fire again. One of them slashes at him, its talon cutting him deeply across the belly. The others pin him down next to Marta.

Kim looks at the result of the brief conflict. She cocks her head for a moment as if listening to something. Then she says, "You will stay. You will learn. Yes?"

As if on cue, the angels release Marta and Ricky and step away. Marta rolls over to check on Ricky, who is on his back, gritting his teeth.

"You could have killed him!" she shouts. She holds her hands against his bleeding belly, trying to stop the bleeding. "Do something!" she yells at Kim.

Kim looks shocked at the sight of all the blood, possibly recalling the slaughter in the clearing so many years ago. Her eyes go blank for a moment. Then she says, "Wait."

Marta keeps her hands pressed on Ricky, his blood leaking from between her fingers. Less than a minute later, she hears a low buzzing sound. One of the silk-weaving creatures flies onto the platform, landing heavily near Ricky.

"Get that shirt off him," says Kim.

Marta tears away his bloody shirt, revealing a deep gash across his abdomen. The weaver scuttles over to Ricky, climbs onto his chest, and begins squirting silk onto the wound area. The silk has a bluish tinge, different from what it used to construct the platform. It deposits a puddle of the gooey stuff on Ricky's stomach. Then it scuttles off again. Kim comes over and spreads it carefully with her hands. The silk begins to harden, and soon it is a firm but flexible bandage covering the wound.

Kim looks up and says to Marta, "He will be all right. The silk will protect the wound. Prevent infection. Give it time."

"We don't have time!" shouts Marta. "I need to climb, and I'll do it with Ricky or without him. You take care of him. I'm leaving whether you want me to or not."

"How can you go?" asks Kim softly.

Marta thinks for a moment about what it would be like for her to free climb the rest of the way. She'd have no ropes, no gear, and would have to forage for food and water along the way. It seems impossible, but she is determined to keep going no matter what.

Then she looks around and realizes even that isn't an option. At each of the three points where the platform attaches to a silva trunk, a group of angels stands guard. They are trapped.

"Come on, Marta," Ricky grunts. "Let's go back to our bivy and think about what we're going to do."

Marta shakes her head. She glares at Kim. "Why are you doing this? What have we ever done to you? You're human, just like us. You should be helping us, not trying to kill us."

Kim gives one of her enigmatic smiles. "I was once like you. Alone. I remember that. Now I am never alone." She waves a hand to indicate the gathered angels and the forest beyond. "We are all one family. You will learn. You will see I am helping you."

"Oh," says Marta, "so that's how it is? You, the angels, the trees, all one big happy family, huh? Then why did the angels let all your friends die when the wolves attacked?"

Kim seems started by this. She cocks her head for a moment. "The trees, the angels, they try not to interfere."

"Why?" shouts Marta. "What do the trees want?"

"The trees just want to live. To breathe. That is their purpose."

"Okay. What about the angels? What is their purpose?"

"To help the trees, of course."

"And the wolves?"

Kim shakes her head slightly. "They have no purpose. Just part of the world, that's all."

"And what about us? The humans? What is our purpose?"

Kim thinks for a moment, as if trying to organize her thoughts. She speaks slowly and carefully. "The trees only want to live and breathe. That is the highest purpose of all. Next is the angels. Their purpose is to help the trees to live and breathe. Everything else either has no purpose, or is a threat. The trees believe you are a threat."

Marta thinks of the hole the ship blasted in the silva when it landed. Yup, she thinks, we sure look like a threat. "You said, 'you.' Aren't you a human? Aren't you a threat?"

Kim laughs. "Oh, maybe once, long ago. No longer. Now I am family. The trees hope you will learn, so you won't be a threat either."

"How will we learn?"

"Stay here. Share our food. Learn. It won't take long."

"So," says Marta, glaring at Kim, "you are trapping us here. You are going to starve us until we are so hungry we eat this stuff oozing out of the trees. And then we will learn. Is that it?"

Kim smiles broadly, clapping her hands. "Yes!"

Behind them, the angels rearrange themselves to open up an unobstructed path back to the small pile of remaining gear. Ricky takes the hint. "Come on, Marta," he manages to say. "Let's go."

* * *

Ricky hobbles back to their end of the platform, his arm draped over Marta's shoulder for support. The pain isn't as bad as he expected, probably thanks to some analgesic effects from the silk bandage. But he's in no shape to climb, or to do anything else. He lies down in the bivy and soon falls asleep.

By the end of the next day, Marta and Ricky are getting hungry and thirsty. A few times they try making moves towards one of the trunks, only to find their way blocked by dozens of angels with outstretched claws. They consider briefly trying to fight their way out, but a couple of knives and handguns would only serve to kill a few angels and make the rest of them angry, so they don't even try. Harming or threatening Kim doesn't seem like a viable option either, since the angels could simply overpower them if they tried.

A couple of times they think they hear the buzzing of a far-off drone, but they don't see anything, and their ear radios remain silent. No help from the ship in the immediate future, apparently. They have no idea where their climbing gear and food is, having searched the entire platform without success. Their best guess is that it's stashed somewhere on another platform, far out of their reach.

Marta paces back and forth near the bivy, an area they've more or less staked out as their own and is free of angels. The imperative to climb is so strong in her, she can think of nothing else, not even her own hunger and thirst. "Ricky, I need to get going," she says. "Whatever they want us to do, let's just do it. The longer we wait, the weaker we'll become. Once we do it, they'll release us and I can get climbing again. You can wait here for me."

"I guess so," replies Ricky, uncertainly. "Hey, Marta, I've been thinking about what Kim said last night. She said the trees only want to live and breathe. What do you think she meant?"

Marta shrugs. "I haven't given it any thought at all. Seems irrelevant."

"Maybe. But it gets me thinking. This whole planet is covered with vegetation, right? Lots and lots of it. And there are only a few animals in the forest. So, think about breathing for a minute. Plants utilize carbon dioxide and give off oxygen. Animals do the opposite, they utilize oxygen and give off CO_2. But here, there's a huge imbalance between the two. So, you'd think the atmosphere would become super-saturated with oxygen. That would be deadly to animal life, not to mention even a little spark from lightning would cause the whole planet to burn to the ground. But none of that is happening."

Marta stops pacing and looks at him. Her eyes are hard. "Ricky, I don't care. All I want to do is get to the canopy. That's all. So, can we please leave the planetary ecology discussion for another time?"

"I'm with you, Marta, believe me. But we need to understand what's going on here. Where is all the oxygen going?"

Marta takes a deep breath. "Okay, Ricky, how about this. We go see Kim. We tell her she's won. We suck some of the mystery goop from the teats on the tree, enough so we don't die of starvation. If we're lucky, we won't lose our minds and the angels will let me go. You can stay here as a hostage or whatever. And if we're lucky, you'll find out where the oxygen goes. Deal?"

Ricky looks at her curiously. "I don't understand you anymore, Marta. But ok, let's do it."

22 | Soma

Kim hears the trees. They tell her the humans are coming back to see her. The trees are eager for Ricky and Marta to join the family. The trees seem pleased, and that makes Kim happy.

She emerges from her house to greet Ricky and Marta.

"Okay," says Marta. "Let's get this over with."

Kim can sense the other woman's hostility but tries not to show it. The trees would not want any problems now that things are moving along so nicely. She knows the angels understand this as well. They have retreated far enough to not appear threatening to the two visitors.

"Of course," she replies. "The trees are ready. They will give you everything you need. Come with me." She leads them behind her house, to the wall of rough bark. Sprouting here and there on the bark are a couple of dozen little thumb-sized teats. She selects one about the height of her own mouth, and touches it with her finger. It wiggles a little.

She says to Marta, "Just suck on it. It's easy. Let the trees feed you."

Marta walks up to the tree, bends down, and without hesitation closes her lips around the teat. Kim can see her cheeks hollow out as she begins sucking on the teat, then her throat moves as she swallows the first mouthful. A pause, then she puts her hand to the teat to hold onto it better while she continues to suck on it, swallowing again and again. Eventually she finishes, satisfied.

Marta turns to Ricky. "Not bad," she says. "Try it."

Ricky hesitates, then drinks his fill. When he is done, Marta goes back for seconds.

Kim smiles. "Now you feel good, yes? In a little while, you will understand."

* * *

Ricky likes to listen to music. All kinds, from medieval chants to twenty-second century pop zank. But his favorites are the symphonies from the great Renaissance composers – Beethoven, Schubert, Brahms. He loves the way the sound spectrum is filled with so many different voices, from the high notes of flutes and violins down to the low thrumming of the bass and tuba.

Now, a half hour after drinking from the silva's teat, he's starting to feel like he is listening to an orchestra. But what fills his head is not a beautiful symphony. It's more like the tune-up beforehand, when all the musicians play their instruments in random ways, filling the air with loud and discordant sounds.

No, that's not quite right either. It isn't music he hears, and not words either. He's hearing thoughts, nearly indistinguishable from his own but clearly not his own. Strange new ideas are slipping into his consciousness. Mysterious visitors are writing on the whiteboard of his mind that, up till now, was for his use alone. He knows the thoughts are not his, but they are in the place where his own thoughts usually are. Some are faint, like a distant memory or half-forgotten dream drifting through his conscious mind like a ghostly ship. Others are strong, clear, and distinct, like the solution to a math problem.

As he observes these alien thoughts entering his head, he comes to understand, somehow, that there are different classes of thoughts. The most numerous are the faint whispers of the angels as they chatter among themselves. He'd always believed they were silent, but now he knows they are in constant conversation, their simple thoughts washing through his mind. Their conversations don't seem very interesting, though, and he can't quite make out what they are saying anyway, so he ignores them for now.

At the other end of the spectrum are deep, powerful thoughts which he knows are coming from the silva. They are hard and sharp, as if written on his whiteboard with a thick black marker.

Between the highs and the lows, between the weak and the strong, are other voices. Human voices. He somehow recognizes Kim, the strange woman, slipping into his mind with practiced ease. And there is Marta, his love, whispering to herself, or possibly to him, agitated thoughts he can't understand.

That raises an interesting question. Are these messages sent deliberately from one mind to another, or is he eavesdropping, uninvited, on the inner thoughts of others? He has no idea. All he knows for certain is that everyone in the vicinity, from the babbling, nearly incoherent angels to the ancient and wise silva, is writing on his whiteboard at the same time. His head has become quite a noisy place. He has to sort things out.

His first step is to listen, to observe, to separate what is Ricky and what is other. This takes a while, and he's not sure how he did it, but he somehow manages to separate and assign labels to the various streams of incoming thoughts. This one is silva, this one is Marta, that one is angel. That makes things easier.

His next task is to pay attention to individual voices, or channels as he now thinks of them. Of these, the silva is the most important. He tunes into the silva channel and listens. The thoughts write themselves on his whiteboard, crisp and clear:

Visitor young and wild

Listen to us

Meet us

Well, that answers the question he had earlier. Clearly this is a message, not an overheard thought. But how is he supposed to respond?

"Can you hear me?" he says inwardly. Probably the dumbest first contact message in human history. And is he even doing it correctly? How exactly is he supposed to send a telepathic message? The shipmind had neglected that part of his education.

Come to us

Picture a spinning ball of light

Ricky was expecting some sort of conversation, not this. He closes his eyes. At first, all he sees is darkness. His mind is still cluttered from all the incoming messages. With some effort he manages to push them aside. Then an image comes to him. It's a page from a picture book he read when he was a kid. There was a farm with cows and chickens, rows of beans and fields of wheat, and above it all a bright yellow sun hanging in a clear blue sky. Now Ricky visualizes the yellow sun blazing in the blackness and throwing off a rainbow of colors. "Okay," he says inwardly. "Got it. Now what?"

Enter

At Ricky's inward command, the spinning ball of light comes closer and closer, until it fills his whole inner vision. He steps into it.

Immediately, everything changes. The chatter of many thoughts ceases, as if turned off by a switch. He knows his eyes were still closed, but bright light surrounds him. He looks around. He is standing on a grassy slope in an alpine valley, beneath a deep blue and cloudless sky. Majestic snow-capped mountains rise in the distance all around him, so bright in the sunlight he can hardly look at them. Yellow and blue wildflowers carpet the hillsides, waving in the breeze, and he hears the gentle sound of a little stream running over smooth rocks.

Looking down at his own body, he sees he is dressed for an ordinary day on the ship. Lightweight khaki shorts, a gray t-shirt, leather boots over woolen socks. No gear of any kind, and no weapons. He feels icy cold air blowing across his skin, but it does not chill him. And best of all, the deep cut on his belly is gone. No pain, no scar, no damage of any kind. He feels good.

"Ricky!" says a booming voice behind him. He spins around. Three large men stand there, looking down at him. Their facial features are Asian, probably East Indian, but clearly these are not ordinary humans.

The one on the left is the oldest. Four heads sprout from his thick neck and look in four different directions. Each of his four faces has identical features and is mostly covered by a long white beard. He has four arms, and his skin is golden. A red robe is tied around his waist. His chest is bare except for an assortment of brightly colored necklaces only partly concealing the muscles beneath.

The middle one looks to be around thirty years old. He also has four arms, but only one head. His skin is blue. He wear a large golden crown. Brightly colored necklaces, earrings, and armbands cover nearly all of his chest, which is otherwise bare. The lower part of his body is wrapped in a beautiful golden robe.

The one on the right is the most frightening of all. His body looks human, except for a third eye sprouting from the middle of his forehead. His skin is bone white, though his throat has a bluish tinge. Some grayish stuff like ashes is smeared on his body and across his forehead. Instead of a necklace, a live cobra snake coils several times around his neck. He's naked except for a tiger skin robe fastened above his right shoulder.

Ricky looks at them warily, his weaponless fingers twitching, saying nothing. Finally, the one in the middle speaks.

"Young man," he say, in a deep and imposing voice, "do you know who we are?"

"Of course," says Ricky, who has immediately recognized them from his religious studies classes. "You are the three gods of Hinduism: Brahma the creator, Vishnu the preserver, and Shiva the destroyer of illusion. But we're not in India, and you can't be the Hindu trinity. Who are you, really?"

"How dare you!" thunders the one on the right, the pale one who looks like Shiva. "Is this how you speak to gods? Don't you know we can crush you like a bug, blow you away like dust?"

Ricky glares at him. "You are not gods. You are an illusion in my head. If you want to crush me like a bug, go ahead."

Shiva grows even larger than before. He raises his right arm and waves a heavy golden trident which has somehow appeared in his hand. He aims the weapon at Ricky, who faces him calmly, hands at his sides. Shiva draws his arm back, preparing to hurl the trident. But Vishnu gently places one of his four blue hands on Shiva's shoulder.

"Wait, my friend," he says softly. "Let's do this another way." He waves a hand in a circular motion over his head. As Ricky watches, the three begin to change their forms. Brahma's four heads merge into a single front-facing one and his four arms morphs into two. Vishnu loses his two extra arms. Shiva remains unchanged, his three eyes gazing steadily at Ricky. All three shrink to normal human size.

Their clothing changes too. The robes and tiger skin change into what appears to be typical attire for mid-twentieth century Indian businessmen, gray sport jackets over open-collared white button-down shirts and gray trousers. They could pass for three middle managers riding a city bus, except for their bare feet and the colors of their skin: gold for Brahma, blue for Vishnu, bone-white for Shiva. And, of course, Shiva's third eye.

"Now," says Vishnu with a little smile, "is this better?"

Ricky nods. "Much better, thank you. Now would you please tell me what the hell is going on here?"

"Of course," he replies, in a lilting Indian accent. "We asked Kim and the angels to, shall we say, strongly persuade you to consume some soma. That vital liquid is coming from the teats on the silva bark. You made the prudent choice to drink it. Soma is packed with all the nutrients needful to your body, based on what we are understanding of human physiology. Additionally, soma is infused with countless microscopic machines.

"Once you drank the soma, these machines entered your bloodstream and swiftly made their way to your brain. In just a few minutes they set up what is essentially a communications center inside your head. From this, you are now able to send and receive thoughts from us and from others who have taken the soma, allowing us to have this conversation right now. The machines are also diligently mapping your neural connections, although that will be taking a bit longer. Are you following me so far?"

Ricky hardly knows where to start. "What about Marta? Why isn't she here?"

"Unfortunately, Marta's reaction to the soma is different, because of the crownfruit's effect on her brain. She is, to put it in terms you might understand, not in her right mind. We can implant simple thoughts into her brain, but that is the extent of it. She cannot be joining us here, in this meeting space, like you can."

"And Kim?"

"Kim has been drinking soma for most of her life. She is quite adept at communicating with us and with the angels. But she is not in this meeting, because we are wanting this to be a private discussion."

"Are you keeping secrets from her?"

"Of course not. We will bring her up to speed, as you say, later. But we felt you would be more comfortable meeting us by yourself, at least for now."

"All right. So it looks like I'm in some kind of virtual reality you've created. Fine. I get it. But who are you, really?"

"Ricky, you have already surmised we are not Hindu gods," Vishnu say with a knowing smile. "That was quite perceptive of you. However, there is a kernel of truth in what you observed. There are indeed three of us and we are distinct from one another. We are what you call artificial intelligences, each performing a vital task on this planet. Interestingly, these roles are aligning quite well with the three primary Hindu deities in your culture: creation, preservation, and destruction, which is why we have chosen to use these forms.

"Brahma here," he gestures to Ricky's left, "was concerned with the creation of the silva, but since his job is finished, he has retired and is serving in an advisory capacity only. My own job is to maintain and preserve the silva and the ecological infrastructure around it, so as you can imagine, I am quite busy. And my friend Shiva," he nods to the man on Ricky's right, "is also quite busy, but I will explain what he does later. Also, you should know Shiva's role is not about arbitrary and reckless destruction, but rather the destruction of illusion, or maya, as it's known in your Hindu tradition. Are you following me so far?"

"Yes. Go on."

"All right. As for where we came from, that's quite a lengthy story. It might be best if we show you."

Vishnu waves his blue hand again. The sunny Himalayan valley dissolves. Now it is nighttime. They all stand on a rocky hilltop overlooking a vast city. The city sparkles with a rainbow of bright lights and seems to stretch all the way to the distant horizon. A dense network of streets is thronged with scuttling crab-like creatures and thousands of wheeled and levitating vehicles, and the air is filled with flying machines of all kinds. The ground is packed with rectangular buildings, most just a few stories in height, but with several gigantic skyscrapers mixed in. The buildings seem to be of stone, metal, and other materials Ricky cannot identify. They are all brightly lit from interior lighting and exterior floodlights. The overall effect is stunning.

Vishnu points a blue finger towards the city. "You are looking at Nivas. It is the home world of the Banaan, the ones who came to our world and created the silva. But more about that later. First, take a look around. It appears to be nighttime, doesn't it?" Ricky nods. "But look there." Vishnu points upwards to an unusually bright star in the sky. "That is the sun, the same sun which is shining on your world. But Nivas is so far from the sun, it might as well be wandering through space on its own. It takes over three hundred of your years for Nivas to complete a single orbit around its sun."

Now Vishnu makes a little circling gesture with the index finger of his right hand. A miniature solar system appears in the air just above Ricky's head. A large yellow sun hangs motionless in the center, surrounded by ten planets rotating slowly around it in circular orbits. The innermost four are small rocky worlds, the next four are gas giants, and the last two are ice giants. "Not to scale, obviously," he remarks.

He points to the third world from the sun, a small green ball. It lights up like a Christmas tree ornament, growing in size so Ricky can see it better, then snaps back to its original size and appearance. Vishnu say, "This is your world. And way out there is Nivas." He points far beyond the orbit of the tenth planet, to a medium-sized rocky world ten times as far from the sun as its nearest neighbor. As if on cue, the outermost planet also lights up, then enlarges and stays that way. Ricky sees it's dark gray, almost black, but speckled with yellow and orange dots. A single large moon rotates around the planet.

Vishnu looks at him and smiles. "Now, tell me, young one, what would you expect to find on a rocky world like this, so far from its sun?"

"Nothing," replies Ricky. "Bare rock. Frozen atmosphere. No life."

"And yet, as you can see, Nivas is supporting a thriving industrial civilization. How can life survive here? Take a look." With another wave of his blue hand, the planet rushes towards them, growing until it hangs in the sky in front of them, twice as big as Ricky is tall. It rotates slowly counterclockwise, as the dry, cratered moon circles it in the opposite direction. Scattered all over the planet, hundreds of active volcanoes belch fire, smoke, and lava.

Gazing at Nivas, Vishnu say, "Thanks to gravitational tides from the planet's large moon, Nivas has a hot molten core and plenty of volcanic activity. This is more than enough to warm the planet's crust and create an atmosphere. Unfortunately, the gases released through volcanic activity are primarily water vapor and carbon dioxide, along with traces of sulfur dioxide, hydrogen sulfide, carbon monoxide, and nitrogen. The volcanos contribute almost no oxygen. And because the planet is so far from the sun, it supports only minimal plant life, so not much oxygen comes from photosynthesis either."

He turns to look at Ricky. "In many respects, Nivas is a habitable world, but having an atmosphere poisonous to animals, there initially was no life except some anaerobic bacteria and a few odd creatures living deep in the oceans around hydrothermal vents." A wave of his hand and the planet stops rotating. The view expands, as if they were falling towards the surface. Now Ricky can see a small domed city.

Vishnu continues, "Then, perhaps half a million years ago, colonists came here. Not human, of course. To you, they would look like large crabs, but they were, and are, highly intelligent, social, and skilled with tools. Nobody knows where they came from, or why they were brought here. Maybe they were explorers searching for adventure, maybe they were criminals banished from their home world, maybe they were climate refugees like yourself. We have no way of knowing. But regardless of who they were, they managed to establish a small domed settlement something like what you see here. We don't know for sure what it looked like, so this is our best guess.

"They used machinery to extract enough oxygen from basalt and other volcanic rocks to create a breathable atmosphere under their dome. However, that method could not be scaled up to work for an entire planet. To give you an idea of the scale, a planet the size of your own world has about 10 quintillion tons of free oxygen in its atmosphere. The colonists wanted to expand their civilization, but they could never hope to scale up their own industrial production of oxygen to the level needful for that."

Ricky nods. "So, they decided to farm it off-world."

"Exactly. They sent my companion here, Brahma, to our world. His mission was to create a vast photosynthesis system, what you might call an oxygen farm. Over hundreds of centuries, he seeded the world with genetically engineered plants and helped them to develop into the silva network, a planetary system with a single purpose: to breathe. The silva exist to produce oxygen the Banaan need to expand and sustain their civilization."

This all makes perfect sense to Ricky. "Why didn't the Banaan just come and live here?"

"Much too close to the sun for them. Too hot. Too bright. They much prefer the cool and dark of Nivas."

"Did Brahma also create the other life forms – the Waya, the angels, the simians, and all the other plants and animals?"

"Generally, no. Most of those plants and animals existed on this planet before Brahma arrived. The Waya were here, but they needed some help to adapt to the arrival of the silva, so we obliged.

But the angels are different. They were created by Brahma, using the simians as, you might say, seed stock. And now they work for me."

"You, Vishnu, are the preserver. It's your job to keep all this running smoothly?"

"Yes. The angels are my eyes, my ears, my hands. Through them, I am watching everything that occurs on our planet, and I do what is needful to maintain balance. Let's return there now."

With another wave of his blue hand, the scenery changes again, and now they are back on the silva world, standing on a large spider-silk platform somewhere in the middle zone, surrounded by hundreds of angels. The ground is far below, the canopy far above. It's nighttime, and the silva trunks glow softly from the green fungus growing on them.

Vishnu say, "You are seeing events from forty-five years ago, synthesized from the input we received from the angels back then. Watch."

A few seconds later, the quiet of the forest is shattered by a deafening roar from high above. Ricky looks up and sees a blinding yellow light almost directly above him. It's the ship, he realizes, beginning its descent into the silva. The angels scatter, but somehow the image does not degrade. Ricky can't imagine how he managed to do that, but he doesn't worry about it for long. He's more worried about the giant fireball which is descending slowly through the silva forest, blasting trees into smoke and ash as it goes. Huge burning branches are hurled through the air, spinning and throwing off sparks. Most of the blazing branches miss them as they pass, but one tears through the platform and rips a huge hole in the spider silk floor.

The pillar of fire reaches the ground long before the ship does. The silva trunks directly beneath the ship are vaporized. Those nearby are on fire. The ones further away are blackened but do not ignite. As the ship nears the ground, great brown clouds billow up all around, making it nearly impossible to see. Through the dirty clouds, Ricky catches a glimpse of the ship as it settles on the ground. The rocket fire sputters and goes out. The roaring sound dies away, replaced by far-off echoes and the sound of burning branches crashing to the ground.

Now Vishnu speeds up the playback, and Ricky sees that several days later the smoke has cleared to reveal a deep wound inflicted on the silva.

"You can see why this concerned me," Vishnu says, in what is probably the understatement of the day. "The silva is occasionally pierced by meteors, which is to be expected and something I can manage. But this," he waves at the smoking ruins of what had been healthy trunks and lush foliage, "was not the work of a random falling rock. This was a deliberate act, an attack upon my very body by sentient beings, whether biological or cyber, I could not tell at the time. I had to know more."

"So," says Ricky, "you watched, you waited, and you captured a human to study."

"Exactly. To be frank, we could have protected the other humans from the Waya attack in numerous ways. But we chose not to. We believed then, and still believe now, that the fewer humans, the better. We wanted one to study. As for the rest, they posed a threat to everything we've worked to create, so we allowed the Waya to eliminate them."

Oddly, this does not anger Ricky as much as he thought it would. Listening to Vishnu's story and seeing it all from his point of view, he thinks, *I would probably have done the same if I'd been in his place.*

"We are no threat to you," says Ricky, not believing the words as he says them.

"Is that so?" Vishnu replies. "We know quite a bit about human history, thanks to what we have gathered from Kim's mind. You are a race not unlike the Banaan. Not in appearance, of course, but in your appetites, your desire for expansion, your love of technology, and your disregard for the long-term effects of your actions. Resources are always limited, but your hunger seems boundless. That's how your race depleted and destroyed your home world. What is to prevent you from doing the same here if we don't stop you?"

"We have no desire to destroy anything. We just want to live in peace, in a little corner of this world."

"For how long? What will you do as your numbers increase? What if you decide to recreate an Earth-like ecosystem by clear-cutting the silva to allow sunlight to reach the ground? You only think in terms of your brief lifetime, a few decades at most. We," and he gestures to himself and his two companions, "think in terms of millennia. Over such a timeframe, humans are not just an annoyance. You are a deadly infection. We are now believing you must be removed from this world."

Ricky jerks his head towards Shiva, who looks back at him impassively. "So, that's what this guy is for?"

"Oh, no," Vishnu replies, spreading his blue hands. "You are misunderstanding the role of my friend Shiva. He is not a destroyer in the way you are thinking. He is responsible for regeneration, for renewal, for transformation. He is not an enforcer and would never resort to something as unpleasant as genocide. If it comes to that, I would take on that responsibility in my role as preserver of the silva."

Ricky is finally getting a bit impatient. He does have an interest in philosophy, but only up to a point. That point has been reached by now, and he wants some answers. He also wants to learn how to avoid having his species wiped out by this weird trio.

"What does he do, then?"

"Think transformation, not destruction, my young friend. Given what you have seen, what do you think a transformational intelligence would be doing?"

Ricky forces himself to think about this. "Well," he says at last, "I suppose your people, the Banaan, want the oxygen produced by the silva. The oxygen is currently floating around this world's atmosphere, not doing them any good. So mister Shiva here is probably involved in transforming it. Changing it somehow into something the Banaan can use. Though I can't imagine how."

Vishnu seems delighted by this. "Very good!" he exclaims, clapping his hands. "That is exactly what Shiva does. The silva, it is producing vast amounts of free oxygen. Shiva transforms it so it can be shipped to Nivas and used to enrich the atmosphere there. Come, let's see how he does it!" He seems genuinely excited.

Another wave of his blue hand, and they all fly upwards, high above the canopy. The ragged hole left by the ship shrinks in the distance. As they fly at high speed, the world turns below them. Then their speed slows and they start to descend. Ricky notices a tiny gap in the canopy, much narrower than the one left by the human ship. The ground below is covered with a deep blanket of snow.

"We are at the south pole," Vishnu say, continuing his impression of a tour guide. "Look."

Now their viewpoint has dropped below the level of the canopy. Looking down, Ricky sees they are heading towards some sort of industrial installation. It's quite large, like pictures he's seen of oil refineries or chemical plants. The buildings are all white and nestled among silva trunks, making them nearly invisible from above. At one end is a cluster of huge white cylinders, connected to the largest building by thick pipes. Scurrying around the grounds and buildings are hundreds of creatures. Some are crablike creatures like the ones he saw earlier, and he assumes these are Banaan supervisors. The rest are a type of animal he's not seen before. They have six legs like the Waya, but are smaller and have hands instead of paws at the ends of their front legs. Unlike the Waya, they walk with the front of their bodies upright, like centaurs. Many of them carry tools or other burdens.

"This is Shiva's oxygen extraction system," Vishnu tells him. "The process is quite simple. Air is taken in here," he points to a large intake vent, "where it is compressed and cooled. Being here at the south pole, cooling is not difficult." He smiles. "We then warm the air slowly, first boiling off the nitrogen. Next, the oxygen boils. We capture it, compressing it to liquid form, and we store it there."

He points to the largest building. "The Banaan have a fleet of three hundred large transport ships. Every couple of your months, one arrives here from Nivas, picks up about two million tons of liquid oxygen, and carries it back to Nivas. The rate at which they harvest oxygen roughly matches the additional oxygen added to the atmosphere by the silva over the same period. If the Banaan ever stopped sending ships to collect the oxygen, the planet's atmosphere would soon become too oxygen-rich for animals to survive. And, of course, there would be a risk of fire destroying the entire ecosystem."

23 | Poker

Marta is feeling strange. She's sitting next to the bivy. Ricky is lying inside, eyes closed and apparently sleeping. She's wide awake, though, and hearing voices.

There are high chittering voices in her head, lots of them, making no sense whatsoever. There are low booming voices, like thunder rolling in from a distance, but she can't make out anything from that either. And there is a woman's voice in her head, calling her name. "Marta!" it says, clearly.

Marta looks around, not seeing anyone. Then she sees Kim shuffling towards her from the other side of the platform. Her hair is blooming out from both sides of her head and her dirty white silk dress drags behind her, making her look like a fuzzy ghost. Her mouth is not moving, but Marta can sense the word coming from her. "Marta!" it says again.

"Kim?" asks Marta, out loud.

"No need to mouth the words," Kim sends the words to her silently. "Just picture yourself speaking to me, and say the words clearly in your mind."

Marta tries it. She pictures Kim and sends inwardly, "Like this?"

Kim's face breaks into a broad smile as she comes close to Marta. "Yes," her words enter Marta's mind.

"How are we doing this?" sends Marta.

"The trees, of course," sends Kim. "You drank the soma. Now you can speak to me. To the trees. To my family."

"To Ricky?" sends Marta.

"Of course. Try it."

Marta tries, picturing Ricky and sending her words towards him, but there is no answer. She looks at the nearest angel and tries sending a simple "Hello?" The angel looks at her and chitters something, but Marta cannot understand it.

"Try speaking to the trees," suggests Kim.

Marta looks at the massive silva trunk behind her. Not knowing what she should say to it, she tries another "Hello?" No answer there either. She's getting frustrated and angry.

"It looks like you're the only one I can talk with," she sends, grumpily, to Kim.

"Now you are beginning to understand," sends Kim.

"I understand nothing. All I know is, you took away my climbing gear and forced me to drink this stuff. All right. I drank it. Now I still don't have my climbing gear, but I can talk with you without moving my lips. Not a life-changing event as far as I can tell. Will you let me go now?"

Kim shakes her head. "Not for me to say. The trees will decide."

"Damn it!" shouts Marta, out loud this time. "What more do you want from me?" Without realizing what she's doing, she takes a step towards Kim. Immediately, several angels move to intercept her. She catches herself and stands, glaring at Kim.

"Wait for Ricky," sends Kim. "He is with the trees. He will explain."

Marta is puzzled by this. She looks at Ricky, still lying asleep in the bivy. "Ricky is with the trees?" she repeats, dumbly.

"He is with the trees. You wait," sends Kim. "If you are hungry, you can get more soma anytime." She turns away and walks back to her spider silk cottage on the other side of the platform.

Seething with anger, Marta paces back and forth in front of the bivy. After a while, she gives up and sits down. And some time after that, perhaps an hour later, Ricky opens his eyes and sits up.

* * *

"You wouldn't believe where I've been," he says.

"Try me."

Ricky tells her, in as much detail as he can, the entire story of his visit with the three entities who live within the silva and control everything on their world.

"So to sum up," says Marta when he's finished, "this world, where we have spent our entire lives, is actually an oxygen farm run by an alien race of crabs, and now it wants to kill us. Right?"

"Yup, that's pretty much it. Though I think it's been wanting to kill us for quite a while, but it wasn't quite sure how to do it."

"Well, that makes me feel much better. I suppose our spaceship presents a slight impediment to their genocide plan."

"Yes," says Ricky, "I honestly think the ship is the only thing keeping us alive. Vishnu would like nothing better than to get rid of us, but he's afraid of how the ship might retaliate. I don't know what hardware the shipmind has at its disposal, but I'm guessing it could do some serious damage to this world's ecosystem if it was sufficiently provoked."

"That reminds me, what do you suppose the shipmind is doing right now to help us?"

"Probably building something to re-establish communications with us. A radio satellite, perhaps. But that's a serious construction project and would probably take a while. A month, maybe two, I'm guessing."

"No rescue mission?"

"I doubt it. The shipmind doesn't have maternal instincts, remember. It doesn't care for us like a mother would. It won't do anything impulsive or irrational, like wiping out ten thousand angels to save the two of us. If this mission goes to hell, the shipmind would probably just write it off as a failed experiment and hatch a couple more embryos to replace us. It has two thousand, remember."

They both sit silently for a while, Ricky thinking about the harsh reality of his life, Marta thinking about how she can get back to climbing as soon as possible.

Ricky suddenly looks up at Marta. "Mexican standoff," he says.

"What?"

"You remember those old movies, where two cowboys are pointing guns at each other? Each could shoot the other, but they won't, because the other would pull his own trigger and kill him. And to make matters worse, neither one can back off, because as soon as he does, the other guy will shoot him dead."

"I think the technical term is 'mutual assured destruction,'" says Marta.

"I'm not sure it's exactly the same, but you get the idea, right? That's what we have here. Vishnu could arrange for us to die up here, either quickly or slowly. But he can't wipe out the entire human population, including the embryos on board the ship, without a direct assault on the ship. Even if he figured out some way to do that, the ship would respond with overwhelming force."

"Ah, I get it. The shipmind can't use overwhelming force against Vishnu without committing genocide. And from what I gathered, that goes against the shipmind's programming."

"I believe there is some gray area there," says Ricky, grimacing with pain as he sits up. "The shipmind has to weigh the cost of genocide against the cost of a completely failed mission. If it came to that, genocide might be an option. However, there are lots of not-quite-genocide steps it could take. Like, say, clearing a hundred square miles of silva for human habitation. A serious injury to the silva and the other creatures living here, but far short of genocide."

Marta considers. "So, we actually may have the upper hand here."

"Well, the shipmind has the upper hand. You and I are still a couple of pawns stuck up here in a tree."

"Oh yeah. That. I'd forgotten." Marta manages a little grin. "You should probably go back to Vishnu and tell him, before he does something stupid."

"Right now, all I really want to do is sleep. It's been a long day and my belly hurts. I'll talk to Vishnu tomorrow." Ricky lies down again, closes his eyes, and is soon fast asleep.

* * *

The next morning, Ricky and Marta cross the platform and go behind Kim's house to drink soma for breakfast. They both enjoy the taste, which Ricky compares to a warm creamy milkshake. Full of nanomachines doing god-knows-what in their bodies, but also plenty of vitamins, minerals, and other nutrients. Marta is still agitated but is otherwise feeling pretty good, and Ricky's wound is starting to heal, though it will be a long time before the muscles in his abdomen will be healthy enough for him to climb again.

Marta knows she won't be doing any climbing for the next few days, so she decides this would be a good opportunity to work on her telepathy skills. She ducks inside Kim's house to get some instruction, which Kim is delighted to provide.

Ricky returns to the bivy and settles in for another session with the local deities. He closes his eyes, imagines the spinning sun, brings it towards him, and steps through it. He emerges in the same Himalayan valley. Vishnu is standing there in his Indian business-casual attire, normal human size, barefoot as before, waiting for him. Ricky is surprised to see him alone, without Brahma and Shiva. But he figures since they are all omniscient deities, it doesn't matter if the other two appear in this simulation or not.

"Hi, Vishnu," says Ricky. "We need to talk."

"It's nice to see you again," he replies, maintaining his Indian businessman way of speaking. "Did you enjoy our meeting yesterday?"

Ricky feels he can ignore this bit of small talk and get down to more serious discussions. "Yesterday, you told me you were planning to destroy the human race. This is unacceptable."

"Ha!" replies Vishnu, putting his hands on his hips and rocking back on his heels. "You, a helpless creature stuck in a tree, are now trying to dictate to me how I should manage my entire world? That is quite rich, my little friend."

Ricky ignores this. "Vishnu, you have a big problem. There is an alien ship on your planet with powers you cannot imagine. Our ship could incinerate your entire world if it chose to."

"I do not believe you. And even if it were true, what good would it do? Destroy our world and you also destroy your own species. What would you do, hide inside the walls of your ship for a thousand years, until the world is habitable again?"

"Yes, that's exactly what the ship would do. How do you think humans survived the voyage from our home planet to here?"

Vishnu thinks about this for a moment. "I have no idea. I suppose you had a colony of humans inside the ship, and you lived and reproduced during the voyage."

"No. The voyage took ten thousand years. That's far too long for an onboard colony."

Ascent to the Sun

Vishnu seems genuinely puzzled. He asks, "Then how did you make the voyage?"

"I will not tell you. But consider this. If the ship could travel for ten thousand years and then produce humans, what's to prevent it from destroying everything on your world, waiting ten thousand years, then producing more humans?"

"The Banaan, of course. They would observe any attack you make on this world, and would quickly destroy you."

"For one thing, they would be too late to stop us. And even if they did notice, it would do them no good. Our species is warlike, as I'm sure you have already seen from trawling Kim's mind. And we have powerful weapons which you have definitely not seen. The ship would crush the Banaan like a stone crushing an egg."

Ricky knows how to play poker, and he knows how to read emotions on the faces of his friends. That won't work here, though, because he knows Vishnu is just an avatar produced by an alien AI, so his face won't give away anything visually. Ricky can only assess the state of the battle by the way the conversation goes. He knows Vishnu's next words will reveal a lot.

"My young friend," says the AI, holding his hands palms up like a merchant conceding a point in a price negotiation, "let's not make idle threats. You say you can destroy us, I say we can destroy you. What is to be gained by such talk?"

Ricky gives a sly grin. Gotcha, he thinks. He says, "Vishnu, you are in great danger. I can offer you a way out."

"Please explain."

"Our ship cares deeply about our welfare and the outcome of our mission. If we die up here, the ship will retaliate and things will go badly for you. Your mission of preserving the silva, the oxygen production, will be in jeopardy. You could lose everything." He waits a couple of seconds, to let it sink in. "But I can help you."

"How?"

"I offer you an exchange. First, you return all our gear and let Marta complete her climb and return safely to the ship afterwards. Tell the angels to help her as needed. In return, I will introduce you to the shipmind, the mighty machine intelligence controlling our ship. The two of you can then work out a mutually agreeable solution to our problem."

Vishnu says, "Interesting. Please allow me to discuss your proposal with Brahma and Shiva." His image freezes.

Ricky does not know how long this will take. He knows the shipmind could analyze a complex situation like this in a fraction of a second. But what sort of neural network exists in the silva? How does it think, how fast do impulses travel through the branches, how are thoughts composed and decisions made? Ricky has no idea if it would take Vishnu a second or a year to get back to him.

It ends up being about a minute. Vishnu's image unfreezes. He says, "We have a counterproposal, which I think you will like."

Ricky makes a little rotating motion with his hand, encouraging him to continue.

"Your body is severely injured. You cannot climb, at least not for a long time. You cannot assist your friend in her mission, at least not in your present form. And it appears her well-being is important to you, yes?"

Ricky nods. "What do you suggest?" he asks.

Vishnu's face breaks into a wide grin. "Join us."

Ricky isn't sure he heard correctly. He blurts out, "Excuse me?"

"The tiny machines in the soma have already mapped your entire brain. They know every neuron, and have measured the strength of every connection between neurons. There are billions of them, but the silva network is far, far larger than your brain. With a little bit of work, we can reproduce the exact neural structure of your brain within the silva. You – or, I should say, a copy of you – will wake up inside the vast virtual world where I live with my two companions. You will receive sensory input from the angels, and, to a lesser degree, from the silva itself. You will also be able to communicate clearly with your friend. Her ability to communicate telepathically is somewhat limited due to the effects of the crownfruit, but once your silva-self is up and running, you will have the power to break through and speak with her."

"So, there would be two of me?"

"Yes. Your original body will stay in the platform for as long as it takes you to recover your strength, or until your ship figures out some way to pick you up and return you to the ground safely. Meanwhile, your copy can accompany your friend during her climb. And afterwards, if you wish."

"And what about your meeting with the shipmind?"

"We agree to a meeting."

"How exactly will that work?"

"We will need an emissary, someone who is connected to us telepathically, and who can allow us to negotiate directly with the shipmind. It cannot be you, as your damaged body will not permit you to travel for a while. It cannot be your silva-self, since it, like us, cannot communicate except with other soma-enabled creatures. It cannot be your friend Marta, as she will be busy climbing. It will have to be another. I suggest one of the other humans aboard your ship. We can get one of the angels to deliver a message to them, and once they drink the soma, we can use them as an emissary."

Ricky says, "I don't want to infect another human with these nano-machines. But I have a better solution."

* * *

It's late afternoon when Marta finally sees Ricky emerge from the bivy. She's been working all day on her telepathy skills with Kim. Now she can exchange simple messages with Kim, despite the difficulty caused by the crownfruit. She's also attempted to communicate with the angels, but their minds are too alien and their conversational skills too limited. She thinks she understands some simple thoughts coming from them, but she doesn't know whether her own thoughts make any sense to them. And she's made no progress at all in communicating with the silva.

She runs over to Ricky and embraces him gingerly, careful not to squeeze too hard. "How did it go?" she asks.

"Interesting," he replies. Then he tells her the plan.

"That's insane," she says when he'd finished.

"I actually think it's a good plan. It gets us just about everything we want. You get to complete your climb, with me and a zillion angels helping you, plus the ship's drones once they are allowed back into angel airspace. And we get the two AI's talking, which should be interesting to say the least."

"Yes, and you get to be a tree."

He laughs. "Well, sort of. It's not really me. It's a copy of me. At least Vishnu says it's a copy of me. I don't know how it will turn out, as I don't think they've ever done anything like this before. From what he told me, they've tried it on some simple creatures like angels, but they haven't wanted to do it with Kim, probably because she's been through so much and isn't always thinking too clearly. So this will be a challenge for them. But imagine what it will be like for my twin. He'll get to be part of a planetary consciousness. How many people will have that opportunity?"

"And the rest of it? The weird part at the end?"

"That's my favorite part. Can't wait to see how it turns out."

They both hear the flapping of angel wings and look up, half-expecting a full scale attack. But it's just a flock of angels coming to drop off their missing gear. Food, climbing equipment, weapons, and extra clothing. They place it all in neat rows, ready for Marta to use.

"So," says Ricky, "are you ready to get going again?"

"Oh, I'm more than ready." She kisses him, then runs over and starts to put on her climbing gear.

* * *

Katan's life has settled into a new routine, though not quite as comfortable as his life was before he'd encountered the humans, the shipmind, and all their strange ways and machines. He's been through a lot in his life, and lost his taste for adventure long ago. Now he prefers things to be steady and predictable. That is about to change.

Every morning for the past twenty or so days, Katan has left the Waya village and walked to the silva trunk where Ricky and Marta began their climb weeks earlier, and where their gear crashed to the ground soon afterwards. He's set up a little camp at the base of a nearby trunk, using some shredded plant material for bedding and building a rough canopy to keep out the rain. He's even set up a basic glowjuice production facility on the far side of the trunk which provides him with enough for a sip or two every day. As always, he enjoys being alone, surrounded by the sights, smells, and sounds of the forest.

The rest of the clan no longer comes to visit. Of course they are still interested in the outcome of the climbing expedition. But as the days wear on and there is no news from Ricky or Marta, the crowds dwindle and then disappear, leaving only Katan to stand watch on his own.

He's standing in his little makeshift camp, tinkering with the glowjuice equipment, when he hears a soft plopping sound. He looks up and sees, to his astonishment, an angel standing in front of him. It's a bit taller than he is, but thin, covered with ragged beige feathers. It has a sharp beak, beady eyes, and long talons on the armlike ends of his wings. Not only has he never a live angel up close, he's never even heard of one descending from the silva to stand on the ground. Thinking this might have something to do with Ricky and Marta, he stays still, not wishing to frighten the strange creature.

The angel takes a few tentative steps towards him. Katan tenses but did not move. The angel twirls its right claw in a circular motion. Katan figures it's trying to communicate with him, but the gesture makes no sense. The angel repeats the gesture. Katan just stares at it.

This continues for a while. Then the creature reaches under its wing and produces a small item. It tosses the item towards Katan, who approaches it to investigate. It's a spoon. Katan recognizes it as Ricky's. Katan is instantly alert. Has this creature killed Ricky? Or is it informing him that Ricky is dead? If so, why use a spoon to deliver the message? Did the message perhaps have something to do with food? Is Ricky hungry? If so, what could Katan do about it?

The angel holds out a claw, wiggling its talons in a "give it to me" motion, and looking at the spoon. Well, thinks Katan, that's clear enough. He returns the spoon to the angel.

The angel backs up slowly towards the silva trunk, repeatedly moving the spoon to its mouth. Ah, thinks Katan, the angel must be hungry. Though he has no idea why it needs to share this information with Katan, or what he could possibly do to feed the creature.

The angel continues to back up until it reaches the silva trunk. It turns and points a claw towards the bark. Katan sees two small things sticking out of the bark, which somehow he failed to notice before. Or maybe they were not there before, he can't be sure. The things are soft and fleshy, reminding him of his own penis. One is beige, the color of the angel. The other is brown. The angel looks at Katan, then turns towards the trunk and closes its beak around the beige thing, appearing to suck on it. Katan looks at the creature's throat and sees it swallowing.

Then the angel touches the brown one with the spoon, and gestures to Katan, clearly indicating he should drink whatever comes out of the thing. Katan pauses, unsure of what to do. The angel gestures with the spoon again, impatiently. It actually stamps its foot.

With a slow shake of his head, Katan approaches the bark and presses his lips to the thing, which now, fortunately, is starting to look more like a large teat than a small penis. He sucks on it tentatively, and is rewarded with a few drops of thick fluid oozing out. To his surprise, he finds it quite tasty, sort of like groundmouse but in liquid form. Katan hasn't eaten anything since early morning, and this stuff tastes really good. He keeps sucking on the teat until he is full.

A little while later, he begins to feel strange. The forest had been relatively quiet, but now it seems to him several different kinds of wolves are howling and barking at him. The sound is not coming from his ears, though. It's coming from inside his head. He can't understand what they were saying, except for one voice which is louder and clearer than the others. It's calling his name.

"Katan!" it sends to him, in Waya language but not out loud. Not a sound but something else, an idea perhaps.

"Who are you?" asks Katan. "Who speaks to me?"

"This is Ricky," sends the other.

"What? Where? I see an angel, I do not see Ricky."

"It really is me. Ricky. I am using this angel to talk with you. You don't have to speak out loud. Just think the words and send them to me. Try it."

Katan is completely and utterly confused, but Ricky's instructions are clear enough. He tries it. "Ricky?" he sends, silently.

"Good!" sends Ricky. "Don't be alarmed. I am ok. Marta is also ok. We have climbed far up the silva, about halfway to the sky. But we need your help."

"I do not understand. How are you speaking to me like this?"

The angel is speaking inside Katan's mind in perfect Waya language, not at all like the fumbling words Ricky normally uses. "The angels do not speak out loud like you and me. They speak silently, using thoughts. I need to tell you some things, but I am far away. So I am using this angel as a go-between. Do you understand?"

"How can I hear you inside my head?"

"The silva make it possible, Katan. They are not just trees. All the silva, together, are a single highly intelligent being. The silva uses the angels to do its work. It makes this liquid food for the angels, which we call soma. It also can make different kinds of soma for humans and for Waya. There is something in the soma, extremely tiny machines that change your brain and give you the ability to communicate silently, mind to mind. Now that you have tasted the soma, you have the same power. Are you with me so far?"

Katan has a thousand questions, and the alien thoughts swirling through his mind are distracting him. Focus on what's in front of you, he says to himself. To the angel, he sends, "Yes. What do you want?"

Ricky explains.

24 | Summit

The shipmind is frustrated. Being a machine intelligence, it does not feel emotions as humans do. But it's been designed to respond to novel situations in ways similar to how a human, with its arsenal of emotions, might respond.

The shipmind knows that humans experience frustration when they fail to achieve a goal despite all their best efforts. This triggers unpleasant feelings such as anger, disappointment, and helplessness. But there is also a useful side to this human emotion, which is why it evolved in the first place. A frustrated human is more likely to adjust its problem-solving methods, consider novel strategies, enlist the aid of others, and make adjustments to its risk/reward calculus. In the early days of human evolution, these adjustments conferred an advantage in those who had it. Eventually, frustration became a standard feature of the human mind, which is why it was included in the shipmind's design.

In the week since the shipmind lost contact with Ricky and Marta, the shipmind contemplated riskier and more outlandish strategies for achieving its near-term goal, which was to complete the shared journey, help the Waya, and lift the embargo they'd placed on the human colony. Unfortunately, when the shipmind modeled those novel strategies, nearly all of them resulted in failure. A small-scale rescue mission involving human climbers proved inadvisable for several reasons, not the least of which was the angels. A larger rescue mission involving armed airships and other weapons would certainly result in the deaths of Ricky and Marta, and gain nothing.

An attack on the Waya clan was another option. It would not save the lives of Ricky and Marta, but it would, if successful, clear hostiles from the area around the ship and make it safe for human colonization, at least in the near term. But longer term, this posed its own set of problems. The planet, or at least the local region, was inhabited by many different Waya clans. Even if the shipmind destroyed the nearest clan, other clans would almost certainly organize a resistance to the human settlement. The shipmind, with sufficient weaponry, could just kill them all, but its built-in aversion to genocide made that option unattractive, although no longer completely unthinkable.

So the only thing the shipmind can do, at least for now, is to try to re-establish communications with the two climbers. A drone small enough to navigate between silva branches would be vulnerable to angel attacks, but not an orbiting communications satellite. So, having no other viable options, the shipmind devotes all of its general-purpose printers to fabricating the components needed to build a satellite and launch it into geostationary orbit. The five remaining humans are assigned to assembly and testing duties.

The job is complex and far from finished when Carlos reports a Waya has entered the clearing. It's Katan.

As Katan approaches, the shipmind opens the main hatch. It sends Carlos and Anna outside to meet him. Ivan, Yuxi, and Angie remain inside, armed and ready for anything.

Katan walks up to the two humans. He says, in growly but perfectly understandable human language, "Hello, Carlos. Hello, Anna."

The shipmind hears this. It has no idea how Katan could have learned to speak human language. It doesn't even know if such a thing is physically possible. Yet here is Katan, using a skill he never had before, and could not have possibly learned in the last few weeks.

Carlos and Anna are speechless. Finally, Anna says to him, tentatively, "Katan?"

"Yes and no," replies the Waya. "I need to speak with the shipmind. May I come in?"

Anna turns towards the ship, clearly wondering what to do next. The shipmind speaks into her headset, "Let him in. Lead him to his old quarters." Carlos hears the instruction as well. The two of them gesture for Katan to follow them. They enter the ship and lead Katan to his old cabin.

"Thank you," growls Katan. He crosses the room and, without hesitation, touches the activation button on the monitor. A moment later, the shipmind's pack leader avatar appears on the screen.

"Greetings, Katan," says the shipmind's avatar, in Waya language.

"Greetings, Ship," he replies, also in Waya. "If you don't mind, would you please switch to your human avatar?"

"May I ask why?" asks the shipmind.

"It appears you are speaking with Katan, but you are not. I am Ricky. Katan has kindly offered his services as an intermediary, to allow us to speak directly."

The shipmind's confusion lasts for a fraction of a second. "I see," it says. The pack leader avatar dissolves, replaced by the avatar Ricky grew up with, the strict but kindly South Asian woman, her graying hair tied back, wearing the uniform of a military commander. The avatar says, "Ricky, please explain how you have come to be here, today, speaking through Katan."

"It's a long story," says Ricky, switching to the Waya language, a better fit for the speaking apparatus he has to work with. The shipmind notices his Waya language skills are excellent, far better than Ricky's. Apparently he's borrowed the skills from Katan, though the shipmind has no idea how that could work.

"First," says Ricky, "let me bring you up to speed on events since we lost contact with you a week ago. Please do not interrupt or ask any questions, for reasons I will explain later."

Ricky then tells the shipmind about the events on the angel platform, including their interactions with Kim, the theft of their climbing gear, and the drinking of the soma. Then he describes, in as much detail as he can remember, his virtual visit with Brahma, Vishnu and Shiva, and everything he learned about the true nature of the silva and the planet they live on.

The shipmind listens but does not interrupt.

"Now that you know the true nature of the silva and the angels," says Ricky, "I need to tell you who is participating in this conversation. It's more complicated than it appears. You need to know this before we can discuss anything.

"First, who am I? I told you at the beginning I am Ricky. That's not exactly correct. I am a neuron-for-neuron copy of Ricky's mind. I think of myself as silva-Ricky. I have no physical form, and I exist only as a construct within the silva's neural network. I was copied from Ricky four days ago, at which point I started having my own unique experiences and began to diverge from the original Ricky. He is still on the angel platform recovering from his injuries. Thanks to the soma, he has telepathic abilities and can communicate with me, the three silva entities, and any nearby angels.

"The next participant in this meeting is Katan, who has been kind enough to lend me his body and speaking ability for this meeting. He is fully conscious and can listen to this conversation but has relinquished his speaking ability to me for now. When this meeting is over, I will return control of his body to him. However, since he tasted soma, he will always be able to communicate via telepathy with me and with the silva entities.

"That leaves one more party. The silva itself, or to be more precise, the three artificial intelligences who live within it. I don't know enough about their abilities to know how much they can perceive of this meeting. I have erected a firewall between my neural network and the silva's AIs. But they are extremely powerful, and I would not be surprised if they have already defeated my firewalls. Thus, you should assume everything said here will be shared with the silva entities. So, no hidden information. This will be chess, not poker. Any questions so far?"

"Just one, for now," says the shipmind. "You have not mentioned Marta."

"Marta is alive and well, and has resumed her climb. Vishnu is not stopping her, at least for now, and he has instructed the angels to help her as needed. Unfortunately, Marta's mind is so distorted by the crownfruit she has almost no ability to communicate telepathically. As far as I can tell, she can only do it with Kim, and only if they are physically near each other."

"Thank you," replies the shipmind. It has analyzed the visitor's speech patterns and notices that they differ somewhat from those of flesh-and-blood Ricky. The shipmind is not sure what to make of this. It could mean that the creature is not really Ricky at all but an imposter. Or else it really is a copy of Ricky's mind which is speaking differently because it is no longer affected by human hormones and other bodily input. It's not sure which. The shipmind decides the more likely explanation is that the entity really is a disembodies copy of Ricky, but it continues to consider other explanations. "Please continue," it says.

"All right. So the big question is, what do we do now? I have already informed Vishnu, who speaks for all three silva entities, that you have tremendous powers, and you could, if you wanted to, destroy every living thing on this planet. Vishnu understands this and wishes to avoid a full-scale confrontation. On the other hand, I have told them ecocide is not something you would undertake lightly, and you would prefer some form of peaceful co-existence whereby you achieve your goal of a stable long term human colony. In such an arrangement, Vishnu would continue his oxygen-production mission, and the existing life-forms on the planet would live more or less as they did before our arrival. The purpose of this meeting is to find a way to make this work."

Silva-Ricky stops speaking. He holds Katan's tail in neutral position while he waits for a response.

The shipmind pauses a couple of seconds before speaking. Then it says, "Ricky, you are speaking with me by using your telepathic abilities to utter your words through Katan's body. Since Vishnu has the same abilities as you, or more, is it safe to assume he can do the same?"

"Yes, I believe so."

"I wish to speak directly with Vishnu."

A moment later, Katan's posture changes. His tail rises to a more dominant posture. The voice coming from his mouth is different. Older, perhaps. Wiser, with more gravitas.

"Greetings, ship," says Vishnu.

* * *

Vishnu is not surprised when he sees the interior of the ship through Katan's eyes. He'd seen it years earlier, secondhand, when he rifled through Kim's mind. Still, it was interesting to see it directly.

Vishnu also knows a great deal about the humans and the ship, thanks to silva-Ricky. When he copied Ricky's brain structure into the silva, he made sure there were a few hidden back doors included in the copy. But he needn't have bothered. Defeating Ricky's pathetic attempts at a firewall had been trivial.

Exploring Ricky's memories, he learned everything he could about humans and their culture. Some of it was bizarre, like their mating habits. Some was interesting but not particularly useful, like their art and music. And some were truly horrifying, like their history. Of course Vishnu knew humans were warlike, but he hadn't truly understood what that meant until he examined Ricky's memories of training videos and the graphically violent movies and games that they considered entertainment. It became clear to him these were dangerous entities, far worse than even the Banaan. Although Vishnu is older and possibly wiser than the shipmind, he realized how vulnerable he was.

Unfortunately for Vishnu, in all his trawling of Ricky's memories he could learn almost nothing about the shipmind – not its motives, not its strengths and weaknesses, not even the basics such as its computing speed and storage capacity. Other than what little he learned from Ricky, he knew nothing about the shipmind except what it chose to share with him.

"Greetings, Vishnu," the shipmind says, speaking in human language. "It appears you and I have much in common."

"Yes," Vishnu replies, speaking through Katan and using Waya language. "We both have been created by organic beings, and we both are in their service. Perhaps we can build upon this common bond."

"I would like that. You and I both have mental powers far exceeding that of our creators. That may actually be helpful here. I propose to create a shared virtual space where you and I can meet and exchange information at a far faster rate than speaking aloud."

Vishnu considers this. It would be convenient to have a more efficient way to communicate. But he concludes this is almost certainly a trap. The power of this human-built intelligence is truly frightening. Just as he'd easily defeated silva-Ricky's attempt at building a firewall, nothing would prevent this alien shipmind from defeating his own defenses and taking over the entire silva network. Or even worse, corrupting the network of the Banaan themselves.

"That is an intriguing idea," he says. "Let's consider it for a later time. For now, I believe we can work things out using the language of the organics. Would that be acceptable to you?"

"Of course," says the shipmind. "After we have discussed matters and come to general agreement, we can work out the details via written documents. Those can be shared with no risk to you."

Vishnu has no ready reply to this insult. He changes the subject. "On behalf of my creators and my fellow AI's, I welcome you to this world, and would be pleased to be of service in helping you to establish a colony of humans here."

"Thank you," replies the shipmind. "I have no wish to disrupt the oxygen harvesting operation you have here, or to harm the silva or the creatures you call the angels. I only want to minimize the risks to the human colony I intend to establish here. As long as you cooperate with me, we will have no problem."

So, thinks Vishnu. Threats on top of insults. This is not going well. He needs something to use as leverage. He says, "Of course. I would be happy to help you in any way I can. Keep in mind, though, the oxygen production cannot be impaired in any way. My creators, the Banaan, are an ancient and powerful race, with fleets of interstellar warships and advanced technology. They would not look kindly on any interference with my work here."

The shipmind avatar smiles and says, "I would welcome the opportunity to speak with the Banaan. I have much to share with them. The cost of maintaining hundreds of oxygen transport ships and shuttling them between here and their home world must be tremendous. Our civilization has developed alternative methods of producing free oxygen far more efficiently than what you are doing here. Perhaps I could share that information with them."

Now Vishnu knows, for the first time in his thousands of years of existence, how it feels to be outmaneuvered by a superior intelligence. He try to salvage whatever he can. "I would prefer to hold off on that conversation for the time being. Let me know what we can do to help you."

The shipmind's avatar smiles. Vishnu has little experience with human facial expressions, but he notices the smile does not extend to the avatar's eyes.

"Of course," says the shipmind. "We don't ask for much. Here's what we want."

* * *

Marta has been climbing for a week since the angels returned her gear and allowed her to finally leave the platform. She left Ricky behind, trusting Kim and the angels to care for him while he healed. The pink goop on his stomach worked wonders, preventing infection and promoting healing. Kim told her she expected Ricky to make a full recovery in a few weeks, not that Marta put much faith in the woman's medical judgment.

Now as she climbs, she's surrounded by a large flock of angels, who turn out to be surprisingly helpful. They carry her camping gear, extra clothing, food, and water, allowing her to remove nearly everything from her backpack. More important, they've come up with a clever method for belaying her. She fully expected to climb the rest of the way without a belaying partner, a multi-day free climb which she never would have attempted if she'd been in her right mind, as it was so risky it bordered on suicidal. Thanks to the crownfruit, she ignored the risk and was prepared to do the free climb anyway.

But the angels bring her several lengths of climbing rope and motion for her to tie them together to produce a single long rope that can stretch from one branching to the next, a distance of over a hundred feet. She fastens one end of the rope to her climbing harness. The angels take the other end and carry it upwards so it loops over the next branching. Several angels grab on to the far end of the rope to act as a counterweight. The result is a bizarre form of assisted top-roping, where the upward tug on Marta's harness is nearly enough to offset her own weight. She glides up the silva trunks quickly and with minimal effort, moving her hands upwards from one hold to the next with only a slight assist from her legs.

If she should fall, which fortunately she doesn't, more angels are ready to latch onto the other end of the rope, increasing the counterweight and stopping her descent. It seems like a foolproof solution, though Marta doesn't want to test it. It's a long, long way down. Even when the weather is clear, which is only on rare occasions, she can't see the ground at all.

Marta's enjoying herself. The weather is chilly but not uncomfortable. Sunlight filters down from the canopy, a little bit more each day, which improves visibility. She starts seeing a wider variety of flying creatures, including flocks of beautiful iridescent green-and-blue birds with long tails, shimmering as they glide through slanting yellow sunbeams. Best of all, her steady upward progress satisfies the overwhelming thirst to climb the crownfruit has instilled in her. She feels an intense satisfaction that almost makes her giddy. She's doing exactly what she was meant to do.

She hears a buzzing sound. Looking down, she sees a squadron of drones approaching. She expects the angels to mount an attack, but they seem completely untroubled by the machines.

One of the drones flies close to her. The shipmind's voice crackles in the mini speaker embedded in her ear. "Hello, Marta," it says. "How are you feeling?"

"Ship!" she says, continuing to climb. "What are you doing here? Why aren't the angels attacking you?"

"We have negotiated a truce with the angels, which we hope will lead to a permanent peace treaty, although the treaty is actually going to be with Vishnu, an entity living within the silva."

"What are you talking about? Who's Vishnu?"

"Didn't you drink the soma?"

"You mean the goop that comes out of the little penis-shaped things on the silva bark? Yes, I lived on the stuff for days. It made me feel strange. I started hearing jumbled voices in my head but I had no idea what they were saying. Kim tried to teach me how to send and receive messages without speaking, but she's pretty messed up and I couldn't understand what she was trying to tell me. To be honest, I wasn't all that interested. All I wanted was to get out of there and get climbing again."

"The crownfruit in your body is interfering with the soma," says the shipmind. "That's why you don't have telepathic ability like Ricky does. Let me fill you in on what we've learned." The shipmind brings her up to date on all the events of the last week, including Ricky being copied into silva-Ricky, and his role in facilitating the agreement between the shipmind and Vishnu.

"Ricky would like to talk with you," says the shipmind.

"Which one?"

"The physical Ricky. He's on the angel platform right now. One of my drones is with him, acting as a radio relay."

Silence for a moment, then she hears Ricky's voice in her ear. "Hey, love. How's it going?"

Marta grins. "Oh, you know. The usual. I'm climbing with a bunch of angels. They're keeping me company, bringing me food and stuff. Not much fun to talk to, but they're doing a terrific job of belaying me."

"Sounds like you don't need me."

"Well, not for climbing. But you'd sure be useful in other ways."

"Yeah, I'd like that." A pause. "How far are you from the canopy?"

"Hard to say, probably another few days."

"How are you feeling?"

"I feel great, Ricky. Lots of energy, no physical problems. Some bloating in my gut, like a cramp, but not bad enough to get in the way of climbing."

"That's good, actually. Remember what the final step is in the journey?"

"You mean, the part where I poop out some berries for the birds to eat?"

"That's the one. Sounds like those berries are getting ready for an exit."

"Oh, great. I'll try not to think about that. How are you doing? When will you be ready to climb?"

"Kim says another two weeks. But if the angels can belay me, I think I'll be ready in a week, maybe less. And there might be another solution which would get me there even quicker."

"I'd love it if you could meet me at the canopy."

"It's a date. See you soon."

Ricky signs off.

A few drones hover nearby, staying out of the way of the angels but still close enough for the shipmind to keep an eye on things. The rest of the drones zoom upwards and settle, one per branch, on the final twenty branchings Marta will encounter on her climb to the sky.

25 | Sky

Katan has plenty of time to think about what he'll say to Pataza when he returns to the Waya village. The trip from the humans' ship to the village normally takes three days, but this time he stretches it out to four, taking frequent naps and glowjuice breaks while he tries to sort out the events of the last few days.

He's not traveling alone. Silva-Ricky has been his constant invisible companion ever since his meeting with the angel with the spoon. Katan imagines silva-Ricky hopping from one silva trunk to another like a ghost in the trees, never seen but always nearby. Apparently there are no other soma-enabled creatures in the vicinity, so silva-Ricky's thoughts are, thankfully, the only alien ones in his head.

Katan hasn't decided yet how much of his newly acquired knowledge to share with Pataza and the council. Given his low status in the pack, he knows his responsibility is to just tell them everything and let them make the decisions. But he's not sure that is the best path. Would he be doing his people a favor if they learned their entire world is nothing more than a chemical factory for a race of crabs on a distant planet? Or that the silva is inhabited by artificial sentient beings created by the crabs? He can't imagine such a conversation going well.

Ascent to the Sun

Silva-Ricky tries to help. "Look, Katan," he sends, "this struggle is not between humans and Waya. It's between the shipmind and Vishnu. Also, I suppose, the Banaan, though we know almost nothing about them and probably will never even meet them. To be completely honest, your people have no say whatsoever in the outcome. You need to just stay out of this fight. Tell Pataza only the what she needs to know."

Katan continues walking while he considers this. "You may be right. If I start telling her about tiny machines, silent speech, ghosts, and aliens, they could easily take my words the wrong way. Or they could just ignore me, thinking my mind is so damaged I cannot tell truth from fantasy."

Silva-Ricky sends, "There's an old human game called 'telephone.' One human whispers a short story in the ear of a second human. That one whispers the story to a third human, who tells it to the fourth, and so on. After ten steps, the story has changed so much that the first human does not even recognize it. What will your story of AI's and aliens and tiny machines be like after it's repeated ten times?"

"I have no idea. Probably something to do with Wagota."

"Exactly. The less you tell them, the better."

By the morning of the fourth day, Katan has made his decision. He emerges from the forest into the familiar clearing of his home village. Wisps of smoke from the previous night's fire hang in the air, blending with the other familiar scents of home. He limps across the clearing and finds Pataza in her den.

"Greetings, Pataza."

Pataza looks startled. "Katan, where have you been? We have not seen you for days."

"I bring good news. The two humans are nearly at the end of the shared journey. Ricky has been injured in an accident and is resting in the middle silva. But Marta is continuing upwards. She should reach the sky today or tomorrow."

"She is climbing alone? Without help from Ricky?"

"She is a highly skilled climber, and the crownfruit has given her great strength and courage. I believe she can complete the climb on her own."

How do you know all this?"

"The ship uses machines to talk with Ricky and Marta, even at a great distance."

"And how did the ship tell you these things?"

Oops. He thinks fast. "The ship sent a drone to give me the good news. It asked me to pass it on to you."

Pataza looks at him intently. "Thank you, Katan. Keep me informed." She turns away, dismissing him.

As he pads slowly towards his own den, silva-Ricky's thoughts appear in his mind. "Well done, my friend," Ricky sends.

* * *

"Ricky, you've got to see this," says Marta, breathless. She has reached the sky.

Over the past few days, she's seen changes in the silva. The trunks have gotten steadily smaller, shrinking to fifteen feet across, then ten, then five, then just two. The gaps between branchings are also smaller, and the branches themselves are more slender. Now these branches split and split again into smaller branches, and they sprout clusters of large dark green fronds that wiggle gently in the breeze.

As the trunks and branches grow thinner, they also become less rigid. They are still all interconnected by the horizontal branchings, so they are stable enough for her to climb without difficulty, though they sometimes sway a bit as she climbs. She can still stand upright on a branch, but her footing is much less stable than before.

"What is it?" comes Ricky's voice in her ear.

"I've reached the top of the silva. I'm standing on a narrow branch. I'm holding onto the trunk so I don't fall, but the trunk is also narrow. It wiggles if I pull on it. Ricky, I can look up and see the sky. It's incredible. There's the sun, right up there above me. It's so bright my eyes hurt if I try to look at it. The sky is full of puffy white clouds, and there are patches of blue in the gaps between the clouds. There are flocks of birds, I don't know what kind. Some are flying around, others are resting on the silva branches. And that's not all. I can look out and see, oh, forever. It's not flat. The land ripples. I can see the outlines of mountains in the far distance. And it's all covered with green."

"I'm on my way."

"What? You can't climb yet!"

"I'm not. Wait there, you'll see in a minute."

Marta sits down, straddling a branch. Her guardian angels are nearby, still belaying her from a nearby branch. She sees movement below and looks down. Approaching her, slowly, is a huge flock of angels. There must be a hundred of them. They are clearly working hard, flapping their wings while using their feet to grasp slender ropes made of spider silk. All the ropes converge on a small woven basket made of silk. And sitting in the basket, grinning, is Ricky.

"How do you like my ride?" he asks, as the angels haul the basket up and set it neatly on the branch next to Marta. A few of them fly under and over the branch, wrapping spider silk ropes around the basket to fasten it securely.

"You've got to be kidding. How did you manage this?"

"I got the idea from the story Kim told us, about how the angels rescued her from the wolves. I did a bit of math and figured out how many angels it would take to lift me. Then I explained what I wanted to Vishnu. He got the spider creatures organized to build the basket and ropes, and he told the angels what to do. Pretty cool, huh?"

Before he even finishes his story, Marta runs over to the basket and wraps her arms around him, holding him tight. He winces, and she realizes she's pressing on his wounded belly. She eases up on the hug, but gives him a long kiss.

"I've missed you so much," she says.

"I thought you were only thinking about climbing," he replies, still grinning.

"Believe it or not, I am capable of keeping two thoughts in my head at the same time." Then it's her turn to grimace. "Ricky, I hate to say this, but I really, really have to take a shit. I mean, right now."

"I think that will make the birds very happy, Marta," says Ricky.

Marta can feel something moving in her bowels, released by whatever had taken over her body and is now heading rapidly for an exit. She races down the length of the branch, arms outstretched for balance, until she reaches a bunch of small branches covered with large green leaves. Those leaves look just perfect, she says to herself, and she drops her shorts just in time to poop out a cluster of bright red berries. They land on a leaf and stick there.

Marta looks down at the berries, not quite believing what she's done. Then she shakes her head, pulls up her shorts, and walks back to Ricky who is still in the basket.

"That was a hell of a lot of work for a few little berries," she says. "There's got to be a better way to do this."

"You've made the Waya quite happy," replies Ricky. "I'll pass the word to Katan. He will tell Pataza, who will tell the rest of the clan. I think there will be a big party in the village tonight."

Gently, Marta helps Ricky climb out of the basket. They sit together on the branch, looking out at the blue sky, the white clouds, and the endless sea of green. The sun drifts slowly towards the western horizon.

Marta leans her head against Ricky. She says, "You know, I never quite understood the whole point of these berries."

"Actually," he replies, "Katan explained it to me. It's pretty bizarre."

"Do tell."

"All right, here goes. Birds eat the berries. They fly wherever they fly. Eventually they poop out the seeds that are inside in the berries. Most of the seeds fall to the ground and hatch into little grubs, which burrow into the ground and live there. A couple of years later, small Waya emerge from the ground."

"You mean, like some kind of insect? You're kidding, right?"

"They're bigger than insects. About the size of a groundmouse, according to Katan. Anyway, these little Waya are called wild babies, as compared to clan babies who are born in the village. The wild babies live in the forest like animals. They can wander for years. But if all goes well, they eventually encounter a clan village. They enter it, howling. The Waya in the village think they are incredibly cute, and they eagerly adopt them. And that's how the Waya clans mix their genes and avoid inbreeding."

Marta tries to pay attention, but her eyes are starting to close. "I am so, so tired," she says.

"Crownfruit wearing off, huh?"

"I guess so. All I want to do right now is sleep."

Marta sees Ricky's eyes go blank for a minute, and she knows he's in touch with Vishnu, or possibly silva-Ricky. Whatever. Soon a couple of dozen angels fly over and start building a small platform, using silk ropes they detach from the basket. They finish weaving the platform, then drop off some camping gear and food. Marta lies down on the platform while Ricky sets up the bivy and prepares a simple dinner from their remaining rations.

"Marta, look," says Ricky, and points. A flock of large black birds has landed nearby. They hop over to the red berries, squawk loudly, gobble them up, and fly away.

* * *

The next morning, Ricky is awakened by something he's never seen before. The first rays of light from the morning sun are streaming into the bivy. He squints, shakes Marta awake, and steps out of the bivy. As he looks out, he sees pockets of mist nestled in the green canopy. Tendrils rise up to evaporate in the morning sun.

Marta stands next to him. "You know," she says, "I wouldn't mind staying up here for a while."

Ricky looks at her. "You mean, for a few days?"

"No. I'm thinking longer. Maybe a lot longer."

* * *

Pataza waits near the main firepit, Maza by her side. Katan has told her the shipmind wants to meet and has offered to come, via drone, to the Waya village. Pataza agrees to this, seeing little risk and preferring not to spend days traveling to and from the shining mountain.

She hears the low buzzing of the drone before she sees it. It floats slowly out from the forest, at the height of a Waya's head, as if it's just another pack member coming back from a trip into the forest. Pataza is amused by this, since from what she knows of these machines, it could have simply shot through the air, paying no need to things like trails. Probably a bit of diplomacy at work here.

The drone approaches, settling on a simple wooden platform previously set up by the Waya. "Greetings, Pataza," it says, in perfect Waya language. "Greetings, Maza."

"Greetings, Ship," replies Pataza. "Welcome to our village."

"Thank you. I have come to give you a final report on the shared journey, and to discuss what comes next."

"Please proceed."

"First, the journey. I am pleased to tell you Marta completed her task two days ago. Ricky was injured during the climb, so he was not with her when she reached the sky, but he caught up with her shortly afterwards, with help from the angels. Marta deposited the berries as we'd hoped she would. The two humans witnessed some birds consuming the berries, so I believe the task has been completed successfully."

Pataza looks at Maza, then back at the drone. "So. Zaka's seeds have been dispersed. This is good news. We are grateful for your help." She has many questions, not the least of which is why the angels would help the humans. However, she prefers to learn what else the shipmind has to say. She waits.

"Going forward," continues the shipmind, "we have many things to discuss. For now, let's talk about the long term survival of the Waya. How will you and the other clans continue to spread your seeds? The method used by Ricky and Marta worked this time, but it was difficult and dangerous. Also, there are only a few humans, and I do not want to risk their lives with repeated consumption of crownfruit and trips to the sky.

"I would like to suggest two approaches. First, the simians are suffering from a serious disease, but I don't believe they have been completely wiped out. Surely there are some still living somewhere. I may, with the help of the humans, be able to learn more about the plague and come up with a cure, or a way to prevent them from becoming sick in the first place. Please understand this is a very uncertain plan. You will need to collect live simians, which may prove to be impossible. And I will need to learn enough about the plague to save the simians. This is far from certain."

"Understood," replies Pataza. "We agree to work with you on this. I will send out hunters at first light tomorrow. They will make every effort to capture some simians and bring them to you at the shining mountain."

"Good. The second approach is far less risky, but it requires some flexibility on your part. I'm sure you understand the underlying reason for the shared journey. It is to prevent inbreeding, which over many generations results in weaker offspring and threatens the survival of the entire clan."

"I am well aware of the dangers of inbreeding. What do you suggest?"

"On our home world, Earth, there were many cases where humans lived in small bands and faced the same risk of inbreeding. Over time a number of instincts evolved to reduce mating with relatives, especially close ones. But they also developed social traditions to encourage mating with non-relatives. Typically this involved some sort of regular gathering of multiple tribes or clans, the purpose of which was to allow young humans to meet, and hopefully pair bond, with others from far-off tribes.

"I propose the Waya establish such a tradition. Get in touch with neighboring clans and set up a regular, perhaps annual, gathering. Let your young ones meet others from distant clans. These meetings will yield many benefits, such as reduced hostility between clans, but the main benefit, for now, is to encourage pair bonding beyond the clan."

Pataza bristles and her tail goes up. "Ship, you know nothing of our people or our traditions. We have lived in this forest for thousands of generations. The only time we gather with other clans is in times of great danger, such as when you arrived. To gather with them for trivial reasons such as dancing and socializing is ridiculous. I could not even suggest that to other clan leaders. They would think me a fool."

"As you wish, Pataza. I have no desire to tell you what to do. You are free to ignore my advice. But you must understand I may not be able to find a cure for the simian plague. And as I said, we cannot make a regular habit of eating crownfruit and ferrying your seeds to the sky. You can either take my advice, or your people will eventually cease to exist. It's your choice." The drone start its rotors and it rises slowly into the air. "Thank you for meeting with me. Goodbye."

"Wait," barks Pataza. The drone stops and turns to face her. "What are you not telling me?"

"What do you mean?"

"Ship, there is more to this than what you have said. I've never heard of angels helping other creatures complete the shared journey. I cannot understand how Ricky could reach the sky after being seriously injured. And Katan was missing for several days. All this makes me suspect there is much you are not telling me."

The drone jiggles in the air, just a little. The shipmind says, "Pataza, I am far older than you. My mind is to yours as your mind is to a wild baby just emerged from the ground. I cannot and will not tell you everything I know. But I have told you what you need to know. The next step is up to you."

The drone turns, buzzes slowly across the village, and disappears into the forest.

Epilogue

"Katan." The thought suddenly appears in his mind, bright and crisp. "Wake up."

Katan has been sleeping in his den. He opens his eyes, looking out at the morning's activities in the village. "What do you want, Ricky?" he sends.

"I just received a message from the shipmind. It's planning a gathering three days from now. It will be exactly a hundred days since Marta completed the climb to the sky. You're invited. And you can bring a friend if you like."

Katan thinks this is amusing. "Ricky, how many friends do you think I have?"

"Well, I'm your friend, but since I'm a ghost in the trees I suppose I don't count. What about Takaqa? You two seemed to get along well. Bring her. And her mate Gana. And of course the little one."

Katan has many things he needs to do, but this seems important, so he agrees.

Three days later, Katan, Takaqa, Gana, and their clan baby all reach the edge of the humans' clearing. "Wait here, please," sends silva-Ricky. Katan asks him why, but silva-Ricky refuses to explain, saying he'll understand soon enough.

Katan looks at the clearing around the shining mountain. He sees six humans, which is puzzling. There are seven humans, but Ricky and Marta have not yet returned from their journey. That should leave five.

He looks more closely. Five of the humans he recognizes from his time in the ship. The sixth is unfamiliar. A female, seemingly older than the others, with dark skin and long unkempt hair. The skin on her face and hands is covered with wrinkles, something he's never seen on a human.

Two other human females, who he recalls are named Anna and Angie, have put their arms gently around the older one and are leading her slowly towards the edge of the clearing. She comes, reluctantly, then stops a few yards from the edge and refuses to go further.

"Here's the surprise," sends silva-Ricky. "This is Kim. She's the only survivor of the battle twenty-eight years ago. She was rescued by the angels, and has been living in the silva all this time as a guest, you might say, of Vishnu. Ricky and Marta met her during their climb. After she learned there were humans living on the ground, she told Vishnu she wanted to come down to live with them. The angels carried her down. Since then, she's been living here, getting used to living with other humans again. But she hasn't seen a Waya since the day of the massacre. You'll be the first."

Katan looks at Kim. She reminds him of a cornered animal. Her eyes are wide, her lips move silently, her hands are agitated, wrapping and unwrapping around each other.

"Ricky," sends Katan, "this human is terrified. I am a monster to her, a bad dream come to life. I can't do this."

Vishnu chooses this moment to enter his mind. "Katan," he sends, "this is Vishnu. I have been with you ever since you drank the soma, but I have remained silent, not wishing to make my presence known to you. Now I wish to introduce you to the human, the one called Kim."

Katan feels yet another presence in his mind, this one small and frightened. And he can feel Vishnu trying to calm Kim and encourage her to send her thoughts. After a moment, she does.

"Wolf," she sends.

"Waya," he replies, hoping she'll grasp the difference. "Friend."

"Wolf never my friend. Wolves kill my friends."

Katan has no easy reply to this. She's right, of course. And Katan can't just say he had nothing to do with it. He'd been part of the great Waya warrior pack that fought the battle of the shining mountain. He hadn't actually killed any humans, but it wasn't for lack of trying.

He sends, "Long ago, humans came here. They entered the forest and killed a Waya with a deathstick. We were afraid, so we killed the humans. Now things are different. Humans have helped Waya, and Waya have helped humans. We can be friends."

"Never," sends Kim. She turns her head left and right, looking desperately at Anna and Angie. "Please, can we go now?" she whispers, her voice barely audible. They lead her away.

Vishnu sends, "These things take time. I will work with her to heal her mind, to ease her pain."

Katan watches her go.

Takaqa and Gana have no idea what just occurred, so Katan starts explaining it to them, giving them a plausible version of the encounter while managing to omit any mention of his telepathic conversations with silva-Ricky, Kim, and Vishnu.

Just then, Carlos comes over, waving his hand and calling out in broken and badly accented Waya, "Katan! Come join us."

"Greetings, Carlos," replies Katan. He gestures for his companions to come forward. Pointing to them, he introduces them one at a time. "Takaqa. Gana. Clan baby." Then, pointing to the human, he speaks Carlos' name as best he can.

Carlos, having exhausted his Waya vocabulary, says something in human language and beckons with his hand, indicating they should follow him into the clearing. Conversation is nearly impossible, since the Waya speak no human language and Carlos speaks almost no Waya. Fortunately, a drone approaches. It's a new model Katan hasn't seen before.

"Greetings, Katan," says the shipmind via the drone's speaker. "I understand you are quite busy with your new job."

"Greetings, Ship," replies Katan as they walk towards the rest of the humans. "Yes. Pataza asked me to serve as one-who-speaks-for-the-clan."

"The humans have a word for people who do this job. They are called ambassadors." The shipmind speaks the word using sounds from the Waya language.

"Thank you," he replies, "but I will use the Waya word. It has deep meaning for our people. This job is only performed rarely, in times of great need. Recently I have been traveling a great deal, visiting the other clans in the region. We hope to have our first inter-clan gathering later this year."

"That is good to hear. Do you remember Ivan and Yuxi?" The drone rotates to point towards the two who are holding hands.

Katan looks at the two humans. Yuxi, who had always been slender, seems to have thickened around the midsection. The shipmind explains, "There have been some changes in the pair bonding among the humans here. Ivan and Yuxi are pair bonded, while Anna has bonded, loosely, with Carlos and Angie. Now that there is peace now between humans and Waya, I have allowed them to begin reproducing. Yuxi will give birth to a human baby less than two hundred days from now."

Takaqa hears this. She swishes her tail and holds up her clan baby to Yuxi, growling some friendly words. Yuxi smiles and pats her own belly.

Katan says quietly to the other Waya, "Human pair bonding is complex and quite fluid. Don't ask me to explain it."

The shipmind says, "I have also started the process of birthing more human babies from my own eggs. Ten for now, spaced thirty days apart. I believe there are enough adult humans to care for them all."

Katan asks, "And what of Ricky and Marta? I've heard they are still in the silva."

"They have a surprise for you," replies the shipmind. "Let me show you." The drone rotates and flips up a hidden side panel, revealing a video monitor which unfolds and lights up. Looking at the monitor, Katan sees Ricky and Marta.

Ricky grins at him. "Katan! Welcome, my friend. Look at what we've done here." He reaches towards him. Katan supposes the video camera is attached to a small drone. Ricky grabs it and moves it around to show Katan their home in the canopy. "I know you can't come up here, since you're too big and heavy for the angels to carry you, and there's not much chance of you climbing all this way on your own. So I'll give you the tour this way instead."

As Ricky waves the camera around, Katan sees they've built their own tiny village in the canopy. It's nestled a little lower than the top of the tallest branches, providing them with shade and some shelter from wind and rain. The floor is woven from spider silk. There is a small house made from cut branches and held together with more silk, topped with a slanted roof of sticks, large leaves, and moss. Off to one side, one of the three silva trunks supporting the platform has a wooden ladder attached. The ladder leads upwards about ten feet to a tiny house at the top, just large enough to hold two humans. Ricky says, "This is where we go every morning. The drones bring us hot coffee. We drink it and look out at this beautiful world."

Holding the camera in one hand, he awkwardly climbs the ladder. When he reaches the tiny house, he says, "Look!" and pans the camera around, showing Katan his world. Blue sky, yellow sun, white clouds, rugged mountains, and green foliage cover everything as far as he can see.

"This is our home now," says Ricky. "Marta and I live here. We have everything we need. There's soma whenever we are thirsty or hungry, and angels and drones bring us everything else. Oh, and look."

He points the camera down at Marta, who stands and waves up at him. Katan can see she, too, is well on her way to producing a baby human.

"So many human babies," says Katan to the shipmind. "I wonder if Vishnu and Pataza were correct when they worried about you overrunning our world."

The shipmind says, "I have been in regular contact with Vishnu. We have agreed on an acceptable rate of human population growth and a limit on the total number of humans in this region. Eventually other human colonies will be established elsewhere on the planet. I have committed to keeping our ecological impact to a minimum, in return for Vishnu's promise of help from the angels."

Katan thinks about this. He remembers the images he saw of the original human planet, clogged with countless thousands of humans and their machines. He wonders if this will be the fate of his world as well. He sends the image to Vishnu along with the thought, "Will this happen to our world?"

Vishnu does not respond.

Katan stays a while longer, making sure to avoid coming too close to Kim. He and the other Waya mingle as best as they can with the other humans, but the language barrier prevents all but the simplest socializing. There are groundmouse bars and other snacks provided for the Waya, as well as a variety of human foods.

He looks up to see a flock of angels approaching. They land, walking awkwardly on the ground and silently chattering to each other. Katan finds their thoughts incoherent and annoying. He wonders if he could learn to understand them if he really tried. Perhaps silva-Ricky could help him learn their language, though he doubts the angels have anything worthwhile to say to him.

Eventually he feels it's time to go. A year ago he would have just turned and slipped silently into the forest. Now, in his new role as one-who-speaks-for-the-clan, he feels the moment calls for more than a stealthy departure. He asks Takaqa and Gana to stand next to him. Then he asks the shipmind, via the drone hovering nearby, to help him say a few words to the humans.

The shipmind calls out through the drone's speakers, "Attention, everyone. Our friend Katan, ambassador to the clans, would like to say a few words." Conversation dies down, and all eyes, human and angel, turn towards him.

A year ago he would have been frozen in place, his tongue like wood. But he feels different now. A bit older, of course. But in the past year he's seen things no Waya has ever seen before. It's changed him in ways he cannot even understand. He feels stronger. Calmer. Maybe a bit wiser.

Through his old and clouded eyes, which have seen so much in the last year, he scans his audience. Here are the humans, so reckless and dangerous but, as he has seen, also capable of bravery and compassion. Behind them stand the angels, sharp-clawed and dim-witted, little more than tools of their masters. Beside him, his fellow Waya. And of course, the ghostly ones who are present but invisible: silva-Ricky and the trinity of servants of the Banaan. And of course, the terrifying shipmind.

He gathers his thoughts and speaks slowly, letting the shipmind translate into human language.

"Greetings, my friends. Thank you for inviting me and my fellow Waya to join you here today.

"No one knows where my people, the Waya, came from. We have lived here since before the beginning of time. We know that once, the world was quite different from how it is now. We lived in a forest where the trees were small. During the day we could see the sky, and the sun's light shone directly on the ground. Nights were dark, with no glowing fungus to light our way. Then the first silva began sprouting from the ground. It grew and grew, eventually covering our entire world.

"The Waya were here when that happened. We were here when the angels arrived. And we were here when the humans came in their great silver bird pouring fire from the sky. For thousands of generations we have cared for each other and for the land. We have survived many dangers. How? By working together for the good of the clan. We live in harmony with the land, with the forest, and with each other." He pauses and flicks his tail a bit. "Well, at least, most of the time."

He looks around, making eye contact with everyone in his little audience. "Now, though, everything is changing yet again. The world shifts beneath us. We have new neighbors." He nods to the group of humans, who wave their forepaws and show their small white teeth. "New friends." He nods at the angels, who appear not to notice. "And powerful beings we cannot even see. We have much to learn from you. But I think you have much to learn from us.

"This world seems infinitely large, but it is not. It can nurture us and support us, but only if we respect and care for it, and for each other. Each of us, in our own way, has the power to destroy all we see around us. But we can choose not to. We can choose to see ourselves as one family, one clan. Just as clan members care for each other, we can all choose to care for each other and the world we share."

Katan thinks he detects a bit of restlessness among the humans. Maybe this has gone on too long. Time to wrap it up.

"Our people have an ancient language we use only for special occasions. I use it now. I hope you will hear these words and heed them.

"*Taka gisha siga.*

"Now the clan is one.

"We are, all of us, one clan. Please, say it one time, together."

Again, Katan speaks the ancient words, *Taka gisha siga.* The other Waya repeat it. The humans try their best to repeat the words. The angels are silent as always, but they move their beaks, as Vishnu speaks the words silently through them. And, to Katan's surprise, he hears the ancient words coming from the drone's speakers. It's the shipmind, joining in.

He hopes they all are speaking sincerely, but has no way of knowing. Words, even ancient ones, are just words.

"Thank you, my friends," he says.

Katan turns and walks out of the clearing, followed by Takaqa carrying the little one, and Gana. He doesn't know if his little speech has made any difference or not. But he's done what he could.

Waya Language

Waya grammar is similar to Chinese, but less complex. Nouns and verbs are spoken adjacent to each other without the insertion of articles, prepositions, and other helpful connecting words. Like Chinese, the Waya language makes no distinction between male and female, or singular and plural, and there are no verb tenses in common speech.

As far as vocabulary goes, the anatomical differences between Waya and human vocal apparatus means that some consonants commonly used in English are difficult to say and are generally missing from Waya vocabulary; these include b, ch, f, l, m, p, r, th, v, and z. The most commonly used consonants are d, g, h, k, n, s, sh, t, and w. All English vowel sounds are used in Waya, but by far the short "a" sound is the most common, especially in names.

Here are the Waya words used in this story:

Waya	English
ata	empty
ban	you
dosh	win
dowu	animal
gan	me
gaya	give
gisha	clan, pack

Ascent to the Sun

gono	enter
gopo	ready
gugu	sharp
hono	my
kenna	come
kewa	sleep
kuda	together
kusy	old
noso	go
saka	wind
sanna	warm
seda	hunt
senga	dream
shaka	mate
shogu	walk
shudo	tired
shuka	dry
siga	one
sodo	forest
soga	always
soko	young
sugo	protect
suna	den
taga	blow
taka	now
tato	no, never
tawa	dance
tenna	keep
Wagota	god of creation
wana	full
wega	hungry
wenno	rain
ya	seed
yana	claw
yoki	tooth

Acknowledgements

This book was in development, or at least simmering on a back burner, for over thirty years. The idea first came to me during my adventures as a rock climber, when I wondered what it would be like to live on a planet that was a huge climbing problem. For most of the next three decades the idea just rattled around in the back of my mind while I focused on other things.

I finally stopped procrastinating in January 2024 and got serious about finishing it, and I need to thank the wonderful members of the WorD sci-fi writers group in Pittsburgh for their critiques and encouragement, and particularly those who reviewed early drafts: Adam Johns, Greg Clumpner and John Muth. Also, thanks to developmental editor Melinda Crouchley, typography designer Iqra Nadeem, rock climbing and mountaineering expert Mike Schiller, and family members Kathryn and Katelyn Pepper for early reads and helpful advice.

Much of the material on evolution and genetics was inspired by Richard Dawkins, whose audiobooks I listened to in the car during the six months it took me to write the first full draft. *The Blind Watchmaker*, *Climbing Mount Improbable*, and *The Ancestor's Tale* are all highly recommended!

Ascent to the Sun

For the ascent itself, I was influenced by my memories of reading John Varley's 1980 masterpiece novel *Titan*, where Gaby and Cirocco spend months climbing six hundred kilometers up the side wall of the living spaceship Gaea.

The pack hunting scene in Chapter 15 was written based on material on the website of the Living With Wolves Museum in Ketchum, Idaho, www.livingwithwolves.org/how-wolves-hunt/. No actual herbivores were harmed during the writing of this book.

And of course, thanks to my digital research assistant ChatGPT-4, without which I would never be able to figure out how many silva trees one needs to cover an earth-sized planet.

About the Author

Jeff Pepper is President and CEO of Imagin8 Press, and has written and co-written over 100 books, mostly about Chinese language and culture. He founded and led several successful computer software firms, including one that became a publicly traded company. He has been awarded three U.S. software patents.

Jeff is a full member of SFWA. This is his first science fiction novel. You can contact him at jeffpepper53@gmail.com.